THE LIAHONA LEGACIES

Waters of Mormon

VOLUME IV

A Novel by TINA MONSON

Acknowledgements

This book is a result of the sustaining inspiration, unselfish service, support, faith and love from my children, Carson, Carter, Sierra and Bristol, who also helped with the artwork for this book. No words can adequately express my thanks, love and gratitude for them. And to my husband who, through his love, support and talents, makes me better than I am.

Many thanks go to Doyl Peck, Kay Curtiss and everyone from Sounds of Zion—I hold these friends in great esteem! This book is a result of your efforts, encouragement, sacrifice and time on my behalf. Thank you.

Words cannot adequately thank my sisters, Suzette Jensen and Tiffani Thunstrom. Their willingness to support me through editing and refining the book, and their passion for perfection, are greatly appreciated. This book is truly better because of their efforts.

A special thanks to Toni Lock and Tina Falk at tmdesigns, who designed and typeset this and all my other books to perfection.

And last but not least, I express my deep appreciation to all my readers, who take the time to write and encourage me. You make it all worthwhile!

Chapter One

Pale moonlight from the sky above cast an eerie glow through the swaying branches and leaves in the dark and foreboding forest. As the moon's subtle glow reached the edge of the trees, the light softly and mysteriously disappeared into what looked like a dark emptiness beyond. Mrs. M., surrounded by weeds, trees, and bushes, was positive she was no longer in the Treehouse. Silently glancing at the surroundings, she was baffled as to where she was and how she suddenly found herself somewhere other than the Treehouse. She was shocked and overwhelmed, surprised by what she saw and heard.

The noise of an all-encompassing river gurgled just beyond the light, causing Mrs. M. to wonder how far they were from the water's edge. Animals of all kinds chirped and chuckled loudly, seeming to laugh at the Team's plight. There were no lights from the city, no noises from passing cars, no loud or obnoxious music playing on a radio—nothing felt right.

Mrs. M. was terrified that the unbelievable story Hero had told her back at the Treehouse about Moroni's Treasure could possibly be true. Fear spread across her face at the very thought.

"Where are we?" she wondered nervously. "Hero's story couldn't be true. I can't possibly be in another time! Could I?"

As several shadows around her moved, Mrs. M. was instantly aware that several of the children from the Treehouse were with her. She breathed a cautious sigh of relief, glad that the sparse light in the forest kept the nervous and terrified expressions on her face concealed from their sight. She glanced down at the Liahona, still in her hands, not convinced that the small, ornate ball might have actually done what Hero had suggested.

"There's no way I am in Book of Mormon times!" she thought to herself. "This has to be a trick. These kids must be playing a trick on me. But how? How could they have tricked me? How did they get me in the forest without me even moving?"

The scattered light in the forest abruptly disappeared as a dark, ominous cloud spread swiftly across the sky, blocking the moon's soft, eerie glow. Mrs. M., Squeaks,

Tater, and Butch were left in complete darkness. Uncertain where they were and what kind of trouble they might be in, they were completely surrounded by the mysterious unknown.

Squeaks, frightened by the sudden darkness, threw her arms around her mom's waist, buried her face into her back, and squeezed as tightly as she could, quietly praying she could be back in the Treehouse. She hoped the creepy darkness would be a dream when she opened her eyes. She began to whimper in fear. When she opened her eyes, she realized the darkness was not a dream.

As Mrs. M. listened to her daughter, she worried for the kids' safety and grew more anxious about figuring out exactly where they were. Concern and worry filled her every thought, growing more uncontrollable with every passing second.

"There's no way this is a trick. The Team couldn't do something this elaborate," she thought to herself. "And I know they couldn't make Squeaks act scared if she really wasn't. So...am I in Book of Mormon times?"

"Mom, where are we? I'm cold," whispered Squeaks, interrupting Mrs. M.'s frantic thoughts. "And I'm scared. I can't see anything. Why is everything so dark? Where are the street lights?"

"I don't know, Squeaks," replied Mrs. M. "I'm trying to answer the same questions."

"I'm cold too, Mrs. M.," added Tater. "Do you think it would be safe for me to find some kindling and build a fire to give us some warmth and light? I don't think Squeaks would be so scared then."

"That would be great," answered Butch. "I'd love to see where we are and where that water is that I can hear so clearly! I really don't want to get wet tonight."

"You know what? I'm cold too, kids, and I have never liked the dark much. But, until we know where we are, and if we are in Book of Mormon times, I don't think we're safe to build a fire yet," replied Mrs. M.

"But Mom, I'm freezing, and it's windy. I only have on shorts and a t-shirt," argued Squeaks. "Please, please, let Tater build a fire. I promise everything will be all right."

"I'm sorry, Squeaks. Because of what I'm seeing and the fact that Hero suggested that the Liahona takes you somewhere in Book of Mormon times, I really don't think we're safe to build a fire until we know for sure. Unless, of course, you kids are playing a trick on me," replied Mrs. M., as she listened anxiously for the kids to tell her everything that was happening was a joke.

"You're right, Mrs. M. We could be in the war times of the Book of Mormon," Butch said seriously, nodding his head as though she could see him. "Who really knows what period in time we could actually be visiting."

"I thought you were going to tell me this was a joke," Mrs. M. whispered disappointedly. "I was really hoping all of this was an elaborate trick."

"Sorry," replied Butch matter-of-factly. "But this is no joke. I really think we could be in war times from the Book of Mormon; that's where Hero and Bubba traveled."

"Moroni's Treasure isn't a joke, Mrs. M.," added Tater. "The Liahona has already taken parts of the Team on adventures."

"War times?" whimpered Squeaks. "What do you mean, 'we could be in war times'?"

"War times, like when Captain Moroni led the great armies, or like Helaman and the two thousand warriors," replied Tater, frightening Squeaks even more.

"There are plenty of war times," added Butch, joining in the fun scaring Squeaks. "My favorite leader is Teancum. Now that was a scary time."

"So could we really be in the war times of the Book of Mormon?" Squeaks asked in a terrified voice. "Do you think our lives could be in danger?"

"Hold on, calm down. Everyone, wait a minute. Let's not jump to conclusions. Let's not worry about war times and where we are until we know for sure if we are even in Book of Mormon times," insisted Mrs. M. "Now why don't you two boys stop trying to scare Squeaks and do your best to quietly move closer toward us. We can try to keep warm cuddled together until we have more information about where we are," suggested Mrs. M. in a calm, quiet voice, even though her heart raced in fear.

"Good idea. With this wind, I'm about to freeze to death," replied Butch, as he stumbled over the bushes in the dark.

"Be careful, Butch!" insisted Tater. "Can't you hear that water close by? You don't want to fall in."

"I can hear the water, but with the dark and cold, I'm having a hard time moving through the bushes," replied Butch.

"Mrs. M., will you keep talking so that we can follow the sound of your voice?" suggested Tater, as he shuffled cautiously through the weeds. "I don't want to fall into the water or get hurt."

Quietly, Tater and Butch pushed through the bushes toward her voice. They inched closer toward Mrs. M. and Squeaks, hoping to find some warmth in the cold, dark, scary night.

Once the boys reached the girls, several anxious moments passed in silence. They huddled together, to get warm, waiting for the dark clouds to pass and for the moonlight to return. Mrs. M. was straining through the dark night to see anything in the area that might be familiar, when strange noises suddenly began to fill the air.

The unfamiliar and unnerving sounds of rattling leaves, animals' cries, and wind rang through the forest of trees, like music from a creepy, old horror show. Squeaks was sure that, just like the old Scooby Doo cartoons she always watched, at any moment, the villain would jump out of the darkness, chase her, and then catch her. Nervously, she continued to whimper at all the unrecognizable and frightening sounds.

"Can anyone else see those small lights in the distance?" questioned Butch.

"I can," replied Tater. "They look like they're getting bigger and bigger."

"Kinda like they're coming right at us," said Squeaks.

"I think they are, Team. I think someone is coming right at us," Mrs. M. said nervously.

"What do we do?" asked Squeaks, as she anxiously squeezed her mom's hand tighter and tighter.

Mrs. M. looked nervously around the dark area. Unable

to see very far, she spotted a fairly large bush just a few feet in the distance. "Everyone hold on to each other, and let's move a few feet to my right. I think we can hide in that bush," she suggested. "Follow me, and move quickly."

Without a word, the kids followed her to the safety of the bush. Then they swiftly crouched down into the thick bushes and weeds.

"Do you think they saw us?" Squeaks questioned worriedly.

"I don't know, but here they come," whispered Tater. "So be quiet. I don't want to be caught today."

Squeaks squatted down as low as she could between a fallen log and the bushes. She closed her eyes and hoped that if she couldn't see who it was, then they wouldn't be able to see her. She listened carefully as the voices moved closer and closer. Afraid to open her eyes, she whispered, "Can you see who it is?"

"Sssshhh," warned Mom. "They're close, and they look like soldiers."

Mrs. M. watched as nearly two dozen men approached. They carried torches, and were dressed in what looked like ancient soldiers clothing.

The soldier that seemed to be in charge held up his torch and called, "Halt men. The traitor has to be close by. We have been tracking him for nearly two days, and I feel that he is hiding somewhere in this part of the forest." The soldier then walked to where mom and the kids had just been standing. He bent over and picked up a broken tree branch. He mischievously smiled, turned toward the men, and called, "We must be very close. I hold a broken limb from the careless foot of the traitor. Commander, take three men and back track to the area we just came from. See if the traitor has doubled back on us. The rest of you, get ready. I feel we are very close."

With that, the soldiers waved their torches and swords in the air. Then they quickly disappeared into the dense foliage of the forest. Mrs. M. and the kids watched quietly as the light from the wooden torches disappeared into the night.

"Are they gone, Butch?" whispered Tater.

Butch slowly stood up, cautiously peering around the area for any sign of lingering soldiers. He replied, "Yes, I think they're gone; at least the main group is gone. But I don't see the man that the soldier in charge called the 'Commander'."

"A traitor—I wonder who they were talking about," said Mrs. M. uneasily.

"Whoever it is, I'm glad I'm not him," replied Butch. "Does anyone know a story from the Book of Mormon that talks about a traitor?"

"I don't," replied Tater, straining to remember a story like that from the Book of Mormon.

"In Book of Mormon times, anyone who did not believe the way that the king or person in charge believed, could have, and most of the time might have been considered a traitor," answered Mrs. M.

"So the traitor could actually be a good person?" asked Butch.

"I bet the traitor is a good guy," replied Tater.

"Do you think we should get out of here?" asked

Squeaks, still looking worriedly around the area.

"Actually, I think we're safe to stay right here," replied Tater. "We know the soldiers have been here, and if we leave, we could possibly run into them somewhere else."

"I'm cold and really scared, Mom," whimpered Squeaks. "I was sure the soldiers would be able to hear my teeth chattering."

"With all the screaming they were doing, there was no way they were going to hear your tiny teeth chatter, Squeaks," Mrs. M. replied, as she stood up and tried to scan the darkness. Worried about who the soldiers were, Mrs. M. took a deep breath, grasped Squeaks' hand, closed her eyes, and quickly said a silent prayer.

"Heavenly Father, please help me to know where we are and if we really are in Book of Mormon times. Help me figure out why we're here and what I'm supposed to do. Help me to keep these three children safe while we are doing the work you have requested, if this isn't a practical joke the Team is playing on me. And please show me the way to return them home to the safety of their parents unharmed."

Afraid at any moment something terrible could happen, Mrs. M. quickly finished her prayer—adding safety for the unsupervised Team back home at the end—and opened her eyes. Relieved to see sporadic flashes of moonlight in the area, she squinted her eyes tightly as she struggled to see anything in the dim light.

"Squeaks?" she whispered quietly. "Why are you crying? Are you okay, Honey?"

"NO!" Squeaks retorted, pulling her hand from her

mom's tight grip. "I'm not okay. I'm afraid! Where are we, Mom?" she demanded through her tears. "Where are we, and who were those men?"

"I'm not sure," Mrs. M. replied softly. She quickly reached for Squeaks' hand again, took hold, and squeezed her tiny fingers, hoping to comfort her daughter. "Now, don't worry. We'll figure everything out and get home as soon as we can. And Squeaks, please try to be quiet; I have a really bad feeling about all of this!"

"This isn't as fun as Hero and Bubba made it sound, Mom. This isn't anything like what they said. I wanted to go on an adventure like they did. But I don't like the scary dark. I just want to go home. I want to take a warm bath, curl up in front of the fireplace, watch T.V., and know that Dad is in the other room, ready to protect me if I need him to," Squeaks replied softly, as she again began to whimper. "Where are the good people from the Book of Mormon? Where are all the prophets, sons of Helaman, or people like that? And where is the light?"

"I know you're scared, Sweetie," Mrs. M. said in a comforting voice. "We could be in a good time from the Book of Mormon. We don't know that those soldiers were bad. In the light of day, I'm sure we can figure out how this Liahona works exactly. In fact, if your brothers can do it, I know that we can! I also know that the Lord has brought us here in the safety of the darkness for a reason. So, let's not give away our whereabouts by talking loudly and crying, okay?"

"I'm not trying to, Mom," sniffled Squeaks. "I'll try to be quiet, but those men really scared me."

"Butch, Tater, while we figure out what's going on here, you two boys keep an eye out for any returning soldiers," insisted Mrs. M.

The boys scanned the area while Mrs. M. carefully rolled the Liahona back and forth in her hands, trying to find any sort of directions, compass, clues or descriptions of what they needed to do in order to get home. Unable to find any recognizable symbols in the dark, she watched the only thing she could see - the flashing numbers Hero had warned her about just before they disappeared.

Mrs. M. looked up toward the boys and asked, "Hero didn't get a chance to tell me how to use the Liahona. Do either of you boys have any idea why the numbers 1 4 8 B.C. are flashing, and why they scared Hero so badly?"

"I think that when the Liahona flashes numbers, it means there is a mission that needs to be completed. The numbers that are flashing indicate the year we have traveled to in Book of Mormon times," explained Tater. "At least, that is what has happened so far."

"One hundred forty-eight B.C.!" exclaimed Mrs. M. "Are you serious? We're in the year one hundred forty-eight B. C.?"

"Yeah, I think so," replied Tater softly. "Why, is there a problem with the year one hundred forty-eight? Do you know something bad about that time in history?"

Mrs. M. shook her head slowly. She looked silently at the Liahona for several seconds, took a deep breath, and exhaled loudly. Then she startled the Team when she exclaimed. "Tater? Butch? I don't know anything about that time in history! Do either of you two boys know what happened in the year one hundred forty-eight B.C., or where we are that correlates with that date in the Book of Mormon?"

"No, Mrs. M. Neither of us have been out on an adventure yet," Butch replied softly. "And sadly, I don't know the Book of Mormon well enough to recite the dates that certain events happened—good or bad."

"You said Hero has already been on one of these adventures, right?" asked Mrs. M. "And he figured out what to do, where they were, and returned home safely?"

"Yes," replied Tater. "Both Hero and Bubba went on the first adventure, figured everything out, and returned home safely."

"There has been more than one of these adventures?" questioned Mrs. M., shocked at what Tater was telling her.

"Yes, this adventure is actually the third one with the Liahona," Butch replied. "Tater, Squeaks, and I are the only members of the Team that haven't been on an adventure yet!"

"Everyone else on the Team has traveled to Book of Mormon times already?" Mrs. M. asked, astonished.

"Yep!" replied Butch. "Everyone but us!"

"So you three know for sure this isn't a trick the Team is playing on me? And we really are in Book of Mormon times, with a real mission for the Lord to complete?" she asked. She looked at the Liahona—already knowing the truth in her heart—while she rocked it back and forth in her hands.

"Yep, that's right," replied Butch. "This is no elaborate trick by the Team. We really have a mission that we need to complete; otherwise, we're not going to be going home anytime soon."

"Well, did Hero happen to tell either of you exactly what happens or what needs to be done in order to go home?" Mrs. M. asked anxiously. "That's kind of important information."

Tater took a deep breath and started, "From what Hero has told us about his mission, we're going to have to find out exactly where we are, what events are currently happening, and what has gone wrong during this period of time. We will have to figure out all of this from the stories that we've read and know in the Book of Mormon. And when we have figured that out, we have to find a way to fix the problem. And …," Tater stopped suddenly.

"And what?" questioned Mrs. M. impatiently, listening intently to every word that Tater had said.

"And…," Tater hesitated again.

"What is it, Tater?" Mrs. M. questioned nervously. "You know you can tell me anything."

"And…we only have a week of the Lord's time to complete the mission or…," interrupted Butch.

"A week?" asked Mrs. M., anxiously interrupting Butch. She paused just long enough to clear her voice then asked, "This could take an entire week? Do you kids know everything I have on the calendar over the next week?"

"Not a week in our time—a week in the Lord's time," replied Butch, trying to calm her down. "And none of us really knows how long that actually is, or even how to tell time in the Lord's time."

"Was Hero gone very long on his adventure?" Mrs. M.

questioned nervously. "Did this take him a week?"

"Well, according to Bean, several days passed in Book of Mormon times, but back at home, only a day passed," replied Tater.

Mrs. M. covered her mouth with both hands, closed her eyes, and took a deep breath. "What am I going to do?" she thought to herself, trying to hold back the tears. "I can't do this. Hero and Bubba are so much smarter than I am about Book of Mormon events!"

Squeaks watched her mom intently, fearful that all the news of what was happening was too much for her mom to take. Several moments passed before she finally asked, "Are you okay, Mom? Is there a problem? Are you sick?"

Mrs. M. quickly opened her eyes, looked over at Squeaks and replied, "No, no problem. I'm fine sweetie. I was just trying to figure out what we needed to do to go home!" Mrs. M. paused momentarily, then looked over toward the boys and asked, "Butch, you started to say something. We have one week of the Lord's time or... or what?"

"Or we are stuck here in this time forever!" Butch replied matter-of-factly.

"Stuck here forever!?!" Mrs. M. gasped. "What do you mean *forever?*"

"I mean we have to solve the problem in one week of the Lord's time, or we are stuck in the year one hundred forty-eight B.C. of the Book of Mormon, forever!" Butch explained. "Whether we solve the mission or not."

"Forever?" questioned Mrs. M. "Like, as in, never go home?" she stammered.

"Yep, forever," answered Butch, aware he was frightening Mrs. M. "In fact, I think that is what happened to Mr. Jensen's grandfather."

"Hold on. Calm down. Don't worry, Mrs. M., Hero solved his mission in less than a week," reassured Tater. He made a face at Butch and slugged him in the shoulder. "Knock it off," he whispered.

"Ooowww," replied Butch, as he rubbed his aching shoulder.

"All right, boys. Tell me what else Hero said that I need to know," Mrs. M. asked sternly, afraid she still didn't know everything she needed to.

"Nothing that I can remember, that had to do with the mission. But, Hero did tell us that the hardest part of their mission was staying hidden from the people of the time period while figuring out what they needed to do," said Tater. "You know, we don't dress the way they do in Book of Mormon times. According to Hero, we don't talk, walk, or even physically resemble most of the people here. We have to be very careful. It could mean our lives if we don't. We could be mistaken for spies."

"Hero also said that one of the scariest things that happened to them was being chased by soldiers that wanted to kill them," added Butch, still trying to scare Mrs. M.

"Oh my goodness! You have to be kidding. They were chased by soldiers, too?" she exclaimed nervously. "What else do we have to look forward to?"

"Well…Bubba was almost eaten by a jaguar," Squeaks replied excitedly. "And he was attacked by fire ants and almost fell off a cliff or something like that."

Mrs. M. shook her head in dismay and replied, "Boy, we're really gonna have a long talk when I get back home! Those boys are in a lot of trouble. And Butch, you can only try to scare me for so long—but don't think I don't know what you're doing."

Butch's cheesy grin spread across his face, and he replied, "Okay, Mrs. M. I won't try to scare you anymore. I was only playing."

As abruptly as the frightening noises in the forest had begun, they stopped, leaving them again surrounded by silence. The wind blew fiercely, but its presence was silent. For several moments it pushed the dark, ominous clouds through the sky. Then, a dozen or so quick bursts of wind slowly started to scatter the clouds across the sky, allowing the moon's bright beams to splash across the area. At last, the light from the stars lit up the night. Finally able to see a few feet around the area, Mrs. M. quickly peered through the leaves and bushes, hoping to find something in the forest that might indicate where the Liahona had taken the group.

"Can you see anything, Mom?" asked Squeaks, still hiding her face in her mom's back.

"Yes, Squeaks. I can see many trees, bushes, and weeds. I'm sure we are in a forest. What I don't know, Honey, is exactly where this forest is located?"

"Can you see any signs of life, Mrs. M.?" asked Butch.

"I can see what looks like lights or fire—maybe even torches in the distance. But I can't see anyone," Mrs. M. replied quietly.

"How are we going to figure out where we are?" questioned Tater.

"Tater, the clues of where we are in Book of Mormon time are hidden all around us. All we're going to have to do is look for all the clues. You've heard stories from the Book of Mormon all of your life. Don't tell me you can't remember any of them. Besides, Tater, I don't want you to worry. We'll figure out where we are and how to get home. We're just going to have to be patient," Mrs. M. replied confidently, as she placed her hand on his shoulder, hoping to comfort him. "Daylight will surely bring us the answers we are looking for."

"I didn't think about already knowing all of the stories," replied Tater, as he nodded his head slightly. "I know lots of stories from the Book of Mormon."

"Quiet, guys," whispered Squeaks. "I can hear something."

"What is it?" questioned Butch.

"Ssshhhh, that's what I'm trying to hear," replied Squeaks, as she scowled at Butch and held her finger to her mouth.

Squeaks quietly crouched behind a large clump of bushes. She pulled aside several of the branches and searched the darkness for the noises she could hear. Suddenly, in the distance, six armed soldiers appeared.

"Mom, quick, get down!" she whispered frantically, motioning rapidly with her hand for her mom to hide in the bushes. "Butch, Tater, you too! Quick before they see you."

"Before who sees us?" asked Tater, as he fell to his

knees and crawled to where Squeaks was hiding.

"Look!" she replied, pointing cautiously through the bush toward the men.

"Who are they?" asked Butch.

"How am I supposed to know?" replied Squeaks, scrunching up her shoulders and holding up her hands.

"Mrs. M., do you have any idea who they are?" Butch asked nervously.

Mrs. M. crawled to the bushes where everyone was hiding and peered through the small opening. She gasped at the sight of the soldiers not far in the distance and quickly sat back against the base of a tree.

Several seconds passed before Butch finally asked, "Well? Do you?"

"They look like…soldiers," she replied uncertainly.

"Funny, Mom. We can see that," answered Squeaks. "Can you tell what kind of soldiers?"

"I'm not positive, but I'm sure I've seen pictures of men that look like these soldiers before," she quietly replied. "Everyone, stay out of their sight. If they are evil, I don't want to find that out tonight."

"They look like they're searching for something," replied Tater.

"Or someone," added Butch. "Do you think they know we are here? Or do you think they are searching for that traitor that the soldiers were talking about earlier?"

"How could they be searching for us?" answered Squeaks. "We just barely found out we're here!"

"Well, they are looking for something in this area!" Butch irritably answered.

"Be quiet! They're getting close!" Tater warned.

Unexpectedly, a loud screech rang through the forest, as a group of monkeys swung through the trees, frightening Squeaks.

"Uuuuhhhh," Squeaks cried, crushing branches with her body as she scooted away from the noise.

"Squeaks, quiet!" muttered Mrs. M., startled by her daughter's scream. "The soldiers are going to hear you."

"Too late, they're coming our way!" shrieked Butch, as he quickly released the branches of the bush and moved away, turning toward the others. "We better get out of here, quick!"

Chapter Two

Hero sat motionless, holding his head in his hands. He softly shook his body back and forth while he repeated the words, "How could I have let this happen; how could I have been so careless. How could I have let this happen?"

Afraid to say anything, Bubba watched tear after tear drip one at a time down Hero's face. Drawn by gravity, they rolled onto Hero's hand, continued from his hand down his arm, finally reaching his elbow, and then fell to the ground with a tiny splash as each one hit the wooden planks. He knew Hero felt responsible for Mom and the rest of the Team. Bubba just was not sure how to help Hero know that this was not his fault.

"Hero, come on. You know this was an accident," Stick reassured softly, aware of how bad he felt.

Hero looked up, stared at Stick for several moments and sharply replied, "Who are you kidding? This is all my fault. I never should have talked the Team into searching for Moroni's Treasure. Then Mom an the others wouldn't be in this mess."

"Talked us into searching? What are you talking about?" exclaimed Bubba. "You didn't talk me into anything! I wanted to find Moroni's Treasure, with or without your permission."

"That's right!" added KP. "I remember all of us wanting to find the treasure. You didn't have to talk any of us into going on a treasure hunt."

"Yeah, but if I was any kind of leader, I would have said NO! I would have worried about everyone's safety over finding a treasure," Hero meekly replied.

"Come on, Hero. You know that's not true. I'm not sure you could have stopped any of us from searching. How could we possibly pretend that we didn't find a treasure map? All of us were excited!" said Runt. "And you didn't put us in danger. I remember that we all chose to be involved. I don't remember you forcing anyone to go."

"Well, I can tell you, there's no way you could have stopped me!" Red declared. "I wanted to find the treasure and be rich."

"Or me!" added KP.

"Or me!" agreed Bubba. "I wanted to find the treasure, no matter what."

"We can't sit here and worry about what we could

have or should have done. We need to worry about what has already happened and focus on the problems we are currently faced with," Bean insisted. "Now, stop feeling sorry for yourself, get over here, and let's start planning," she demanded, pointing to the table.

Everyone in the Treehouse watched as Hero took a deep breath, looked over at Bean, shook his head, and watched as she began to take charge. Quickly, she cleared several items from the small wooden table in the corner of the room. She brushed her hand across the surface - sliding several small crumbs onto the floor—pulled open the front pocket of her backpack, and retrieved three pieces of paper, a pencil, and two pens.

"Well, what are you waiting for?" Bean snarled angrily at the boys. "Get over here! We've got work to do."

"Bean is right, Hero," Bubba said softly, as he walked toward Bean. "Do you think Mom's all right?"

"I'm sure she is!" Hero answered quickly, looking over at his brother.

"How do you know that?" Bubba questioned, shaking his head back and forth. "I remember how scared we were on our adventure."

"This is Mom we're talking about, Bubba. I don't know anyone who is better at handling difficult situations than she is," Hero replied. "She can do anything!"

"Besides, she has Tater and Butch to help her," added Bean, trying to calm Bubba's concern.

"That's right!" Bubba exclaimed. "Tater's not here anymore, so he must have gone with her."

"Along with Squeaks," said Hero as he scanned the

small room, looking to see who else was missing. "I'm not sure how good that will be."

"Hero, if she doesn't hold it together, they could all be in a lot of trouble," Bubba said worriedly. "Squeaks is afraid of everything. She could cause some really big problems."

Silence filled the Treehouse for several moments before Red tried to ease the nervous tension in the room. "Squeaks' own shadow could scare her to death, you know!" he joked.

"Let alone a spider," chuckled Stick.

"What are you talking about, Stick?" started Hero, as he walked through the area toward Bubba. "You don't have any room to talk. Everything scares you, too!" he teased.

"Nuh-uh," argued Stick, as he scrunched his nose and made a face.

"Yeah-huh," teased Bubba, smiling. "Do you remember the snakes, bats, spiders, and let me think what else in the last few days that you have been afraid of?"

"Well, that's only because they startled me," interrupted Stick. "Usually I'm not afraid of anything!"

"Come on, Stick. It's all right to admit that creepy-crawly things scare you," added Bean, chuckling. "We all know that they do."

"Yeah, we all still like you!" said KP, grinning uncontrollably. "Even if you do act just like little girls do!"

"Oh, very funny, KP," Stick snapped.

"Hey, wait a minute. I'm a girl," chimed in Bean, glaring at KP. "And I'm not afraid of creepy-crawly things."

"You're not a normal girl, Bean," KP replied quickly.

"You're stronger than most guys I know."

"I hope that's good," said Bean, frowning.

"Yeah, real good!" exclaimed KP. "With Stick and Squeaks, we have enough girls on the Team."

"All right, guys!" interrupted Hero, sure at any moment Stick would get mad. "We need to worry about the others out on the mission right now, not who's afraid of what!"

"You're right, Hero," agreed Bean. "We need to worry about Mrs. M., Tater, Butch and Squeaks."

"What can we do? It's not like we can help them at all," responded Red. "We have to sit here and wait for them to contact us…if they can."

"Sure we can help them," Bubba insisted.

"That's right," added Hero. "We can figure out what to do with our biggest problem—making a plan for what we're gonna tell Dad."

"We need to check the supplies from the group that just returned from the mission and see if we can figure out what Tater might have had in his backpack that could help them on their mission," reasoned Bean.

"You're right," agreed Bubba. "What if they have a walkie-talkie? Maybe we could get a hold of them and help them."

"Tater did have his backpack with him, didn't he?" asked Red, as he wandered around the Treehouse, looking at the packs on the floor.

"Oh, I sure hope so," Hero replied nervously. He jumped to his feet and followed Red around the room, anxiously looking at all the packs. "Hopefully he has a

Book of Mormon in his pack, they'll need that to get home as well."

"Hey guys, we better figure something out really quick," insisted Bear, as he looked out the Treehouse window. "I think I just saw your dad pull into the garage."

"There's no way," argued Bubba, as he looked down at his watch. "He doesn't get home from work until five-thirty or six," he said, as he walked to the window and peered outside. "He couldn't be home this early."

"I have an idea!" exclaimed Red, looking over at the window.

"What is it?" asked Hero. "We need all the ideas we can think of right now! Especially if my dad has come home from work early."

"Okay, then. I know that some of you won't like this idea, but what about Bear's mom? Hero, aren't your mom and Bear's mom sisters?" asked Red.

"Yeah, why?" asked Hero.

"Well, maybe we could tell Bear's mom what happened and get her to help us?" suggested Red.

"NO WAY!" shouted Bear, with a terrified look on his face. "If she knew that I traveled to another time and place without telling her first, I...I...I'm gonna be grounded for the rest of my life or longer!"

"Oh, Bear," laughed Bubba. "I think Red's on to something here. Aunt Maggie is tons of fun. I think she would help us if we ask her to."

"Oh, I'm sure my mom will help us!" replied Bear sarcastically, the terrified look on his face turning to anger. "It's what she's gonna do after that, that scares me!"

Suddenly, a loud buzz filled the Treehouse, startling the group. Bean screamed, frightened by the noise. Bubba, of course, fell off his chair.

"What was that?" Bean asked fearfully.

"Relax, Bean," teased KP, pointing toward the small, black box on the table. "It's only the walkie-talkie base."

"Hero, Bubba, Bear, are you boys up there?" asked a woman's high-pitched voice.

"It's okay, Bean. That is only my mom," Bear said casually.

"Your mom?" asked KP. "Why is she here? I thought she gave you permission to stay for a few days? How are we going to explain to her where Mrs. M. is?"

"It's my mom! Why is she here?" Bear screamed frantically, realizing who had just pulled in the driveway, and was calling from the walkie-talkie inside the kitchen.

The Team raced to the window and looked into the backyard, sure that any moment Bear's mom would be headed for the Treehouse. Several anxious minutes passed as they watched for any sign of Bear's Mom exiting the house. Finally Bean spotted her moving around inside the house. The Team watched her walk through the kitchen into the front room. Then she suddenly disappeared down the hall.

"What are we going to do?" squealed Bear. "I'm gonna be in so much trouble, and I really don't want to get in trouble."

"We're only going to get in trouble for doing something wrong," KP replied calmly. "And since we really haven't done anything wrong, your mom will understand everything we have to tell her. Come, on Bear. You'll be fine."

"Oh, yeah, right," replied Bear sarcastically. "She's never going to believe us! And if she does, that's when she'll get really angry with me."

"Well, we have to try something," said Red. "And I really think our best option is telling an adult that we can trust. And I know that we can trust her to help us."

"How do you know?" asked Bear, still not convinced.

"Come on, Bear. I don't know many people better able to handle stressful situations than your mom—other than maybe our mom," replied Bubba, pointing toward Hero.

"What about Cheri? Why can't we just tell her what has happened?" asked Bear, trying to come up with another solution.

"Cheri? All Cheri will do is tell Dad. I bet Aunt Maggie will be better at that then Cheri will," insisted Bubba.

"I agree, Bear. Aunt Maggie will be a lot better at telling Dad then Cheri would be," agreed Hero.

"Alright guys, we can tell my mom. But I'm sure I'm going to be grounded for the rest of my life," whispered Bear. "And if I am, then you are going to be grounded for the rest of your lives with me!"

"Come on, Bear. Telling her won't be that bad…will it?" asked Stick. "She's nice to me."

"My mom is always nice, but she's gonna be mad—just wait and see," replied Bear, as he shook his head.

"Bear, are you up there?" the walkie-talkie rang again. "Where is everyone?"

"Where's the walkie-talkie at?" screeched Bean.

"Someone better answer her fast, or she's gonna be out here in the Treehouse any second."

"I can't find it," replied Bear. "The handset is not on the base."

"Where is it?" questioned Hero. "Where could it be?"

"Well, the handset is not in the Treehouse anywhere," yelled Bubba. "I can't find it. All I can see is the base unit."

"Come on, guys. It has to be here somewhere," replied Hero. "Someone better answer before she does get angry."

"Do you think Tater has it in his backpack?" asked Bean, as she continued to search the area for the walkie-talkie. "I'm almost sure he had it in his backpack."

"I guess it's possible," replied Hero. "He did have it with him when we were waiting for the last group to finish the mission and get home."

"Oh, I sure hope he does," declared Red. "That would be great!"

"Great," roared Bean. "If Tater has the walkie-talkie, then every time Bear's mom screams into it, without knowing, she could be putting their lives in great danger."

"Oh no! I forgot about that!" exclaimed Hero. He ran to the Treehouse door and threw it open. As fast as he could, he climbed down the rope ladder and raced toward the sliding glass door in the kitchen, yelling for his Aunt Maggie, and praying she would stop yelling into the unit.

"Aunt Maggie, Aunt Maggie, are you in here?" called Hero, as he raced into the kitchen. "We can hear you, but we can't find our walkie-talkie."

"I'm in the family room, Hero," Aunt Maggie called.

"Where is Bear?"

Hero raced into the family room and watched as Aunt Maggie laid the walkie-talkie on the coffee table. Relieved, he took a deep breath and sat down on the couch next to her. "Bear is on his way down from the Treehouse," he replied, trying to catch his breath.

"Why didn't you respond when I called the first time?" Aunt Maggie asked suspiciously.

"We could hear you on our base unit, but we couldn't find the handset. I ran down here as fast as I could, so you wouldn't worry," Hero explained, trying to pretend everything was fine.

Suddenly, the sliding glass door in the kitchen slammed shut, and the Team filed into the front room one by one.

"Hey, Aunt Maggie," called Bubba. "How are you?"

"I'm great, Bubba. How are you?" she replied.

Bubba nodded and smiled. "Oh, I'm great. Just messing around with the Team, you know."

"Mom," Bear interrupted. "You said that I could stay for three more days! Why are you here?"

"Well, hello to you too, Bear. I've been trying to reach Hero and Bubba's mom all morning, and no one has answered here at the house or on her cell phone. She always answers or returns my calls pretty quickly, so I thought there might be a problem—especially with your Team out searching for treasure. So, I stopped by while I was out doing errands to check on all of you," she replied.

"So you didn't come to pick me up?" asked Bear, relieved.

"No, I'm not here to take you, I just wanted to check

on you," she answered. "That is, unless you're ready to go home."

"Waahhooo!" squealed Bear, as he jumped around the front room. "I don't want to go home yet!"

"So, where is your mom, Hero?" asked Aunt Maggie. "Why isn't she calling me back?"

"I'm not sure," Hero softly replied.

"We slept up in the Treehouse, and she was gone before we got up," Bubba explained confidently.

Aunt Maggie scrunched her face, bit at her lip, thought quietly for a moment, and replied, "Why do I think you're not telling me the truth? I can't imagine your mom taking off without at least leaving you a note. Something about your story doesn't seem quite right."

"We're telling the truth. We really don't have any idea where she is right now," added Bear. "She didn't tell us before she left."

"Where is Squeaks? Didn't she sleep up in the Treehouse with the Team last night?" questioned Aunt Maggie, slightly smirking.

"Yeah, she slept up with us last night. She must have come down to the house early and gone with Mom," stammered Hero.

"Really?" replied Aunt Maggie. "And the other members of your Team, where are they?" she demanded.

"They're here somewhere," Bubba replied casually, looking around the room, being careful not to make eye contact with Aunt Maggie.

"Bbooyys, why don't you please tell me what is going on around here, and let's go ahead and start with the truth.

Where is your mom? Neither one of you is a very good liar. Hero, you can't talk without stuttering. And Bubba, can't look me in the face. Now, before I call your dad at work to see what he knows, someone better tell me what in the world is going on around here!" Aunt Maggie demanded.

"I don't know what you are talking about, Aunt Maggie," Hero replied anxiously. He stood up from the couch and quickly walked into the kitchen. He placed the walkie-talkie in the base unit before returning to the front room. "I really, really, don't have any idea where Mom and Squeaks are right at this very moment."

"Is that the story you're all going to stick with?" Aunt Maggie questioned. "Because if it is, I'm gonna make a call."

Aunt Maggie stood up from the couch and headed into the kitchen. Pushing past Hero, she quickly moved toward the phone.

"Tell her! Right now! We really need her help," Red whispered insistently, just loud enough for Aunt Maggie to hear.

Hero looked at Red angrily, held up his finger to his lips and whispered, "Ssshhhhh! I'm not sure if that is what we should do yet."

"No, I'm not going to be quiet," Red replied, frustrated. "Either you tell her Hero, or I'm going to! We need her help."

Bear scowled at Red and ignored his demand. He quietly watched as his mom turned the corner to the kitchen, and seconds later listened to the sounds of the telephone as his mom dialed his uncle's work number.

"Maggie," called Red, as he raced into the kitchen after her. "Wait! Before you call, I need to tell you something important!"

"What is it, Red?" asked Maggie. She held the phone in her hand, pausing momentarily before she pushed the last number. "What do you have to tell me?"

"There is something very important that we all need to tell you," started Red. "And if Bear won't, then I will!"

"No wait, Red," interrupted Bear. "Wait a minute."

"Wait to tell me what?" asked Aunt Maggie. She hung up the phone and placed her hands on her hips. "Someone on this Team better talk to me, and I mean pretty quick! I want to know what in the world is going on around here! And I mean right now!"

Hero took a deep breath, walked to the kitchen table, and said, "Aunt Maggie, you better come and sit down, because what I'm about to tell you is truly an unbelievable story."

"Are you sure this is wise, Hero?" Bear interrupted.

"Bear, you are about to be grounded for the rest of your life! If there is a problem and my sister needs my help, you better let Hero tell me what is going on so that I can help!" replied Aunt Maggie. She walked to the kitchen table and sat down next to Hero. "All right, let's hear it. Let's hear this unbelievable story. I want to know what's going on around here."

"I told you, Team. If we tell my mom, I'm gonna be

grounded for the rest of my life," Bear replied. "And that's the first thing she said!"

"Bear, you're gonna be grounded if they don't tell me what's going on around here," snapped his mom. "Now, join Hero, sit down at this table, and let's hear what it is, that you're all so afraid to tell me."

Chapter Three

"They're coming, Butch," screeched Squeaks, turning away from the soldiers. "The soldiers are back. Mom, what are we gonna do? We're going to be caught!"

"Sssshhhh, quiet Squeaks," whispered Mrs. M., holding her finger to her mouth. "Let's not make it easier for them to find us. I promise sweetie, I won't let anyone hurt you. But I don't want to be caught by those men."

"Who are they, Mom?" whined Squeaks. "Who are they searching for?"

"I don't know, sweetie. But we don't want to be caught by whoever they are," insisted Mom. "Now ssshhh, please."

"What was that loud, scary noise?" Squeaks asked nervously.

"A pack of monkeys, now ssshhh, Squeaks. They're getting close. If we're not careful, we're going to be found," insisted Mom.

※

"I heard something," screamed the commanding soldier as he raced toward the bushes. "Follow me men. Find him! We must return the traitor to the king! Find him, or it will be our heads."

The soldiers were dressed like ancient warriors, wearing white feathers strapped to their heads on dark leather bands. Similar bands were strapped to their arms, and a few inches below their knees were more strips of leather with beads tied to them. War paint was spread all over their chests. Their skirts only an inch or two above their knees, were tightly tied around their waists. The soldiers quickly started searching the area. They swung their spears back and forth through the tall grass like machetes, cutting down almost everything in their path. Slowly and methodically, they searched every inch of the area, moving closer and closer with each passing second and each swing of the machete, toward the hiding group.

"We're gonna get caught if we don't find a better place to hide," whispered Butch, as he looked over his shoulder at Mrs. M. "Those soldiers are getting really close. They're covering the entire area, and they're almost here. They're going to find us any minute."

"Mrs. M., can you see another place to hide?" questioned Tater.

"We gotta get out of here. The machetes are only a few feet away, Mom," insisted Squeaks.

"Okay, kids, follow me, and be quiet," Mrs. M. replied.

Quickly, Mrs. M. turned in the darkness. Not sure where to go, she rapidly started crawling on her hands and knees into the thick brush. She moved beyond the trees, bushes, and weeds to where the Liahona had brought them.

As Tater glanced one last time at the soldiers, he was surprised to see them only a few feet away. He moved from behind the bush—where they had been hiding—as a large, grey, machete sliced through the brush, knocking the branches to the ground and onto Taters' legs. Afraid to look behind him to see if he had been seen, he moved as fast as he could with his large, heavy backpack slung over his shoulder. He moved quietly toward the others as they followed behind Mrs. M., traveling through fifteen yards of tall grass to the long hanging branches of a willow tree.

Mrs. M. stopped suddenly and motioned for the kids to climb under the lower branches of the tree and hide. Looking back to where they had just been, she watched the soldiers tear through the area and felt a sudden cold shiver flash through her body. Once the kids were safely hidden inside the branches of the tree, she made sure that the soldiers were not chasing them. Then she followed the kids into the lower branches of the tree to hide.

"Do you think we'll be safe here?" Butch asked nervously.

"I hope so," replied Mrs. M., "but only if we're quiet."

"What man do you think those soldiers are after, Mom?" Squeaks asked quietly, holding as still as possible.

"I don't know, Squeaks," she replied worriedly. She slid the long branches of the tree to the side, trying to see the soldiers. "But, I don't want the soldiers to find us instead of him. So kids, please do your best to be as quiet as you can."

"I wonder if Hero and Bubba had to do any of this sneaking around and stuff," said Squeaks.

"I'm sure they did!" replied Butch. "Bean told me that they hid in a clump of bushes and trees, and they even slept outside at night."

"We might have to sleep here?" growled Squeaks. "No way! I'm not sleeping outside. What about bugs, snakes, and animals - let alone soldiers that could slash us with their big swords?"

"Ssshhh kids, the soldiers are going to hear us! Let's worry about hiding places and beds later, shall we?" insisted Mrs. M. "When we know they are no longer in the area and they're not going to hear us, we can talk about where to sleep."

Suddenly, a loud buzzing screeched through the tree, followed by several loud unrecognizable words.

"What was that?" Mrs. M. asked anxiously.

"I don't know," replied Butch. "Could the noise be from the monkeys that almost got us caught earlier?"

"If it is those monkeys, we've got to get away from them," added Squeaks. "They're gonna lead those soldiers right to us!"

☼

"What was that noise, men?" yelled the commanding soldier.

"The man we are searching for squeals as though he is in pain," reasoned one of the soldiers. "If he is hurt, we should be able to find him easily."

"Be quiet then, Aiath," demanded the Commander. "Let's see if we can hear where he lies wounded and crying."

The large commanding soldier crouched down to the ground and laid his hand on the freshly chopped grass. He closed his eyes and felt for any movements on the ground. Unable to feel anything, he sniffed the air hoping to smell something.

Only seconds passed before the same loud buzzing noise shattered the fragile silence in the forest, followed this time by a familiar voice. Suddenly, Aunt Maggie was yelling, "Bear, Hero, where are you boys?"

"Oh, no!" Tater shouted frantically. "That's not monkeys! That's the walkie-talkie. They can hear the walkie-talkie! They can hear us."

"Where is it? Where is it? Get it turned off fast. They're going to find us!" roared Butch, scrambling through the branches to help Tater with his backpack.

"Come on, guys. Find it quick. You've got to hurry before she calls again," insisted Squeaks. "The soldiers are trying to follow the noises."

Mrs. M. kept a close watch on the shocked soldiers—patiently waiting for the next noise to guide them to their prey. Tater quickly pulled the backpack off his shoulders, unzipped the main pocket, and frantically rummaged around inside for the Team's walkie-talkie. As fast as he could, Tater located the walkie-talkie and quickly turned the small, round, black switch to the off position.

"I got it," Tater said quietly, as he held the hand unit up for everyone to see.

"I think they know where we are," gasped Mrs. M., anxiously turning to the kids. "The soldiers are moving our way again. We better get moving! We've got to find another place to hide—fast!"

"Where, where are we gonna go?" asked Butch. "It's dark, and we don't know where we are! We don't have any idea where to go that will be safe. Just about the only thing we do know is that there is a river close by, and we could possibly fall into it!"

"Come on, Butch. Don't give up yet," insisted Mrs. M.

"Trust me, I know lots of tricks. Now quickly, everyone quietly follow me! I have an idea."

"I hope it's a good one, 'cause here they come, Mrs. M.!" whispered Tater. He was the last person to drop from the branches of the tree and follow her away from the soldiers.

Mrs. M. quickly scurried into the tall grass beyond the tree and rapidly started crawling into the scary, dark, unknown forest with Squeaks, Butch, and Tater close on her heels.

"I can hear him, Commander!" yelled the soldier, Meles. "I can hear the traitor."

"Well, catch him," replied the commander. "I would love to be the one that takes him back to King Noah for his trial!"

Excited to find the man they were looking for, the soldiers pushed and sliced rapidly through the bushes, weeds, and tall grasses, sure at any moment they would catch the man. They were totally unaware of who they had actually been chasing. They reached the tree where Mrs. M. and the kids had been hiding, and the soldiers nearly destroyed every branch within reach as they searched for the man.

"There's no one here," announced Meles.

"Well, he's got to be close. He couldn't have gotten far, especially if he's hurt," replied the commander.

"Look! Look, Commander, up ahead. The tall grass is moving!" shouted Aiath

"Run men, get the traitor," yelled the commander, as he rushed to follow his men toward the grass.

※❂※

"They've got us for sure now," Tater whispered as he hurried. He was still on his hands and knees, trying to keep up with Mrs. M. and the others.

"They see us moving through the weeds," whimpered Squeaks. "We'll never lose them now."

"What do we do?" whined Butch. "I don't want to meet King Noah, especially if he's angry."

"Is that the time we're in?" asked Mrs. M., as she slowed and turned her head over her shoulder to look at the kids.

"That's what the soldiers said," answered Tater.

Unexpectedly, Mrs. M. came to a complete stop and waited for Tater to catch up with her.

"What are you doing, Mom?" questioned Squeaks.

"Now is the time for you to be very quiet," whispered Mrs. M., as she momentarily placed her hand over Squeaks' mouth.

"What are we doing?" asked Butch softly.

"Tater, this is not a good time in Book of Mormon history, if you're sure those soldiers were talking about King Noah," said Mrs. M.

"I'm sure that's what they said," replied Tater, not wanting to stop. "We've got to get out of here. The soldiers are close."

"Uumm, move just ahead. Keep going just up ahead," Mrs. M. replied. Her thoughts wandered into the unknown, and she pointed into the distance.

"So, come on, Mom," said Squeaks, as she turned and led the way into the darkness. "We can't stay here!"

Suddenly, a shrill scream echoed through the darkness.

"Snakes, they're everywhere," yelled Squeaks. "Ooohhh help, I have snakes on me."

Tater hurried to quiet Squeaks, watching as she struggled not to slip down the steep embankment. Sliding on the loose sand and pebbles scattered over the entire area, she was unable to stop a landslide from pulling her down the edge. Frantically, she scratched, grasped, and clawed, trying to stop her fall over the steep cliff and directly into the river ten feet below. Frightened of the water, she fought hysterically to stop her uncontrollable plunge toward the unknown beneath her. Tater moved at lightning speed, trying to catch her leg and stop her fall. But, despite his best efforts, Squeaks plunged with her arms cut and scraped from her struggles, and finally landed head first in the rushing river below.

Dazed momentarily, she floated several yards down stream before she finally grabbed hold of several tree branches, which stopped her from disappearing down the river. Afraid to scream, she waited several moments, listening for any sounds from the others. When no calls for help came, Squeaks' was sure the soldiers must be close by, and she needed to be quiet. Realizing she had to help herself out of the water to safety, she quickly kicked her legs back and forth to propel her to the edge. She was very careful to keep her feet under the water, so that she did not cause a splash and alert the soldiers to her location.

Suddenly, she felt something slimy slither past her arm. Afraid to see what it was, she closed her eyes and whimpered in fear, "Someone, please help me. Don't let this thing bite me."

Unable to hear anything, she swam as fast as she could to the edge of the river. Slowly, she lifted one leg carefully out of the water, slightly twisting her body. Then she raised her leg higher, straining every muscle she had, to reach her leg to the ledge above. Amazingly, her toe caught the edge, and anxious to get out of the water, she pulled with all her might. Her arms, knees, and legs burned from the weight of her little body. Placing more weight on the ledge as she pulled, the ledge suddenly gave way, dropping rocks, dirt, and boulders into the water. Afraid the falling rocks would attract the soldiers, she carefully allowed her leg to fall back into the water.

Pale light from the moon above shone through the river underneath her. As she stared into the water, she was sure she could see something moving. Frightened, Squeaks struggled to see through the rippling water. She searched for hidden fish, possibly an alligator, or even the rocks and debris that she had knocked down from the edge as she tried to climb out, unable to determine what was swimming near her, but sure something was moving underneath the water's edge. Fearful of what might be under her feet, she again reached up to the ledge. She gathered all her strength and swung her leg, trying to catch it on the edge. Missing the first time, she worked up the strength to try again. But just as she started to lift her leg out of the water, a frantic scream came from the bushes on the ledge above her head, startling her.

☼

"We found him, Commander," screamed Aiath. "We've found the traitor!"

"Where?" called the commander.

"In the river," replied Meles. "He's trying to escape like a sneaky snake in the water."

"Do you have hold of him?" asked the commander, as he reached the edge of the river and looked to see who the soldier was yelling about.

"Yes, Sir. I've got his leg," Meles replied.

"Get him out of the water!" yelled Aiath. "Let's get him back to the king; maybe we'll get a reward."

"Yes, Meles. Get the traitor out of the water. King Noah will be very glad to see him," insisted the commander.

With the help of Aiath, Meles pulled the man out of the water by his leg, still dangling his head over the river and the two men gazed upon the upside down figure.

Chapter Four

❝Have they found Squeaks? Is she who the soldiers found?" questioned Butch. He inched his way closer toward the edge of the river, trying to see who the soldiers had captured.

"Oh, I sure hope not, boys," Mrs. M. answered. She closed her eyes tightly, afraid to see what had happened, and listened to what the boys had to say.

"Well if they did, I'm sure at any moment we're going to hear the loudest, scariest scream anyone has ever heard before!" added Tater. "That might frighten the soldiers just enough to let her go!"

"So, can you see who they have a hold of, Tater?" asked Mrs. M., nervously opening her eyes.

"No, not yet, but if I move just a little…," started Tater as he struggled to inch his way through the thick bushes. "I think I…"

"Can you see if it is Squeaks?" Mrs. M. asked impatiently.

"Okay, I made it!" said Tater, as he finally pushed through the thick bush. "Uummm, it looks like…well the soldiers have caught…I think it's…"

"You think what, Tater?" demanded Mrs. M. eagerly. "Come on, Tater. What do you see?"

"I see an upside-down figure," he replied, smiling. "With its back to me."

"Please," begged Mrs. M., as her voice slightly crackled. "Can you see my girl?"

"I'm sorry, Mrs. M.," replied Tater. "I think they have the man they're looking for, not Squeaks. The figure is too big."

"Hey, I think you're right, Tater," said Butch, as he finally maneuvered his way through the thick bushes. "That dark figure is way too big to be Squeaks."

Mrs. M. breathed a cautious sigh of relief. "Then where is she?" she asked, somewhat baffled. She searched as much of the dark area as she could see.

"I can't see her anywhere," replied Butch, looking back over his shoulder.

"I heard her fall into the water. I tried to grab her legs, but I couldn't get a hold of her in time," said Tater. "Hopefully, she found a safe place in the water to hide until we can come to save her."

"Or she could have drowned," added Butch, not thinking about what he was saying. "Or, in the fresh waters of South America, if that is where Book of Mormon times really took place, there are Piranha, as well as many other very dangerous fish."

"Drowned?" gasped Mrs. M., irritated by Butch's comment. "Eaten by Piranha?! Do you think you could be a little bit more positive for me, please?"

"Oh, I didn't mean that the way it sounded, Mrs. M.," insisted Butch. "Really, I just said it as a possibility."

"That's enough, Butch. You're not helping the situation," growled Mrs. M., as she fought back the tears. "Squeaks is not a very strong swimmer, nor would she know what to do with dangerous fish. We need to find her and save her right now."

"I'm sorry," he replied softly. "I didn't mean to upset you."

"I'm not upset, Butch," Mrs. M. softly replied. "I'm just nervous about everything that is happening around here. I'm really not sure where to go or what to do next!"

"Don't worry, we'll get everything figured out," said Tater calmly. "As soon as the sun comes up, we'll see things a lot more clearly."

"Are you sure those soldiers don't have her, Tater?" Mrs. M. asked frantically, needing reassurance that Squeaks was okay.

"Yes, I can see the man's face now. He is definitely not Squeaks," he quickly replied, trying to calm Mrs. M.'s nerves.

"We've got to find her, boys," insisted Mrs. M. "She is way too little to be in an unknown land by herself. I can only imagine how scared she is right now."

"Don't worry, Mrs. M., I bet she has figured out a place to hide and is quietly waiting there for the soldiers to leave so that she can call for us or come find us," Butch added reassuringly.

"I sure hope you're right, Butch," replied Mrs. M., shaking her head.

※

With the soldiers dangling their prisoner's head just below the ledge, the man could clearly see Squeaks hiding beneath it. Squeaks, afraid the man would tell the soldiers about her, held her finger to her mouth, pleading for him to remain quiet. To her surprise, he nodded his head and smiled softly.

"This is not a smiling matter, Alma," yelled Meles. "When we return you to King Noah, I can guarantee that he will not be smiling at you."

"I'm sure that the Lord will protect me," Alma replied confidently.

"How? How will your God protect you, Alma?" asked Aiath.

"I'm sure that He has already provided a way for that to happen," Alma replied matter-of-factly. "Besides, I have faith in him."

"Faith in what, Alma?" asked the commander. "Can you see your God? Can you speak to your God? What exactly do you have faith in?"

"I do not have to see Him to know that He is real and feel His presence," replied Alma. "And, as for speaking to

Him, I speak to Him in prayer every day!"

"Prayer? You jest! What do prayers do for you?" Meles asked chuckling. "You do not even know if someone can hear them!"

"Yes, Meles, I know that the Lord can hear them. He hears my prayers and answers them. He leads me and helps me to do the right things," Alma replied boldly. "If I ask of Him, and it is His will, all that I ask for will be given to me. I have faith that He is with me all of the time. It is my duty to share the truth and light with others, like Abinadi has done for me."

"I cannot listen to your lies any longer. I would not be so sure of yourself, Alma," scoffed the commander, as he motioned for Aiath to lower Alma's head into the water. "Maybe some cold water will help to clear your head."

Squeaks watched in horror. She was afraid to move or help Alma as the soldiers lowered his head into the water. She prayed in her heart that the soldiers would not keep him under the water for long. After several moments passed, she was sure she would have to show herself and help rescue the man. As a few additional moments ticked by, Squeaks could wait no more. She released the tight hold she had on the spiny leaf branch above her head and dropped several inches deeper into the water.

She took a deep breath and choked back several coughs, then moved toward the front of the ledge to help pull Alma to the surface. Hoping to confuse the soldiers with frantic screaming, she took another breath. Just as she opened her mouth to scream, the soldiers suddenly pulled Alma out of the water.

"Have you had enough, Alma?" Meles demanded. "Are you ready to see King Noah and deny that there is such a God who can do the things that you speak of?"

Alma covered his mouth with his hand, ignoring the questions and coughed uncontrollably for several minutes. Glancing to make certain the soldiers were not watching him, he looked toward Squeaks and whispered, "Below the water is safety. Search for the underground tunnel that will lead you into the hidden Waters of Mormon. The waters will take you to the city undetected. But watch for the dangers that guard the entrance below."

"Where will the water take me?" whispered Squeaks.

"Into the area of the hidden Waters of Mormon, where the Lord can guide and direct you to save his followers," Alma explained. "Before King Noah finds out who they are and arrests them, or worse… puts them to death."

"Are you the prophet Alma from the Book of Mormon?" Squeaks whispered, excited to hear his response. "Are you the prophet who my mom has read me stories about since I was very little?"

"I do not know if I am that man, for I have never heard of the Book of Mormon," Alma replied. "But the Lord has shown me in vision that you and three others are here to help me. I'm sure that is how you found me here."

"Yes, there are four of us, and I know that we are here on a mission of the Lord," Squeaks replied. "But I don't know if that is how we found you."

"Follow the promptings of the Lord and all will be made right here," Alma promised, smiling at Squeaks. "You must hurry, child. If Noah's soldiers find out who believes in the Lord, they all will be put to death. Their lives are in your hands."

"I'm sorry that I led the soldiers to you," Squeaks cried, as a tear dripped down her face. "Saving those people would be a lot easier with your help."

"The Lord's will shall be done here, child," Alma replied in a comforting voice. "The Lord's hand directs all things. There must be something else he needs me to do back at King Noah's palace. I'm sure all will be revealed in his due time."

"But you are not captured in the records that the Lord gave to the people of my time," Squeaks replied. "I'm sure of it. I've heard the stories many times."

"I can feel that your faith in the Lord is strong. He would not have chosen you to come here without such great faith," replied Alma. "Trust in him; He knows what He is doing. Listen to His promptings and He will lead the way."

"Who are you talking to, Alma?" interrupted Meles, as he watched Alma talking to no one. "Are you praying for help from your God who will surely not come?"

"Meles, if you're going to take me to King Noah, then take me," Alma demanded. He wanted to get the soldiers away from Squeaks as soon as possible, fearing they might discover she was there.

"Don't tell me what to do, Alma," Meles warned, as he started to lower his head into the water. "Or I will pass judgment on you myself, and you will never even see the mercies King Noah has in store for you!"

"You can lower me into the water all you want,

Meles. But you won't get me to deny the Lord," said Alma, taunting him.

"We'll see about that, Alma!" yelled Meles, as he plunged Alma's head toward the water a few feet below.

"That is enough, Meles! You've had your fun; now it is time to take Alma back to King Noah. Abinadi has already been captured and is awaiting his sentence. I'm sure the King would like to carry out both men's sentences at the same time. That is, after he gets Alma to tell him who he has tricked into believing there is a God."

"But Commander," argued Meles. "I was just starting to have fun. A few more minutes, please?"

"No, now, Meles! Pull him up now! Aiath, help Meles pull Alma up to the ledge so that we can get him to the King," the commander ordered. "The King will want to see him immediately."

The two soldiers quickly followed the commander's orders and pulled Alma to the top of the ledge, dropping him violently on the ground. Alma let out a moan of pain as his head hit the ground. The two soldiers reached down, roughly grabbed his arms, and pulled Alma to his feet.

"Commander, what about a few well placed punches?" asked Aiath, as he clenched his fist. "King Noah wouldn't mind what he cannot see, would he?"

"Aiath, we will do only that which is ordered by the King," replied the commander. "Control yourself! You are a member of the King's royal army."

"Yes, commander," Aiath replied, as he stood at attention.

"Don't worry about me, child. All will be well. Do as the Lord commands. Follow his promptings, and carefully find safe passage inside, just as I told you," Alma said loudly, hopeful Squeaks would hear his message.

"Who are you talking to? Have you gone mad, Alma?" questioned the commander. "King Noah will not have sympathy for you if you pretend to be crazy."

"No, Commander. I'm not crazy. I'm fine," Alma replied, as he closed his eyes and dropped his head toward the ground. "I'm following the direction of the Lord."

"Don't look so sad, Alma," teased Aiath, as he laughed out loud. "I'm sure King Noah will go easy on one of his very own disobedient High Priests."

"Yeah, maybe all he'll do is slap your hands and send you on your way," laughed Meles.

"I am not worried about King Noah," Alma stated. "I have the Lord on my side."

"Well you better be worried, Alma," replied the commander. "I have served under the King for thirteen years and never once have I seen him show leniency. Not once —whether the men or women he sentenced deserved leniency or not!"

"The Lord will protect me, if that is what he sees fit to do," Alma replied confidently.

"Whether the Lord protects you or not, Alma, King Noah will have his revenge on you," replied the Commander. "You cannot be a High Priest and believe in the things you do. You mock the beliefs of your King who is real flesh—not someone you cannot see."

"Commander, I know the feelings in my heart are real. You may not be able to see Him, but I have faith in the Lord," replied Alma.

Angrily, the commander grabbed Alma's face and stared into his eyes for several seconds. He shook his head slightly, took a deep breath, and yelled, "Men, let's get this prisoner back to King Noah. I do not want this traitor in my sight any longer than he has to be."

Meles and Aiath tightened their grip on Alma's arms and followed the commander as he started back toward the city. They moved up the embankment onto a steeply sloping path nearly fifty yards long. Then it leveled off slightly into a small clearing before steeply sloping again for an additional fifty yards. At that point, the soldiers and Alma disappeared into the thick brush, headed for what had to be King Noah's city.

※☼※

Squeaks stayed motionless in the water. She listened to the soldiers' voices grow faint as they moved further and further away from the river. Afraid to move, but anxious to find the safe opening into the city underneath the water that Alma told her about, she waited until only the noises of the jungle animals could be heard. While she waited, she stared into the water, hoping to spot the entrance or opening to the hidden Waters of Mormon and the city that Alma mentioned.

Unable to see anything in the darkness under the ledge, and unable to hear any voices, Squeaks slowly wiggled and scooted into the moonlight. As she searched through the slow-moving water, she was sure that something was shining and glimmering directly beneath her feet. Fear of what was beneath her made her heart race, but the eagerness she felt to find their way into the city to help Alma pushed her forward. She took a deep breath, used her hands to force her body under the water, and dove, convinced she would find their escape route.

Had the moon's light been covered with any more clouds, Tater, Butch, and Mrs. M. never would have made it to the river's edge without slipping into the water like Squeaks had. They scanned the area, looking for any sign or trace of her. The water was calm, barely lapping against the shore. The wind was almost still. Animal noises filled the air, and the water reflected the moon's light. Nothing in the jungle seemed to be out of place.

"Tater, do you think the soldiers are far enough away?" questioned Butch, interrupting the silence as he looked around the area.

"Yes, I watched them climb the steep hill, then disappear into the trees toward the city," Tater replied.

"Do you think it's safe to call for Squeaks?" asked Butch.

"I think so," replied Mrs. M. "But call quietly, we've got to find her."

Butch nodded and softly called, "Squeaks, Squeaks, where are you?"

"Squeaks, can you hear me?" called Tater, as he stood on the ledge above the water's edge.

"Squeaks are you there?" called Mrs. M. "Come on, Squeaks, answer me. Where are you, sweetie?"

"Helloooo...Squeaks," called Butch. "Come on, answer, before those scary soldiers come back."

They listened intently to every sound in the jungle, but still no reply came.

"I can't hear anything but crickets," said Tater. "Can anyone hear her?"

"Not a word, sound, or squeak," replied Butch.

"Do you think she could have carried farther downstream?" asked Tater, searching for any sign of her.

"I guess she could have. But knowing Squeaks, I thought that she might have fought the current and found a way to stay as close to us, and the edge of the water as she could," replied Mrs. M. "I think she would be afraid to get too far away."

"But, if she couldn't grab hold of anything, I think the current might have floated her farther and farther downstream," added Butch. "Either that, or she's been caught."

"The soldiers didn't have anyone else but the one man that they had been searching for," interjected Tater.

"Could one of the other soldiers from the other group have found her and taken her without us knowing?" Mrs. M. asked worriedly.

"I guess that's possible," replied Tater. "But I don't think so. I think we would have heard her scream if she had been caught."

"You know, Tater's right, I'm sure we would have heard several long and very loud screams from Squeaks," added Butch. "There would be no doubt that she had been caught."

"Not to mention screaming from the soldiers as she kicked, scratched, and bit them," laughed Tater.

"That's true," replied Mrs. M., smiling at the thought. "Boys, why don't you stay here and continue to search for her, and I will move downstream fifty yards or so and see if there is any sign of her?"

"Are you sure that is safe?" questioned Tater. "I'm not sure you should be alone in this jungle."

"I'll be just fine," replied Mrs. M. "Now be very careful. Watch the area closely in case those soldiers return, and stay close to this umbrella tree. This will be my landmark to find you."

"We'll be careful," replied Butch. "And don't worry, I'm sure Squeaks is fine."

"I hope so," Mrs. M. called over her shoulder, as she quickly moved down the river's edge and disappeared into the darkness beyond.

Chapter Five

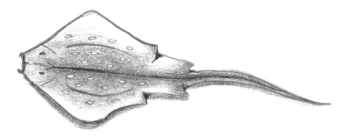

Unable to hear Mom or the boys calling for her from below the surface of the water, Squeaks searched nervously for the underwater entrance to the hidden Waters of Mormon that led to the city that Alma spoke about. With the sixty seconds of air that she could hold in her lungs, she was amazed at what she was able to see. She smiled at the colorful seahorses with their tails wrapped around the floating sea grasses. She noticed several species of fish, although, there were only two kinds that she knew for sure. Under the water seemed so peaceful; no forest noises could be heard anywhere, and there were definitely no soldiers.

A long, flat, thin, black shape slipped through the water along the sandy bottom of the river and floated toward the silver shimmer that Squeaks had seen from the surface. Excitedly, she studied the shiny silver object in the water and was sure it marked the entrance to the underwater tunnel that Alma told her to find. Suddenly, something slimy slithered past her, rubbing its rubbery body against her arm. She quickly glanced to see what it was. Just as she did, the long, thin, flat, black shape turned rapidly through the water, scattering dirt and debris around the area, catching the corner of Squeaks' eye with its movement. The movement forced her attention back to its mysterious shadow in the water, away from the shiny silver object. Again, the long rubber body of what looked like an eel, glided past Squeaks, this time rubbing against her leg as an eerie, tingly sensation sped through her body.

Afraid of the dangerous fish around her, and sure she had found the entrance and the dangers that guarded it, Squeaks quickly raced for the surface as her lungs finally ran out of air. As she frantically broke through the water and gasped for air, she scared Butch as he was leaning over the water's edge, trying to see what was below.

"Aaaahhhh!" he cried, as he fell back from the edge, landing in Tater's lap.

"What's the matter?" questioned Tater, as he pushed Butch away.

"Was that a fish?" Butch asked frantically. "Or was it an alligator coming after me?"

Tater pushed Butch out of the way and leaned over to the water's edge. "If that was an alligator, we've got a lot more to worry about than drowning or dangerous fish," Tater replied. As he searched for the alligator that Butch thought he saw, he spotted Squeaks scurrying toward shelter under the ledge.

"Squeaks," called Tater. "Was that you that scared Butch, or was that an alligator?"

Excitedly, she stopped, looked up, and was relieved to see the boys. "Well, I can tell you that I'm not big enough to be an alligator, so I must be a caiman. Does Butch know what a caiman is?" she asked, smiling.

"I don't know for sure," Tater replied. "Do you, Butch?"

"Yes, I know what a caiman is," he replied heatedly.

"I guess he does, Squeaks," answered Tater, now laughing out the words.

"Then he knows how ferocious I am and how lucky he is to still have his hands," she replied, excited to be reunited with her friends. "Tater, is it really you?"

"Yep, it's me and Butch. Boy is your mom gonna be glad to see you," he replied. "We're here to rescue you!"

"Rescue me?" she giggled. "You mean, I'm gonna rescue all of you."

"Cute, Squeaks!" Tater replied, smiling as he lay down on his belly and reached over the ledge for her hand. "Grab a hold of my hand, and I'll pull you up to safety. You better hurry, just in case there really is a fresh water alligator or caiman."

"I'm not going anywhere!" Squeaks declared frustrated by the boys. "I've got a hidden entrance to the Waters of Mormon and King Noah's city to find. And besides, if you're not careful, I'm gonna snatch your arm off with you hanging it over the ledge like that."

"What are you talking about, Squeaks?" asked Butch, looking over Tater's shoulder. "You're not going to bite anyone's arm off or find a hidden entrance to anything in the water. Let Tater help you out of there, so we can figure out what we need to do and get to work before our time here in Book of Mormon land runs out."

"Where's my mom?" demanded Squeaks. "I know she'll believe me."

"Believe what?" asked Butch.

"Believe me! I have to find a hidden entrance," Squeaks replied nervously. "So, where's my mom?"

"She headed downstream to look for you. She should be back any minute," Tater replied, looking downstream through the trees and foliage. "Your mom's gonna be really excited that we found you. Come on out of the water. We'll find her and then figure this mission out, okay? Please?"

"No, not okay, guys! I told you. I know where we're going, and I know what we have to do. I've already got that handled. Now, if you want to come down into the water with me, I can show you what we have to do," Squeaks said briskly, staying just out of reach of Tater's hand. "Please, trust me. I know what I'm doing."

"Squeaks, this is serious business. We don't have time to play your silly games!" yelled Butch. "Now, who knows what dangers really could be in that water? If you don't get out, you could get hurt."

"If I do get hurt, then at least I'll know I was doing everything that I could to solve the mysteries of the year One Hundred Forty-Eight B.C., unlike you two," snapped Squeaks.

"Squeaks, quit messing around, will ya?" pleaded Tater. "We've got work to do, and there could be piranha in this river."

"Piranha?" she gasped.

"Yeah, piranha. They live all over in South America," replied Butch, grinning wildly.

"Well, if they do and they were in this river, then I would already have been eaten!" Squeaks replied smartly. "I'm not that dumb, you know. Now quit treating me like a baby."

"Come on, Squeaks. Give me your hand, and let me pull you out of the water. If you really found something, you can tell us about it on land. And if we need to, we can get back into the water," Tater reasoned. "We've been looking for you everywhere since those soldiers left, and I would like to see if we can get some of these things figured out before the soldiers come back and we're caught."

"Mom! Mom!" called Squeaks loudly, refusing to take Tater's hand. "Mom, where are you?"

"Quiet, Squeaks! You're gonna get us captured!" demanded Butch. "If there are still soldiers in the area we could get caught."

"Mom, are you there?" Squeaks screamed again, ignoring every word Butch said.

"Squeaks, are you listening to me?" started Tater, as he climbed to his feet and stood on the ledge. "I'm older than you. I am the most senior member of the Team on this mission, and I want you to get out of the water—right now! I am totally not kidding."

"I'm trying not to listen to you 'cause you're not listening to me!" she replied smugly. "I already know the answers that we need to complete our mission, and I'm not going to get out of the water until I talk to my mom. And that's final."

"Come on, Squeaks. How could you possibly know anything?" replied Butch, annoyed with her defiance. "The only place you have been without us so far is in the water. What could you know that we don't?"

"I know that the water is where we need to start our mission, and I have an idea where in the water we need to do it," she replied arrogantly, as she stuck her tongue out at Butch. "I think you're mad because I know something you don't."

"That was really mature, Squeaks," replied Butch. He looked over at Tater and asked, "Do you think she hit her head when she fell into the river and has a serious concussion?"

"No, I didn't hit my head," Squeaks snapped. "And I don't have a concussion."

"That's all I can think of," said Tater, ignoring every word Squeaks said. "She must be delirious."

"I don't have time for your childish games," Squeaks replied. She took a deep breath and again dove under the water, trying to find Alma's hidden tunnel.

"Childish games," muttered Tater, as he watched Squeaks disappear under the surface of the water. "What is she talking about?"

"Yeah, what's gotten into her? I thought she was afraid of everything?" said Butch. He stepped to the side of the ledge, took a few steps down toward the river, and stared into the water.

"Well, she doesn't seem to be afraid of much right now," replied Tater. "Look at her moving around underneath the water. She's even pushing away that fish that kinda looks like an eel."

"An eel?" asked Butch. "Can't they be dangerous? Are you sure we still have the same girl?"

"What's dangerous?" asked Mrs. M., startling both the boys as she walked up behind them.

"You scared me," said Butch, clutching his hand over his chest. He stepped back into the thick weeds at the river's edge, allowing room for Mrs. M. to move in closer and see what Tater had found.

"Aaaaagggghhhh!" screamed Butch frantically, unsure what had just happened. "Mrs. M., Tater, someone, please help me!"

"What are you doing, Butch?" asked Mrs. M., as she turned to see why he was screaming. Upon rotating her head, she saw him dangling upside down by his ankle in a trap swinging back and forth from the tree.

"I don't know," he replied, almost in tears. "I moved back so that you could see the water, and the next thing I knew, I was swinging in the air."

"Sssshhhh, Butch. You're going to be all right. Hang on for a minute, and I will get you down," replied Mrs. M. She reached up to his hand and slowly stopped his body from swinging back and forth. "Are you okay?"

"No, I'm scared," Butch panted anxiously. "What if the soldiers have a warning system, and now they know where we are 'cause I set off the trap?"

"I'm sure they don't have a warning system," Mrs. M. answered calmly. "Now, give me a minute, and I will figure out how to get you down."

Smiling, Mrs. M. asked Tater, "Do you happen to have a knife or something in your backpack that we can cut Butch down with?"

"I'm sure I do," Tater replied, as he started to pull the pack off his shoulder. "I have everything in here!"

All of a sudden, Tater felt the earth rumble underneath his feet. He quickly dropped the pack onto the ground and placed his hand next to it, to steady himself. Again, the ground rumbled underneath his feet, knocking him to his knees.

Mrs. M. turned to Tater and demanded, "Tater, come on! Do you have anything that will work?"

"Could you feel that rumbling in the earth?" Tater asked nervously. "I thought I felt an earthquake."

"What rumbling, Tater?" quizzed Mrs. M., with a strange look on her face. "I didn't feel anything."

"Didn't the ground rumble under your feet?" Tater questioned, confused as to why she could not feel the movement.

"I don't think so, Tater," replied Mrs. M., impatiently holding her hand out for the knife. "You must be imagining things. This forest is kinda scary in the dark."

Tater shook his head, trying to clear the confusion. He looked down at his backpack again. Quickly, he unzipped the main pocket and rummaged through the contents.

"Hurry, Tater! All my blood is rushing to my head, and I'm getting sick," called Butch, still slightly swinging back and forth.

"I'm hurrying," Tater replied, mumbling under his breath.

"So, why don't you boys tell me what you were talking about when I walked up? What's dangerous around here?" Mrs. M. asked. "Besides the soldiers that we saw."

"As soon as we save Butch, I'll show you. You're gonna be so surprised," answered Tater. He finally located his Swiss Army knife and held it out for Mrs. M. to take.

Unexpectedly, the ledge under Tater's feet started to move. This time he was sure of it. Worriedly, he looked at Mrs. M. and threw the knife toward the ground by her feet. The dirt instantly started to cave in under his feet. His legs disappeared below what was left of the ledge, followed by his waist, chest, and then head. The ledge had given way and heaved him toward the dark, cobalt-blue water, waiting for him several feet below.

He screamed as his body prepared to hit ice-cold water, but surprisingly, the water was almost lukewarm. He slipped under the surface and quickly sank to the bottom of the river. His body was followed by a mountain of dirt, rocks, and debris. Because of the dirt in the river, he was unable to see anything in the dark, murky water. Upon touching the bottom, he pushed off the river floor and forced himself back to the water's surface above.

"Are you okay, Tater?" called Mrs. M. She frantically retrieved the Swiss Army knife, opened it up, and worked to cut the rope wrapped around Butch's ankle to get him down from the trap.

"Tater, Tater!" she called, still working on the rope. "Are you alright?"

"I don't think he has resurfaced yet," replied Butch, trying his best to see into the river upside down. "You don't think he's buried in the dirt, do ya?"

"I sure hope not," replied Mrs. M., cutting the rope faster. "Tater, come on buddy, can you hear me yet?" Mrs. M. called again.

"Yeah, Tater, don't be messing around," insisted Butch. "Where are you?"

Several moments went by with no noise from Tater. And then finally, he reached the surface of the water and gasped for air.

"Is that you, Tater?" called Butch nervously.

"Yeah, no worries. I'm all right," he replied, choking and coughing up water.

Mrs. M. finally finished cutting through the thick rope tied around Butch's ankle. Unable to stop his fall, he plummeted downward. He landed in a crumpled ball on the hard, wet, grass-covered ground.

"Butch, come on. I need your help. Get up quick," insisted Mrs. M. "We've got to help Tater before anything else happens."

"Mrs. M., really I'm okay. I'm fine. Look down in the water. Can you see what I found?" asked Tater, casually floating on his back.

Mrs. M. moved to the edge of the dirt near where the ledge used to be and looked into the dark river, trying to find what Tater wanted her to see. "Tater, what am I looking for exactly?" she asked.

"Squeaks! Can't you see Squeaks under the water?" he asked casually. "Butch and I found Squeaks."

"No, all I can see is a bunch of dirty water," Mrs. M. replied. "Are you sure you saw her?"

"She's in here. I promise," replied Tater. He stopped floating on his back and started searching the water for any sign of Squeaks.

"Do you think that when the ledge caved in, she could have been caught underneath and pushed under the surface?" asked Butch, concerned about Squeaks' whereabouts.

"Oh, I hope not," replied Tater frantically. He took a deep breath and dove under the water in search of Squeaks.

"Butch, save Tater's backpack. I have a feeling we're going to need everything inside, and it's floating down the river. I'm going to help Tater search for Squeaks. Hurry!" Mrs. M. screamed, as she pointed down the river to Tater's pack. Jumping to her feet from the ledge she quickly ran to the river.

"Wait, Mrs. M., wait!" called Butch, grabbing at her arm, trying to stop her from diving into the water.

"No, Butch, no time to wait," she replied. She jumped in, and her head disappeared under the surface.

She maneuvered through the water, scrambling to get deep enough to see underneath the ledge that had collapsed. She silently prayed that she would not find Squeaks pinned beneath a mound of dirt and rocks. With her daughter no where in sight, Mrs. M. frantically started digging and sifting through the rubble until, finally, her lungs ran out of air. Racing for the surface, she gasped for breath. Without checking to see if Butch was all right, she took another large breath of air and again maneuvered under the water in search of Squeaks and Tater. Several nervous moments passed while Mrs. M. struggled to turn herself around underwater. As she continued deeper and deeper, she suddenly spotted Squeaks lying face down on the bottom of the river. Her heart raced in fear as she swam as fast as she could towards her daughter. She grasped for anything in her path to help reach her daughter faster, fearful that something terrible had already happened.

Stretching her arm out as far as she could, Mrs. M. grabbed at the back of Squeak's shoe several times until, finally, she caught a hold of her daughter's foot. With the air in her lungs running out, Mrs. M. held on as Squeaks wiggled and moved, trying to get her leg free. Refusing to let go, Mrs. M. raced toward the surface. As she reached the surface, she gasped for breath. Only a second later, Squeaks surfaced, struggled for a breath, and then screamed at the top of her lungs.

"What are you doing, Mom? I had to let go of my reed; I was using it to breath. Everything was working great. Why did you stop me? I think I found what I was looking for! Have Tater and Butch convinced you of their theory—that I have a concussion?"

"What are you talking about, Squeaks? I don't know what you mean. I thought you might have been hit by falling debris when the ledge collapsed. I was worried that you were hurt and lying on the bottom of the river!" explained her mom. She wiped the water from her eyes and struggled to catch her breath. "I didn't know you were breathing through a reed."

"Mom, I'm so glad it's you. Tater wouldn't believe me," Squeaks started excitedly. "I know why we're here, and I know what we have to do to get home."

"First, are you all right?" asked Mrs. M. "And Tater, where are you?" she called.

"I'm over here, Mrs. M." replied Tater as he waved to her from the bank of the river. "I'm holding on and I'm fine."

"Did you get hurt when you fell through the ledges?" she asked, as she watched him rub his head and arm.

"I have a raging headache. But other than that, I'm doing great," Tater calmly replied.

"And you, Squeaks?" asked Mrs. M. "Did you get hurt when you fell into the water?"

"No, I'm fine, Mom. I didn't bump my head when I fell in the water. I didn't get hurt when the ledge collapsed. In fact, that helped to get the eels and stingrays away from the bottom of the river and the hidden entrance. Alma told me I would find it, and I did. I was looking at it when you pulled me back to the surface," Squeaks explained. "I was so close."

"Okay, wait a minute. I don't understand what you are saying, and I can't tread water and think at the same time. Let's climb out of this river, and you can tell me all about what you know," suggested Mrs. M., unable to keep herself above the surface any longer.

"No, we can't wait. The water is where we will find the answers that we need in order to do the work the Lord wants us to do," Squeaks said adamantly.

"Squeaks, my legs are killing me. Can't you tell me what you know while we sit on the river bank, please?" begged Mrs. M. "I promise I won't take my feet out of the water."

"I guess so, Mom," Squeaks replied, following her mom to the river bank. "Tater, Butch, meet us on the other side of the trees. I have something really important to tell you."

"What could she have to tell us that's so important, Butch?" asked Tater, as he held onto several tree branches that were hanging down in the water. "I mean, she was only gone twenty minutes."

"I don't know, but she's not going to stop whining about some hidden tunnel until we listen. We better get over there and see what she has to say," suggested Butch. He handed Tater his backpack and climbed onto the river bank. They maneuvered carefully to where Mrs. M. had climbed out of the river. This time, Butch was careful not to step in another trap and find himself hanging upside down from his ankles again.

Chapter Six

The soldiers marched through a tunnel, which was nearly thirty feet long and twenty feet tall. It was covered by ivy, moss, and large trees. The tunnel curved slightly, hiding the opening at the far end. As the soldiers moved through the darkness, the forest behind them disappeared. Then the tunnel opened up, revealing a spectacular city ahead of them.

Alma looked up at the city in awe. He loved the excitement it offered, the strength it showed to all its visitors, and the sacrifice of taxes all the citizens made for the bettering of their society. He wished that the people of this great city would have stayed righteous, and that Abinadi's call for the people to repent was only needed by a few.

The soldiers moved swiftly across a small open field to the steps that led to the great city. As they reached the top step, to the north they could see the plaza with hundreds of merchants sleeping by their wares. The merchants were waiting for the sun to rise and another busy day to start at the market. To the south was the Temple of Warriors. King Noah used this temple for training his newest soldiers. To the southeast was the sports arena. King Noah loved watching games. There were ball games, fighting animals, and even his bravest soldiers fighting jaguars.

As they walked further into the city, directly east stood the largest building of all—King Noah's Temple. It was adorned with every manner of riches—gold, silver and lavishly carved stone and ivory statues. To the northeast of King Noah's Temple was the High Priests' Temple. Alma knew this was where the soldiers would take him. All courts, judgments, and hearings took place in the center courtroom inside. From there, the soldiers would take him to the prison, which was farther east, outside the High Priests' Temple. This is also where Abinadi was being held prisoner. Despite his circumstances, Alma loved this city. He enjoyed the citizens and was glad he knew the city and the happenings so well. He was relieved to know the laws of the land and exactly what King Noah would do.

Surprised when the soldiers led him in the opposite direction, Alma asked, "Why are we headed to King Noah's Temple? That is not where court is held." Alma became nervous and confused as the soldiers walked up the stairs to the temple entrance.

"King Noah will sentence you without the help of his

High Priests," replied the commander. "He does not know if your teachings have affected any of them. And until he does, King Noah does not trust their judgment."

"I will not even have a fair trial?" questioned Alma in a high, shrill, panicked voice. "I thought I would at least have a fair trial with the High Priests."

"You're lucky to be alive after the stunt you pulled in the court room," Meles answered angrily.

"Yeah, be quiet, Alma. If you interrupt the King, things will be much worse for you," warned Aiath.

"How could things get much worse, Aiath?" Alma retorted. "I'm going to get an unfair trial by a king who believes there is no God, and I'll be thrown into prison if I don't deny the things that I know to be true. I will surely be tied and burned to death with Abinadi in less than three days."

"You have a way out, Alma," replied Meles. "Deny this God that you can neither see nor hear. Maybe the feelings you have are those of stomach sickness," Meles said, chuckling at his own comments.

"I am not sick, Meles. You know in your heart that I am fine. I know there is a God, and I will not deny him - not for you or the king," replied Alma.

"Then you chose your own fate. The king will have no choice, if this is what you will tell him," the commander replied brashly. "Now, be quiet. Men, take him to the king's private chambers. I will find King Noah and meet you there."

"No tricks, Alma! Things will only get worse for you if you try something stupid," said Meles, as he tightened the grip on Alma's arm and led him toward King Noah's private chambers. "I know that as a High Priest, you know about secret tunnels and escape doors, and I don't want you trying to use one of them."

Meles led Alma down a wide corridor that was covered in ancient hieroglyphs, which told the story of King Noah and his family before him. They passed several guards who were protecting the rooms of King Noah's children as they slept, as well as his riches and prized possessions, and other rooms that Alma had never been allowed to enter. Finally, they reached King Noah's private chambers, and Meles lead Alma quickly inside.

Time ticked by slowly as Alma and the soldiers waited for the commander to return with the King. His mind wandered to the last few years when he was chosen to be a High Priest and how excited he was. He often felt that there had to be something more in life than being taxed one-fifth of everything he owned, holding court after court for King Noah, and deciding on discipline for the men and women who either refused to pay the King's unfair or unjust taxes or did not have the means by which to pay them. The feeling that he was involved in something wrong never went away. When Alma heard Abinadi speak the righteous words of the Lord, the experience opened up the desire to have understanding and truth in his heart. Everything he had been feeling for the last few years finally made sense. He knew the words of Abinadi to be true, he knew they were the Lord's words. Alma trusted that if he was put to death, then that was the Lord's will. And no matter what, he wanted the Lord's will to be done.

All of a sudden, Alma remembered the young girl he spoke with as the soldiers pulled him out of the water. Excitedly, he hoped that the Lord would provide a way for him, and possibly Abinadi, to escape the wrath of King Noah. He remembered he had dreamed about a small group sent by the Lord to help him, and knew that somehow the Lord would provide a way for him to continue spreading His word. Lost in thought, he did not hear the commander and King Noah finally enter the King's private chambers. Alma did not even look up, nor did he bow to the King.

"Bow when the King enters your presence!" shouted Meles, as he gruffly pushed Alma's head toward the floor.

Suddenly brought back to the moment, Alma looked up and bowed toward the King.

Slowly, the King walked toward his throne, brushing past Alma's bowed head. Reaching his throne, he lifted his robe and fanned the material out wide for everyone to see its bright, beautiful colors. The King loved to be dramatic, and today was no exception. Finally sitting, he took a deep breath. He stared silently at Alma for several awkward minutes, and then, at long last, he spoke.

"So, Alma, you thought you could brainwash my High Priests and turn them against me with your lies of a God and a better way to live. Do you think that life could be any better than what I have given you? Have I not provided you with the very best that this land has to offer? The best clothes, riches, foods, life? And for my generosity, you attempt to turn my most trusted men against me?" he questioned angrily.

"No, Sir," Alma replied meekly. "I have not tried to turn your men against you. I have only believed the words that Abinadi spoke. I then spoke them myself when prompted by the Lord."

"So, how many of them believe as you do?" the King questioned. "How many of my High Priests have you corrupted with your lies?"

"None that I know of, your majesty," Alma replied. "None of the High Priests have felt the same feelings that I have felt."

"I don't believe you!" King Noah yelled. "And now, because of you, I am going to have to test the High Priests' loyalty and possibly have to kill them."

"No, sir. None of the High Priests have been disloyal to you. In fact, they laugh at me for believing the words of Abinadi," Alma replied, afraid for the High Priests' lives and those of their families. "They laughed at the life that I gave up to teach the truth of the Lord."

"Your version of the truth," snapped King Noah.

"Not my version, your majesty, but the Lord's truth," Alma replied, angering the King.

"Untruths, Alma. All untruths. And now, I understand, you sneak around my city to teach your lies secretly to my people?" the King questioned. "Is that true?"

"Yes, your majesty. I have taught some of the people in the city," Alma answered softly. "But only those who would listen. I have not forced anyone to hear the ways of God. They have chosen for themselves that they want a different life—a life that includes righteousness and goodness."

"And we do not have those things already for the people here? I see a lot of goodness. Take a look around the temple. I have gold, silver, Ziff, copper. I see a beautiful, good city with citizens that loves their King and surrounds him with all their possessions," replied King Noah, smiling. "What is not good and righteous here?"

"Not to show you disrespect, Sir, but what I see is a king who takes all the precious things from his people and surrounds himself comfortably with them, leaving his people to work and suffer with next to nothing to feed themselves," answered Alma.

"That is treason, Alma!" shouted the King. He stood from his throne and pointed toward Alma. "Don't you dare speak to me that way. I am still your King and you will show me the respect that I deserve. I demand respect from my people, and I demand the same respect from you. Do you understand me?"

"Yes, your majesty," Alma replied, as Meles squeezed Alma's arm tighter and pushed him down to his knees.

King Noah regained his composure. He turned his back to Alma and spoke privately with the commander for several moments before he turned again toward Alma.

"Alma, even with your blatant disregard for me, I will forgive you and spare your life, if you will but deny this God that Abinadi spoke of," the King said calmly, as he sat down on his throne.

"You know that I cannot do that, King," Alma replied. "I know that He is real and His ways are that of truth and right. Abinadi does not speak for me, I am speaking the feelings of my own heart."

"Ways of truth and right?" scoffed King Noah. "I decide the ways of truth and right. I do not see your God here now. The last I remember, I was the King in this great land. I decide the ways of truth and right for the people in this city. I decide the laws. I decide all, don't I?"

"I answer to the Lord now, King. I know that the people of this great city must repent, or all will be destroyed," Alma replied boldly.

"You will answer to me," King Noah replied harshly, as anger for Alma's words stirred up hatred in his heart. "Deny the words of your God, and I will spare your life, Alma," demanded King Noah. "Or your fate will be that of Abinadi's. This is the last time I will give you this opportunity."

"You know that I cannot deny my God," Alma calmly replied. "But I can teach you His ways, if you will only listen."

"Listen to your blasphemy?" shouted King Noah. "I will not listen to you or to Abinadi. You both speak words that are of evil origin."

Alma looked at the ground, aware that anything he said would not enter King Noah's heart. Sure the next words would be his punishment, Alma remained quiet. Several awkward moments followed as King Noah whispered quietly with the commander. Several times they laughed and pointed toward Alma, as he knelt on the floor.

Finally, King Noah spoke, "Alma, I will give you the same courtesy that I have given to Abinadi. You will be thrown into prison with the traitor, and I will spend the next day with my High Priests. Together we will determine your fate. But, if I find even one of my priests who support or defends you, I will share with him and his family your fate as well. In this way, I will know who is loyal to me and who is not."

Alma nodded at the King without saying a word, and he slowly rose to his feet.

"Soldiers!" yelled King Noah. "Get Alma out of my sight. I do not want to hear his name or see his face until the priests and I decide what to do with him."

"Yes, your majesty," replied Aiath. He violently grabbed Alma's arm and marched him toward the door.

"Tie him, men," ordered King Noah. "Tie him tight, and throw him into the dungeon with the traitor, Abinadi. And be careful, do not listen to his lies as you take him to prison."

The Commander tightened the ropes around Alma's arms so that King Noah could see they were tight. Then, opened the door to the King's private chambers and bowed his head as he led Alma out the door.

"Why did you have to make him so mad, Alma?" questioned Meles. "He gave you the opportunity for freedom."

"Freedom at what cost?" replied Alma meekly. "Freedom at the cost of my soul?"

"Freedom none the less, and really, what was the cost?" asked Aiath. "To deny someone you have never seen nor spoken with?"

"Only my salvation and integrity," replied Alma angrily.

"Integrity. Salvation. Your God does not even exist," replied the Commander.

"He does exist, I have faith that He does. I know that the words He speaks to my heart are real," replied Alma. "He tells me by my feelings that they are real and true."

"And now you will truly die," said Meles. "Because something in your heart gives you feelings that you cannot confirm."

Chapter Seven

Mrs. M., Squeaks, and Tater, finally reached an area at the river's edge to climb onto the bank. Mrs. M. struggled to pull herself out of the water, completely fatigued by the deep dive into the river. She brushed her hair back out of her face and took a quick look around the area, searching for any sign of more soldiers.

"All right, Squeaks, now tell me what you are talking about," said Mrs. M.

"I've been trying to tell you, but all of you are just wasting time," she replied anxiously. "We need to hurry, Alma's life is at stake."

"Alma? What are you talking about, honey?" asked Mrs. M., as she shook her head, confused by what Squeaks was trying to say. "I don't understand what you are talking about. Alma who?"

"We've got to save Alma, you know - the Alma from the Book of Mormon," she replied adamantly.

"I don't understand either, Squeaks," interrupted Butch. "What are you talking about? How do you know that we need to save Alma?"

"That's what I have been trying to tell you," she replied, annoyed by all the questions. "Alma told me what we need to do to save him and his people."

"How could he have done that, Squeaks? Are you seeing visions?" teased Tater, with a chuckle.

"Oh, very funny, guys. If you are not going to believe me, then I need to get back to work," she replied as she started to scoot off the river bank and back into the water.

"Wait a minute, wait a minute!" insisted Mrs. M. "Am I missing something here? I still don't understand. So please, why don't you start from the beginning, and tell me what is going on."

"You remember when I fell in the water?" asked Squeaks abruptly.

"Yes, I remember," Mrs. M. nodded.

"Well, I floated down stream about ten yards or so and finally grabbed hold of some bushes to stop me from continuing down the river. I stopped about where the ledge was located—where Tater and Butch found me. Are you with me so far?" questioned Squeaks.

"I understand," replied Mrs. M. "The sarcasm can stop now, though."

Squeaks smiled and continued. "Well, I heard the soldiers moving closer and closer. So, I slipped under the ledge that protruded over the water, hoping they wouldn't find me there. At the same time that I hid under the ledge, the soldiers found the man they were looking for. He was climbing out of the water a few feet from where I was hiding under the ledge. For several minutes, the soldiers talked to their prisoner. And then, they got very angry with him. They dunked him under the water - head-first—as they held his legs. When they finally pulled him up, he saw me.

"At first, I thought he was going to tell them I was there. But instead, he told me his name was Alma. He told me to find the secret entrance to the hidden Waters of Mormon and the entrance to the city, so we could enter safely. He wants us to save his followers. He told me to be careful of the dangers. He said the Lord would only have allowed him to be caught if there was something more He needed Alma to do. Maybe something with Abinadi."

"Abinadi?" said Mrs. M., shocked at what Squeaks was telling her. "We are in the time of Abinadi, Alma, and King Noah?"

"I think so, Mom," she replied. "I told him that in our records, he did not get caught. Alma said the Lord had showed him in vision that four people would be coming to help him, and that is why he told me where the secret entrance to the hidden Waters of Mormon and the city was located."

"The hidden Waters of Mormon and the entrance to the city?" questioned Butch. "I thought the city is where the soldiers just took the traitor. How could the entrance to the city be in the water?"

"A secret, safe entrance to the city. One where we can get in unnoticed and save the followers of the Lord, so that they are not arrested and killed by King Noah," answered Squeaks.

"How do you know the story of Alma and King Noah so well, Squeaks?" asked Tater.

"That's one of Hero, Bubba, and my favorites," she replied. "King Noah receives the same fate that he demanded happen to Abinadi—death by fire."

"What about Alma? He's not caught anywhere in that story," Butch said worriedly.

"Now you know why I am so anxious to find the secret entrance and save Alma," she replied. "It is because of us that he was caught. We led the soldier's right to him."

"I guess you're right, Squeaks," added Mrs. M. "So what exactly did Alma tell you that we needed to do?"

Squeaks took a deep breath and replied, "Okay, well, right where Tater caved in the ledge lies a secret tunnel. The tunnel leads safely to the hidden Waters of Mormon, which leads us to the city of King Noah."

"I understand that, but how are we supposed to find this secret tunnel?" questioned Mrs. M.

"According to Alma, the tunnel entrance is located under the water and is guarded by unseen dangers. That's what I was searching for when you pulled me to the surface," Squeaks replied. "The dangers that guard the opening to the secret tunnel."

"So, did you find anything that looked like an opening to a tunnel?" questioned Tater.

"Yeah, I think so," replied Squeaks. "Down along the

bottom of the river there are three large rocks—they are stacked together in the shape of a triangle, with two on the bottom and one placed directly on top. Between them I thought I saw an opening; however, the opening is guarded by eels and stingrays. I was about to push through them and see for sure when the ledge gave way."

"Can you still see the opening?" Butch asked excitedly.

"Yes, but the dirt in the water made maneuvering through the underwater creatures more difficult," she replied.

"So, should we start searching and find this secret tunnel?" questioned Tater, excited to start the mission. "I guess Squeaks did figure out where we are and what needs to be done."

"I think we better," replied Mrs. M. "However, this is a particularly scary time in Book of Mormon history. No matter what, we all need to stay together."

"That's going to be kinda hard in the water, Mom," replied Squeaks.

"Well, we need to stay together the best that we can," answered Mrs. M., with a concerned look on her face.

"So, are you ready to go?" questioned Squeaks excitedly. "We have a prophet to rescue."

"Before we go, where is the Liahona?" asked Mrs. M.

"I have it safely hidden in my backpack," Tater replied, as he carefully patted his pack.

"Do you want me to carry your backpack?" asked Mrs. M., worried about the safety of the Liahona.

"No, I can get it to where we are going safely," replied Tater. He slipped his arms through the straps and tightened the pack on his shoulders.

"Then we better get going," Squeaks insisted anxiously.

Mrs. M. took a deep breath and quickly slid back into the river. "Now, you are sure that you have spoken to the Prophet Alma, right?" she questioned one more time.

"Yes, Mom, I'm sure," Squeaks replied, annoyed by the question. "Follow me and I'll lead the way."

Squeaks jumped into the water and quickly started swimming down stream. Not far in the distance, she found the ledge that had caved in. She quickly grabbed hold of a small tree branch. "This is where Alma said the opening was located."

"So, what do we do?" questioned Tater, struggling with the backpack in the water.

"We have to find the secret opening that leads to the Waters of Mormon and the entrance to the city," Squeaks replied.

"Should we all dive under the water and start looking?" Tater asked.

"I think that's the only way we're going to find anything," Squeaks snapped.

"Okay then, let's start," agreed Butch.

"Hold on, wait a minute," insisted Mrs. M. "I have a few rules."

"What, Mom? We need to get going," Squeaks protested, annoyed by another delay.

"I want all of you to be very careful. Don't bother the dangerous creatures; in fact, stay out of their way completely. Stringrays and eels can be deadly animals and not to be underestimated, okay?"

"Okay," agreed Squeaks. She quickly took a breath and disappeared under the water.

"Guys, please do me a favor, and keep an eye on her while you are searching," said Mrs. M. "I really don't want anything bad to happen while we are in this land."

"Don't worry, Mrs. M. We'll watch her," replied Tater, smiling as he disappeared under the surface of the water.

"I'll watch her as well, Mrs. M.," said Butch.

Locating a small gap between two huge stones, Squeaks wiggled her body through the opening feet first. Cautiously lowering herself down into the unknown, she was sure she had found the secret tunnel of which Alma had spoken. Excitedly maneuvering through the opening, she suddenly felt something hard underneath her feet. Unable to see into the darkness, she reached down with her hand and felt the solid object. She worked her body back through the opening and motioned for the others to follow her to the surface.

"What'd ya find?" questioned Tater, as soon as he reached the surface and took a breath.

"Yeah, what's up, Squeaks?" asked Butch. "Did you find the entrance?"

"Come on, honey, did you find something?" questioned Mrs. M., anxious to hear what her daughter had to say.

Squeaks took several deep breaths and calmly replied. "Yes! I think that I have located the entrance to the tunnel."

"All right then, let's go see what we can find!" exclaimed Tater.

"Wait a minute!" called Squeaks, grabbing for Tater's arm. "There is a problem."

"What is it?" demanded Butch.

"Just inside the opening, I located what I think is a ladder that leads deeper into the river bed. I'm not sure how long it will take us to get through, or if we can hold our breath long enough to get safely to the other side without drowning," she answered.

"Well, the only way to find out is to try," replied Butch. "So, let's get going."

"Now, wait a minute. Squeaks has a good point. I don't want anyone to get hurt or run out of breath," insisted Mrs. M. "So, before we go, what ideas do we have so no one gets hurt?"

"Why don't we go one at a time?" offered Butch. "That way, if there's a problem, we can get back to the surface and make another plan."

"I'll go first," insisted Squeaks. She took a deep breath and started to dive under the water.

"No, no, no, Squeaks," protested Mrs. M. "You're not going first."

"I'm the only one who knows where the entrance is," Squeaks argued.

"Then you will have to show Tater where it is," Mrs. M. insisted. "Tater, Butch, strap your backpacks on tightly so we don't lose them. Tater, you will go first. We'll give you two minutes to return. If you don't, then Squeaks will go next, followed by Butch, and I will be last. Okay?"

"I guess," Squeaks answered sadly.

"Good, then let's all dive down to where you think

the entrance is. After that, we'll all come back to the surface, and Tater will start," suggested Mrs. M.

"Everybody, follow me," said Squeaks. She took a large breath of air and quickly dove under the water's surface.

The falling debris from the ledge had scared the dangerous animals away from the entrance, and Squeaks quickly swam to the huge boulders and pointed to the opening carefully hidden between them. They all quickly located the opening she pointed to and then headed for the surface.

"Wow, how did you ever find that, Squeaks?" asked Butch. "I never would have thought to look inside there."

Squeaks smiled, wiped the water from her eyes, and shrugged her shoulders, glad to be helping the Team.

"Okay, I'm gonna go try out the opening and see what I can find. Wish me luck," said Tater as he took several quick breaths, then a deep breath, and dove below toward the bottom and the secret entrance.

Tater reached the opening between the rocks and crawled through the gap feet-first. He quickly found the stone ladder that Squeaks told him about. Feeling his way down the narrow flight of six stone steps, he was amazed to find a small round hole cut into the stone, marking a passage down a stone tunnel. Unable to see in the darkness inside, Tater let the water current pull him down the tunnel. He was sure it would lead him through the strange, silent underground world to the hidden Waters of Mormon and the city that Alma had spoken about.

Suddenly, he felt the ceiling of the tunnel jet upward. Hopeful it would be an air pocket, as his air supply was running thin, he pushed himself up inside and was relieved to be able to take a breath. After several deep breaths, Tater again filled his lungs with as much air as he could hold. He dove underneath the water and followed the current down the narrow stone tunnel.

Squeaks, excited to follow Tater, started counting out loud. "One, two, three… seventy-one, seventy-two."

"Why are you counting, Squeaks?" asked Butch.

"As soon as I get to one hundred twenty, then I'm following Tater to see where that opening goes," she replied excitedly.

Mrs. M. and Butch listened to every number. Then they watched as Squeaks nervously took a big breath and disappeared under the water's edge.

"I'm not going to count, if that's okay with you," said Butch, smiling. He tried to watch Squeaks' movements under the water.

"Yes, that's fine," replied Mrs. M. "Butch, I think we're probably okay to start. Why don't you go ahead, and I will be right behind you."

Butch nodded. He glanced one last time into the dark-blue water, took a large breath, and disappeared underneath the surface. Mrs. M. looked around the area, making sure they were not being followed. Then she took a deep breath and disappeared into the water.

Squeaks gasped for breath as she located the small air pocket in the dark tunnel. She quickly took another breath and headed further into the darkness of the tunnel. Rubbing her hand along the smooth rock, she followed the tunnel approximately thirty yards, when the darkness of the tunnel finally gave way to light above. Squeaks had exhausted every last ounce of air in her lungs, as she raced for the surface of the water. At last, she broke through the surface of the water and felt the warm sun on her face. She quickly wiped her blonde hair off her face and the water out of her eyes. Then she watched as the sun started to rise above the edge of the mountains.

"I made it!" she thought to herself, as she looked around the area, grateful for the sun's first rays of the day.

Suddenly, she saw a shadow from the corner of her eye. Afraid it could be an alligator coming toward her, she swam as fast as she could toward the lake's edge. She never stopped until she pulled her small water-logged body onto the grass-covered bank.

"Squeaks, where are ya going?" called Tater, as he watched her frantically swimming. "Squeaks!"

Sure she was safe, she looked back over the small lake she had just crawled out of to see what the shadow was and noticed Tater watching her.

"So, what are you doing, Squeaks?" asked Tater, holding his hand above the water and shrugging his shoulders.

"I thought you were an alligator or something," she replied giggling, relieved the shadow was Tater. "Where were you?"

"I swam over to the other side of the lake to see if I could see anything," Tater replied, pointing.

"Did you?" she asked.

"No. Have you seen Butch or your mom yet?" he asked.

"Not yet, but they should be at least a minute or two behind me," Squeaks replied. "Can you believe that we found the right opening?"

"Sure I can. We all have faith in the Lord, don't we?" Tater questioned. "I'm sure the Lord guided you to where we needed to go."

"I hadn't thought about that, but I guess you're right," replied Squeaks.

"This place is really cool!" said Tater, as he looked around. "Especially in the light of day. Everything is absolutely beautiful."

Squeaks quickly noticed the humid air as she struggled to breathe. She stood up and forcefully took a deep breath, compelling her lungs to work in the hot, muggy weather. As she took several deep breaths, she noticed a forest of lush, green trees behind her. She was amazed by the beauty of the area. Ahead of her was a small waterfall that seemed to fall over the mountain's edge and drop about thirty feet, splashing into the river below. The waterfall was completely covered by banyan and umbrella trees, hiding its beauty from the sky above. As she watched the water majestically bubble into the river and flow to the lake she had just climbed out of, Squeaks suddenly noticed how hidden the area around her was.

"We could disappear in this forest," she said nervously. "Trees, bushes, and mountains are everywhere."

"Wait till you see the flowers," added Tater, pointing toward the waterfall.

"And the bugs," added Butch, as he suddenly emerged from the hidden tunnel. "I can see several from here."

"Bugs?" asked Mrs. M., popping up from underneath the water. "What kind of bugs?"

"Well, if you look by Squeaks' right foot, I can see a

colony of rhinoceros beetles. Not far above her head, in the trees, I can see an emerald tree boa snake. Three or four branches above the snake, I can see a beautiful yellow and red toucan. I can hear several species of monkeys, although I haven't seen one yet. And I'm sure there are numerous species of spiders because, on the tree next to Squeaks, I can see three different spider web designs," explained Butch. "That doesn't account for what I can't see yet or all the sounds that can be heard in the forest."

"Am I safer in the water?" questioned Squeaks, nervously noticing the animals around her.

"Not necessarily," replied Tater. "There really could be several different species of alligators in the water, not to mention piranha, eels, and stingrays like we saw earlier."

"You two are scaring me," whimpered Squeaks, unsure what to do. "I've been trying to be really brave, but I'm not sure I can if you keep this up."

"All right, so, where are we boys - any ideas?" asked Mrs. M., trying to change the subject. "And is everybody okay?"

"Well, judging by the dead leaves on the ground, moist foliage in the trees, and the abundant streams and waterfalls around, I would have to say we are in a rainforest somewhere," Tater replied sarcastically.

"I could kinda get that on my own," replied Mrs. M., smiling at Tater. "But is everybody okay?"

"Yes, I think we're all right," replied Butch. "The tunnel was long, but with the air pocket, it was doable!"

"Squeaks, what about you? Did you find the air pocket?" asked Mrs. M.

"Yes, I never could have held my breath all the way through the tunnel without it," she replied.

"So, what do we do now?" Butch asked.

"We've got to find and save Alma," insisted Squeaks. "Who knows what King Noah has done by now."

"Well first, we need to get out of this lake. Then we need to make a plan and see what supplies we have with us. I don't know about you kids, but I am starving," replied Mrs. M. She quickly swam toward Squeaks, who was standing on the edge of the lake. "We need to find some food."

"Good idea," agreed Tater. "If everything is not ruined in my backpack, I know I have some granola bars and a few other treats."

Everyone hurried to the edge of the lake and climbed out of the water. Tater and Butch—the only two with backpacks—quickly pulled their packs off their shoulders. They unzipped the bags and dumped the contents onto the grassy knoll just above the crystal-blue waters.

"I've got a flashlight," said Butch, holding it up for everyone to see.

"And I've got a flashlight, a Book of Mormon, and the Liahona," said Tater. "But everything is totally soaked."

"Here's toilet paper, but, I think it might be ruined," said Squeaks, smiling as she held the dripping paper up for everyone to see.

"Tater, I thought you said you had food in your pack," questioned Butch, not seeing it anywhere on the ground.

"I do," he replied. "But my stash is in a different pock-et. Hold on a second."

Tater quickly grabbed his pack, unzipped another pocket, and dumped the contents onto the grass.

"All right! You put everything in a plastic bag," announced Squeaks excitedly. "Good job!"

"I don't take any chances with food," replied Tater smiling. "I'd never make it if something happened to my secret stash."

"Look what I found!" called Mrs. M., standing ten feet away, next to a palm tree.

"What?" asked Squeaks, looking at her mom. "What did you find?"

"Come over here," said Mrs. M. "Quick! You're gonna be so happy."

Squeaks jumped to her feet and hurried over to where her mom was pointing. A smile engulfed her face when she saw the bananas that were hanging in the banana palm tree above her head. Excitedly, she scurried up the tree and pulled down a bundle of bananas. Unable to hold the bananas and climb down the tree, she dropped them to the ground and slid down the tree. As she reached the bottom of the tree, she grabbed the bananas and headed quickly back toward the others.

"Did you get enough for all of us?" asked Tater, when he noticed the bananas in Squeaks' hand.

"You bet I did," she replied. "There are eight here; that's enough for two bananas each."

"Look what else I found, kids," called Mrs. M., now about twenty feet from the water's edge.

"What is it, Mrs. M.?" yelled Butch, as he peeled a banana and took a bite.

"Berries," she excitedly replied. "I think we're going to have plenty of food here any time we need it."

"I think you're right, Mrs. M.," said Tater. "With my graham crackers, granola, and the fruit you're finding, we're going to be in great shape."

They quietly ate. Mrs. M. looked over the area, awed by the beauty that surrounded them. The lake was in the center of the small valley. The valley was completely overgrown with trees, hiding the area. Only scattered rays of light made it through the area to the group below. The lake was small but exquisite; the water was a clear, azure-blue, with a white sand floor shimmering beneath it in the early morning sun. The lake's beauty was only disturbed by tiny white ripples from the river where the waterfall softly flowed over the cliff's ledge thirty feet above.

As Mrs. M. scanned the area, she found that other than the foliage, they were completely surrounded in the valley by red and orange rock cliffs. They started where the dense trees, shrubs, and bushes ended. The plant life was as diverse as she had ever seen. There was nearly every type of flower that she knew, plus many others surrounding them. The animal life was abundant. There were vibrantly colored fish in the lake, dragonflies flittering through the area, beautiful birds singing joyfully in the trees, and monkeys squawking noisily above their heads. It was apparent that the monkeys were annoyed by the interruption to their playful swinging.

Enjoying the handful of berries that she had picked, Mrs. M. watched as the kids devoured three packages of graham crackers, every banana, and still looked for more.

"Mom, can I have your berries?" asked Squeaks, with a huge, cheesy grin smugly spread across her face. "Please?"

"No way! Pick your own," replied Mom, smiling as she pointed toward the berry plants. "There are hundreds of them."

"Would it be all right if I took a short nap, Mrs. M? Do you think we have enough time?" Tater questioned. "I'm so tired, and I know that the sun is just climbing over the mountains. Maybe I could get an hour of sleep before we start our adventure today."

"No way, we have a job to do," replied Squeaks, not even looking at Tater. "We don't have time for a nap."

"Actually, I think that is a very good idea," replied Mrs. M. "And you can take a nap as well, Squeaks. If we don't get a little sleep, we could end up in a lot of trouble."

"For how long?" complained Squeaks, almost in tears. "We've got stuff to do!"

"No more than an hour," replied Mrs. M. "I think we could all get by on a power nap of an hour. What do you think, Butch?"

Several seconds passed in silence with no response from Butch, before Mrs. M. looked at him and found that he was already fast asleep. Reluctantly, Squeaks lied down on the long, soft, cool grass. Thirty seconds had barely passed before she was asleep as well.

"Come on, Tater, you too," Mrs. M. insisted. "I will keep watch while you try to get a little sleep."

"Do you think we have anything to worry about in this hidden valley?" Tater questioned nervously. "Like soldiers?"

"I don't think so," Mrs. M. replied. "I'm not sure anything could get in or out of here without someone telling them exactly how to do it. Now, rest quickly, and I will wake everyone up in an hour."

Chapter Eight

Hero cleared his throat, looked over at his anxious teammates, looked back at Aunt Maggie and began explaining. "Well, you know how we, I mean the Team, we have been searching for the treasure from the map that we found at Mr. Jensen's house several days ago?"

"Yes, I am aware of the map that the Team called Moroni's treasure map," Aunt Maggie replied, watching Hero's every nervous move.

"That's right, Moroni's treasure map. Well, we searched for a few days, and to our surprise we found clue after clue on our quest," replied Hero.

"Yes, your mom told me," said Aunt Maggie, waiting anxiously for more information.

"We ended up being chased by prison escapees, found hidden warm springs in the mountain, and passageways with a man from another time," explained Hero.

"Even bats—tons and tons of bats," interrupted Stick.

"Okay, go on," replied Aunt Maggie, cautious not to push for too much information.

"Well in the end, surprisingly enough, we actually found a small ancient-looking box that was hidden where the map indicated it would be," said Hero.

"All right, so you found this map, you followed the clues all over the valley, and in the end, you actually found a small wooden treasure box, right?" questioned Aunt Maggie.

"Exactly!" answered KP.

"And what exactly does this have to do with where your mother is right now, Hero?" Aunt Maggie asked, confused by what the Team was telling her.

"I'm getting to that," he replied, as he took another deep breath.

"Tell her about what we found, Hero," insisted Stick.

"Well, after we found the box, of course the first thing we wanted to do was open it," started Hero.

"Yeah, I wanted to be rich!" yelled Red. "And I was sure the box was filled with gold coins."

"And what did you find, Team? Quit stalling," insisted Aunt Maggie, a little aggravated.

"We found a treasure inside the box that we didn't expect," replied Bubba.

"What was it?" Aunt Maggie demanded.

"It was...," Hero paused again, looking at his teammates.

"It was what, Hero?" pressed Aunt Maggie, eager to learn what they found.

"It was a small, beautifully decorated, very ornate, gold, softball-shaped item," blurted Bear, unable to stand Hero's suspense.

"A ball?" replied Aunt Maggie. "Your treasure was a ball?"

"Yes, a ball," answered Hero. "A very special ball."

"Alright, Team, I don't understand the correlation here. What in the world does a small, beautiful ornate ball have to do with your mom's whereabouts?" asked Aunt Maggie, annoyed by all the mystery.

"This ball is one that you would recognize, Mom," said Bear.

"One I would recognize?" Aunt Maggie asked, still confused.

"Yes, a ball that has been described in the records of the church," answered Bean.

"Okay, enough with the drama and suspense," said Aunt Maggie. "Will someone please tell me what in the world is going on around here? Where is your mom? Where are the rest of your teammates? And what does this church ball have to do with where they are?"

"The ball is actually the Liahona," said KP.

"And the Liahona, as you know, is only sent by the Lord for the direction of the saints," said Bean.

"And it can only be used by those who have faith," added Stick.

"And that was the treasure we found," said Bubba excitedly.

"Wait a minute! Are you telling me that you found the Liahona?" asked a stunned Aunt Maggie. "The one written about in the Book of Mormon?"

"Yeah, the one written about in the Book of Mormon, only it's not exactly the same, there are a few differences," answered Red. "This one leads you to a place in history where something has gone wrong."

"Will someone please start from the beginning?" begged Aunt Maggie, as she rubbed her forehead. "I'm not sure that I completely understanding what you are all telling me."

Hero looked at the Team and motioned for them to be quiet, then explained, "Aunt Maggie, during our search for Moroni's treasure, we located a small box."

"I understand that, so far," she replied, still rubbing her head.

"Inside the box we found a ball-shaped object that we have now determined is the Liahona—the one spoken of in the Book of Mormon," Hero continued.

"Okay, I think I am with you so far," replied Aunt Maggie. "Although I'm not exactly sure how any of that has anything to do with your mom."

"After checking the ball out thoroughly, we know for sure that the Lord has sent us this Liahona," Bubba said calmly.

"So, you are telling me that the map led you to this Liahona, which you know for sure is from the Lord?" questioned Aunt Maggie, looking at the boys.

"Yes, that is correct so far," replied Hero.

"Is there more?" asked Aunt Maggie.

"Yes!" exclaimed Bear. "Now we're finally getting to the good part."

Aunt Maggie took a deep breath, letting the air from her lungs puff out her cheeks. Then she replied, "Just getting to the good part?"

"Yes," replied Hero. "We know the Liahona is sent from the Lord because it transports us to a time in Book of Mormon history where something has gone wrong and has to be fixed."

"What?" exclaimed Aunt Maggie. "Are you telling me that your mom, Squeaks, and I don't know who else from this Team, has been sent to a place in Book of Mormon history by the Liahona?"

"No, not sent by the Liahona," replied Bubba. "We are sent by the Lord, to do His work with the aid of the Liahona for direction."

"How do you get to Book of Mormon time?" questioned Aunt Maggie, not sure she believed what the Team was telling her.

"The Liahona flashes a number. Within a few seconds of flashing the number, it takes four people, and suddenly you find yourself in another land and time," replied Bean.

"And how exactly do all of you know this?" Aunt Maggie asked skeptically.

"Because…," started Hero, when Bear suddenly pushed his shoulder.

"This is not the time for secrets, Bear! How do you know this?" she asked again.

"We know this because we have all been on one of the Lord's missions," replied Bubba.

"What?" exclaimed Aunt Maggie. "You kids have traveled to Book of Mormon times without an adult?"

"Yes," replied Hero.

"And we figured out what the problem was, we were able to fix the problem, and then we returned home before we ran out of time," replied Stick.

"Ran out of time? Is there a certain amount of time in which you have to solve the mystery?" questioned Aunt Maggie, somewhat sick to her stomach.

"Yes. We don't know exactly how long it is for sure, but we know that we only have seven of the Lord's days before we are stuck in that Book of Mormon time forever," answered Red.

"Oh my, are your serious? Stuck there forever?" demanded Aunt Maggie.

"We've already been on two of the Lord's missions, Mom. And both groups were able to do what was required in the allotted amount of time, and still return home safely," replied Bear.

"Have you gone on one of these missions, Bear?" Aunt Maggie asked worriedly.

"Yes, I just got back," Bear replied softly, worried about her response.

"And you didn't tell me?" she asked angrily.

"Mom, it's not like you choose when you go, and there is no planning or preparation," replied Bear.

"What do you mean?" she asked.

"At random times, the Liahona flashes a set of numbers," started Hero. "Within about ten seconds, a burst of bright light penetrates the entire area, and suddenly, whoever is holding the Liahona, plus three others, disappear into Book of Mormon lands," explained Hero.

"Have you been on a mission, Hero?" Aunt Maggie asked.

"Yes. Bubba, Bean, KP, and I went on the first mission," he replied.

"Well, how many of these missions are there?" she questioned.

"There could be thousands," replied Stick.

"Or at least as many as the Lord determines," added Bean.

Aunt Maggie sat at the kitchen table, staring into space. She was totally confused by everything she had just learned. Unable to comprehend where her sister might currently be, she suddenly realized that the Team was explaining in detail the fact that her sister, Mrs. M., had been sent on a mission by the Lord to another time. She suddenly looked up with a terrified expression across her face and asked, "How does the group get home?"

"That's the tricky part," replied KP.

"What do you mean?" she asked nervously.

"Once they have solved the mystery and have done what the Lord sent them to do in that time, the Liahona will again flash and bring them home," he replied.

"How do they know if they have done what the Lord wanted them to do?" Aunt Maggie asked.

"They have to wait for the numbers on the Liahona to flash," replied Bean.

"And if they don't?" asked Aunt Maggie.

"Then they have not solved the problem that the Lord

has sent them there to solve," replied Bubba.

"This sounds so complicated. Are you sure that these missions can be solved in the amount of time that they have?" Aunt Maggie fearfully asked.

"Well, if you want to know what I think," started Red, "the time that is allowed isn't always enough. That is what I think happened to Mr. Jensen's great-grandfather."

"What happened?" Aunt Maggie worriedly asked.

"Mr. Jensen told us that his great-grandfather left on a mission, only he never returned," answered Red.

"So you're saying that there is a chance that they won't solve the problem, and they could possibly be stuck in Book of Mormon time forever?" whimpered Aunt Maggie.

"It's possible," replied KP.

"Okay, then how can we help them? Is there any way that we can communicate with them?" Aunt Maggie asked.

"There is one way, but it is very dangerous," replied Hero.

"What is it?" demanded Aunt Maggie, anxious to speak with her sister.

"On the missions so far, we have been able to communicate with the traveling Team using our walkie-talkie. However, if we try to call them, we could possibly put them in a dangerous position," replied Hero.

"A very dangerous position!" said KP. "Squeaks almost got us killed on our mission."

"Do they have a walkie-talkie with them?" Aunt Maggie asked excitedly.

"We think they do," replied Bean. "Mrs. M. was not expecting to go on this mission, it was an accident. So, we're not really sure what supplies they do have.

"When I called for you on the walkie-talkie, could I have possibly put them in danger without knowing?" she asked fearfully.

"That's possible; but with any luck, Tater has the walkie-talkie turned off," replied Bubba, trying to consol his aunt.

"Is there anything else we can do?" she asked.

"Not really," replied Hero. "Not until they contact us."

"So, we just have to sit here and wait?" exclaimed Aunt Maggie.

"Yep, that's all we can do," replied Bear.

"What about your dad, boys? Have you told him yet?" she asked, picking up the phone to call him.

"NO!" exclaimed Hero. "And you can't tell him."

"We have to," insisted Aunt Maggie.

"That's why we told you! So that you could help us," replied Hero.

"Yeah, Mom. Mr. Jensen told us that if people found out, we could be in real danger," said Bear.

"I don't think Hero's dad is very dangerous," replied Aunt Maggie.

"Please, Mom, please," begged Bear. "Can you help us see if we can figure out how to get them home before you tell Hero and Bubba's dad?"

"What if they don't make it home by tonight?" asked Aunt Maggie. "I won't lie to him about where they are."

"Will you at least give us until eight o'clock tonight?" asked Stick. "It's possible that they could be home by then."

Aunt Maggie looked around the room at all of the teammate's faces for several nerve racking moments before she finally replied, "I guess I can help you until eight o'clock. But after that, if their dad asks me, I'm going to have to tell him. Fair?"

"I guess so," replied Bear, looking around at the Team and shrugging his shoulders.

Chapter Nine

"Aaaaahhhhhh!" Squeaks screamed uncontrollably. "Aaaaaahhhhhh! Save me! Save me!"

"What is it, Squeaks?" asked Tater, with his eyes still closed. "I was having a really great dream."

"Aaaaahhhhhh!" she screamed again. "Help me!"

"What is the matter?" demanded Butch, annoyed that she woke him.

"A thing, a thing is sniffing and licking my leg, like it is food," she frantically replied.

"A thing?" asked Mrs. M.

"Yes!" Squeaks screamed. "A thing. Look, quick, before it eats me."

"Oooohhhh!" shouted Mrs. M., surprised by the small pig-like animal that was eating the leftover berries from their breakfast. "What is it?"

Tater finally opened his eyes. Surprised by the animal in front of him, he slowly sat up to get a good look. "I know what it is," he said excitedly. "I saw a documentary on these animals."

"What is it?" questioned Butch. "Is this a long lost dinosaur?"

"No, it's not a dinosaur. I've never seen one of these in person, but I have seen Discovery Channel programs about them," he replied.

"Okay, okay. What in the world is this little thing?" asked Mrs. M. "I've never seen one either."

"Well, they are called tapirs," Tater replied smugly.

"And what do they do, besides lick your legs?" asked Squeaks. She pulled her legs up closer to her body, hoping the tapir would leave her alone.

"From what I remember, mature tapirs can weigh up to six hundred fifty pounds. They are black and white with medium-length anteater-style noses. They live alone, around water, and eat leaves, fruit, and roots. They're great swimmers, runners, and are very good hill climbers. But, they're very aggressive if cornered."

"Wow, Tater, very impressive," said Mrs. M., as she maneuvered slowly to her feet. "I can't believe you remembered so much about them."

The tapir, frightened by Mrs. M.'s movements, suddenly stiffened his body, grunted several times, almost whistled, then sprinted toward the water. It stopped at the river's edge, looked back at them, and then dove into the water, abruptly disappearing behind the waterfall.

"Wow, that was scary," said Squeaks, as she finally dared to move.

"I can't believe I really got to see a tapir," exclaimed Tater. "I've always wanted to see one in real life."

"What time is it, Tater?" questioned Squeaks.

"I don't know for sure. I think my battery is dead because the hands on my watch are not moving," he replied. "Mrs. M., what time does your watch say it is back at home?" asked Tater, as he tapped the face of his watch.

"I'm not sure my watch is working either," Mrs. M. replied, as she shook her hand, trying to make her watch work. "I think something happened to it when we went through the secret underwater tunnel. What about yours, Butch?"

"Nope, mine's not working either," replied Butch.

"Whatever time it is doesn't matter; we've got work to do," insisted Squeaks, standing up and brushing off the dirt on her pants.

"You're right, Squeaks. However, as you three slept, I studied the area. And I found nothing to indicate an entrance or exit. I'm not sure there is a way out of this small, hidden valley. I think you would have to stumble on this area to find it, kinda like we did," replied Mrs. M.

"Well, we're gonna have to check the area to be positive, 'cause I know there has to be something around here that will lead us to the city. Alma said there was a secret way from the hidden Waters of Mormon to the city," insisted Squeaks.

"Squeaks is right. We should split up and search the area," said Butch.

"I don't know if splitting up is good thing to do, but I agree that we need to search this area," said Tater.

"The valley is small," started Mrs. M. "Tater, you and Butch head to the north, and Squeaks and I will start searching to the south. If you find something, holler. I'm sure we'll be able to hear you."

Tater nodded. He grabbed Butch's shirt, pulling him up. Heading in the opposite direction of the girls they immediately disappeared into the thick bushes and trees. Surrounded by steep mountains on all sides, they walked to the closest rocks and studied the rock patterns. The boys wandered for nearly thirty minutes, circling halfway around the small valley, finding nothing - no tunnels, doorways, caves - nothing that would help them find a way to King Noah's city.

"I can't find anything, Tater. Can you?" asked Butch.

"Nothing that jumps right out at me," replied Tater. "I wonder if Squeaks or Mrs. M. found anything. We've almost circled the valley. They can't be too much further away."

"Let's find out," suggested Butch. He placed his hand next to his mouth and yelled, "Squeaks, Mrs. M., where are you? Did you find anything?"

The boys listened for several seconds before they heard Squeaks calling them.

"I can hear her!" shouted Tater. "She doesn't sound too far away."

The boys started calling Squeaks' name, trying to locate the two girls by the sound of their voices. They maneuvered their way through the thickest grasses, bushes, and trees they had encountered so far. They struggled to push through the bushes for about thirty yards before finally reaching a small opening where they suddenly spotted Squeaks and Mrs. M.

"What'd ya find? Anything?" asked Tater, hopeful the girls had more luck than they had.

"I don't know, for sure, if we found anything," replied Squeaks. "But I did find something interesting that was carved into the mountainside close to the waterfall."

"What was it?" asked Butch, annoyed by Squeak's drama.

"Follow me, and I will show you," said Squeaks, excited about her discovery. "Mom is still there looking at the carvings, trying to find a clue."

The boys quietly followed Squeaks along the rock wall, about the length of a football field. Then Tater spotted Mrs. M. running her hands along the wall.

"What'd ya find?" he excitedly called. "Did you find a tunnel?"

"No, not yet. But we did find some really cool drawings on the mountainside," she replied, motioning for them to come and see. "Hurry! Look!"

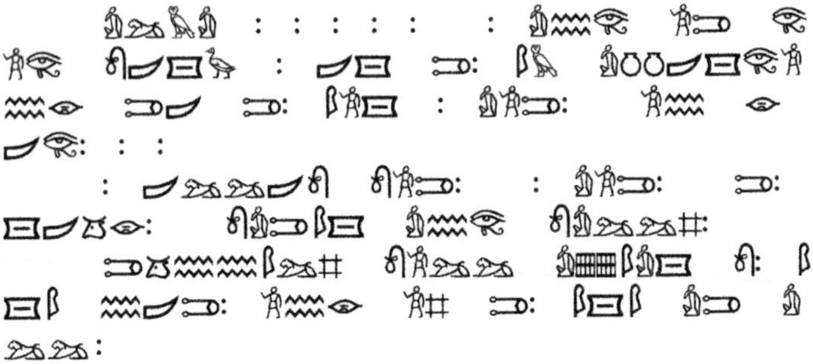

[hieroglyphic text]

"What do you think it means?" asked Squeaks as she rubbed her hand across the hieroglyphs that were engraved on the wall.

"I have no idea," replied Tater. "I wish I knew how to read them."

"Do we have anything from the library that could help us?" asked Butch. "Like we did for Hero and Bubba? We've been to the library a thousand times in the last few days."

"We got help from Cheri at the library, remember?" replied Squeaks. "We never really had a book or anything, except the Egyptian numbers book that Bean checked out."

"Cheri, the librarian, knows about this?" questioned a surprised Mrs. M.

"Uh, yeah, Mrs. M., she's been helping us from the very beginning," Butch replied hesitantly. "We've found all sorts of Egyptian clues and things."

"We're going to have a serious talk when I get back home," replied Mrs. M., smiling. "I can't believe she helped you without telling me."

"She only helped us translate the clues that we kept

finding," said Tater. "And we made her promise not to tell anyone—no matter what."

"And she was able to read this writing?" asked Mrs. M.

"Yeah," replied Butch.

"Wait a minute. When the soldiers were searching for the man, didn't you say that the walkie-talkie went off?" questioned Mrs. M. "Isn't that what made the loud noise?"

"Yes," answered Tater. "I completely forgot about the walkie-talkie. I put it in my pants' pocket after I turned it off."

Tater pulled the walkie-talkie from his right front pocket and turned the black knob clockwise, but he could hear nothing. Anxiously, he turned up the volume all the way.

"Does it work?" asked Mrs. M. nervously. "Can we communicate with the Team back home?"

"We sure can," replied Tater excitedly. "That is how Hero and Bubba deciphered the clues when they were on their mission. They would call us and describe the hieroglyphs. Then we would take the descriptions to Cheri, and she would help us figure them out. After that, we would call Hero and Bubba and tell them what the hieroglyph meant. It's just, right now, either the batteries are dead, or they are…"

"They are what?" demanded Squeaks.

"They're completely soaked with water from the swim we took earlier," Tater replied. "And until they dry out, the walkie-talkie is not going to work."

"That could take hours," cried Butch.

"Hours? We don't have hours!" Squeaks complained.

"We've already wasted enough time as it is."

"Tater, do you think we could try to dry out the batteries?" questioned Mrs. M. "And maybe the interior compartment of the walkie-talkie? Maybe the batteries are unable to make a good connection because the inside is wet."

Tater shrugged his shoulders and replied, "I don't know if it will work, but we could try. I guess drying everything out isn't going to hurt anything."

Tater removed the back cover and popped the three small batteries into his hand. He handed Butch the walkie-talkie, and both boys quickly worked on drying everything. As soon as they were done, they put the walkie-talkie back together, and Tater turned it to the ON position.

"Does it work?" Squeaks nervously asked.

"That's what I'm about to find out, Squeaks," replied Tater, as he turned the knob on and hoped for static on the other end.

"Hey, I heard that!" shouted Squeaks, scaring several birds from the trees above her head.

"Ssshhh," warned Tater. "Just because this valley feels like it's safe doesn't, mean that it is."

"Yeah, but the walkie-talkie, I heard the walkie-talkie. Does it work?" Squeaks asked excitedly.

"Sounds like it might," replied Tater, smiling as he held it up for Squeaks to see. "At least for a minute, or two."

"Well, let's try to call the Team back home," insisted Squeaks, reaching for the unit.

"I'll do it," replied Tater, holding the walkie-talkie out of her reach.

"Mom," cried Squeaks. "Tater's teasing me."

"No he's not," she swiftly replied. "But I am excited, Tater. Why don't you try to see if we can reach anyone back at home?"

"All right, Mrs. M.," he replied, smiling. Tater quickly set the walkie-talkie channel to the Team's secret channel—fifteen, sub-station two. He fiddled with the volume control, then finally pushed the talk button. "Hero, Bubba, anybody there?" he nervously called.

Several awkward, silent moments passed with no response. Anxiously, Tater again pushed the talk button and called, "Team, Hero, Bubba, anybody! Come on, guys! Are you there? Someone, please answer. We need your help."

Again, they anxiously waited for a response. Nearly one full minute passed before finally a scratchy voice muttered several unrecognizable words through the walkie-talkie.

"It works, it works!" Squeaks screamed excitedly. "The Team back home can hear us."

"Sssshhh, Squeaks. I'm trying to hear what they're saying," Butch replied angrily.

"Tater, let me see that walkie-talkie," insisted Mrs. M. She took the small unit from his hands. "Let me try."

"Hero, this is Mom," she called loudly. "Are you there?"

"Mrs. M., you have to push the talk button," said Butch, smiling and pointing toward the front of the walkie-talkie. "You know, right here."

"Oh, I forgot," she said, shaking her head. "My nerves are shot! Thanks, Butch." She pushed the small black button and called again, "Hero, Bubba, is anyone there?"

Again, several quiet moments passed before several recognizable words rang through the small speaker.

"I'm here. Mom, can you hear me?" called Hero, excited to hear her voice.

"Yes, I hear you, and we are all doing fine," she replied. "But I sure wish I knew why I was here. I didn't believe that the Liahona really worked. When we first got here, I was sure this was some trick you and the Team were playing on me."

"This is no joke, Mom," replied Hero. "I tried to tell you."

"I know that now," she swiftly replied. "Hero, I wish you boys would have told me about the Liahona earlier, so I wouldn't have been caught in a very unexpected situation."

"Sorry, Mom. You know I wish I was the one on the mission and not you," Hero replied. "We were going to put the Liahona away so that no one would have to go on another mission for awhile."

"Well, that didn't work so well, did it?" Mrs. M. asked sarcastically. "Now, Tater, Butch, and Squeaks have filled me in on what we have to do. We've found a clue, but we're going to need your help to figure out what the hieroglyphs mean and what they are telling us to do."

"Okay, Mom," Hero replied. "What is the clue you've found?"

Tater grabbed the walkie-talkie out of Mrs. M.'s hand, fiddled with the volume, and replied, "Hero, we've got to hurry. Our walkie-talkie isn't working very well, and I'm afraid we're going to lose the signal-like we did during your mission."

"It's good to hear your voice, Tater," replied Hero. "I've got paper. What's your clue?"

"Okay, it is a series of ancient writings and pictures. They start with a picture of a kneeling man, then the side view of a jaguar, an owl, and then a kneeling man again. Then there is a break, followed by three upside down U's, seven lines, another break, then four upside down U's. Do you have that so far?"

"Yep, is there more?" asked Hero.

"Tons," replied Tater.

"Keep going then, quick," insisted Hero, writing as rapidly as he could.

"All right, the next series of pictures starts with the kneeling man, two zigzag lines, the all seeing eye, a break, then a standing man, the prongs on a plug, another break, then the all seeing eye, the standing man, and then another all seeing eye. Hero, are you still there?" questioned Tater, afraid the walkie-talkie had gone dead.

"I'm still here," Hero replied. "Keep go…"

"Hero, Hero, are you there?" Tater called nervously.

"Oh no! Did we lose him?" cried Squeaks. "We'll never figure this clue out without their help."

"Relax a minute, Squeaks," said Tater calmly. "Let me see if I can make it work again.

Tater quickly popped the batteries out of the walkie-talkie, dried them and the interior off with his shirt, and placed them back inside. He reset the channel and quickly tried to call Hero again.

"Hello, anybody there?" Tater called anxiously.

Several nervous seconds passed before Tater heard,

"I'm here. We better hurry, Tater. It doesn't sound like your walkie-talkie is going to last very long, so get going," suggested Hero.

Tater quickly found where he had left off and started describing the ancient hieroglyphics. He explained every symbol as fast as he could, sure at any second the walkie-talkie would quit working.

"Okay, Tater, we'll get back to you as soon as we know something," replied Hero.

"Don't take too long," insisted Tater. "We've already had a run in with some soldiers. And because we don't know exactly what we're doing yet, I don't want to take any more risks than we have to."

"We'll hurry, I promise," replied Hero. "But Tater, do me a favor, will you?"

"What's that?" Tater asked.

"Take care of everyone and get them back here safely, will ya?" Hero asked in a nervous, scared voice.

"I'll try," Tater answered. He switched off the power to the walkie-talkie, and breathed a cautious sigh of relief.

Chapter Ten

"I can't believe all of this is real!" exclaimed Aunt Maggie.

"Did you think we were kidding, Mom?" asked Bear.

"Well, all of it is a little far fetched, don't you think?" she replied.

"Not really, but then I have been on a mission," Bear answered smiling.

"Okay, Team, you heard Tater. He sounded scared and nervous. I guess we're all in this together," said Aunt Maggie. "We better get to work. How do we go about deciphering the clues he explained to us? Do you have a book or something that you have used before to find the information we need to solve the clue?"

"No. Actually, Aunt Maggie, we've got to go to the library," replied Bean, as she threw her backpack over her shoulder. "And we better get a move on."

"The library? What are we going to find there?" asked Aunt Maggie. "Will a book, give us all the information that we need?"

"No, not a book. Cheri, the librarian, has been helping us since the very beginning. We never would have been able to find anything without her help," said Hero. "She can read and translate hieroglyphs, so she's able to decipher all of the writings for us. If there is something she can't read, then we turn to a book."

"You told the librarian about Moroni's Treasure before you told your own mom, Bear?" Aunt Maggie asked, with a concerned look on her face.

"I didn't, Mom—the Team did," replied Bear smiling. "Besides, we really needed someone that could read the ancient writings. We're really lucky to have found someone like her; she's been a lot of help so far."

"Is the library still open?" asked Stick. "I think it closes at four o'clock tonight, doesn't it?"

"Oh no!" exclaimed Bubba. "I think you're right. Cheri told us they were going to start renovations on the old building, and for the next few months, they would start closing early. We can't make Mom wait until morning to get the answers to the clue. She could end up stuck in Book of Mormon time forever."

"We'll never make it to the library on our bikes in time!" yelled Bear. "We need help."

"We'll make it if we hurry," said KP, looking down at

his watch. "Try to be positive, Bear. Let's get moving."

KP grabbed his backpack and threw it over his shoulder. He picked up the paper with the symbols written on it and headed for the front door.

"Wait a minute, KP," called Aunt Maggie. "Why don't all of you jump in my car? I can get you to the library in a matter of minutes. That way, we can make sure the missing Team members get the information they need."

"I told you we were telling the truth, Mom," said Bear. He lifted up his backpack and followed her to the car.

"I never doubted you, Bear," replied Aunt Maggie. "I was more upset that you didn't let me in on this earlier. I could have helped you with your last mission with anything else you might have needed."

"But, Mom, I couldn't tell you. We promised Mr. Jensen we wouldn't tell anyone. He said that if certain people found out, our lives could be in great danger," Bear explained.

"Your lives wouldn't be in danger—by your mother," Aunt Maggie said smiling. "I guess the only danger you're in from me, is knowing that you might be grounded for the rest of your life for going on one of these missions without telling me first," added Aunt Maggie, as a smile completely covered her face.

"Mom!" exclaimed Bear. "Be serious. Are you really gonna bust me?"

"I'm only kidding," she replied. "Now get in the car, and let's get going; we only have a few minutes. But Bear, next time you have something come up where you need an adult, I'm always here for whatever you need—no matter what."

"I know, Mom. I'm sorry," replied Bear, as he opened the car door.

The Team jumped in Aunt Maggie's car and buckled their seatbelts. Aunt Maggie drove as fast as she dared down the small main road in town. They passed the hair salon, the athletic club, retirement home, then swiftly pulled into the parking lot of the library. Aunt Maggie squealed her tires as she raced around the parked cars, slamming on her brakes in front of the door.

Hero was the first one to push open the car door and run inside the library. He quickly scanned the room frantically looking for Cheri, but saw no sign of her anywhere.

The librarian standing at the check-out counter looked up at Hero and the others as they entered. "You only have a few minutes before the library closes," she whispered. "Please make your selections quickly, or you will need to come back another day."

Not wanting to waste time, Bubba asked, "We just need to talk to Cheri. Is she here today?"

"If she is still here, she's probably gathering her belongings in the back room. She should be out any minute."

"Could we walk back to where she might be?" asked Bean in a soft, sweet voice.

"You can walk back to the employees' lounge, but, you can't go inside," replied the librarian behind the counter. "You'll have to wait there for her to come out."

"Thanks," called Bubba, as he took off swiftly toward the back of the building.

"I sure hope we haven't missed her," said Stick, as he followed closely behind Bubba.

"Me, too," replied Aunt Maggie, coming inside the library after parking the car. "I'm interested to see what system the Team has for translating these clues."

Bubba stood by the door marked Employee Lounge for several moments, before he could stand waiting no longer. He turned, looked at the Team, and said, "I can't wait any longer. You know how slow Cheri is. I'm gonna go inside. Wait here. Cheri, are you in here?" he called quietly, as he pushed open the door. "Cheri, we really need your help. Please answer. Are you here?"

Bubba listened intently for any noise, waiting nervously for her soft, quiet voice to reply. Only moments passed when he heard her laugh explode throughout the room.

"Cheri? Is that you?" Bubba called again. "Cheri, it's the Team. We need your help. Are you here?"

"Hold on a minute; I'll be right there," she called.

Excitedly, he pushed open the Employee Lounge door and called to the waiting Team, "She's in here, and she'll be out in just a minute."

Cheri and Bubba walked out of the break room moments later, and Cheri quickly rushed them to their favorite table in the quiet back corner of the library.

Cheri looked around at the Team and suddenly noticed Aunt Maggie. "Team, have you finally told an adult?" she asked relieved.

"Oh yeah, Cheri, this is Mom's sister, Aunt Maggie," announced Hero, pointing toward her.

"I'm so glad. I wasn't sure I could handle the pressure of being the only one to know everything for much longer!" Cheri exclaimed. She walked around the table and held out her hand to shake Aunt Maggie's. "It's nice to meet you."

"It's very nice to meet you—the lady who can read hieroglyphs, and made it so the Team could find the treasure," replied Aunt Maggie.

"I am blessed to have had the opportunity to help them. These kids are truly wonderful," Cheri replied.

"Hello! Ladies," interrupted Hero. "We don't have much time, here. Now that you two have met each other, Cheri, we have a new problem. Tater, Butch, Squeaks, and my mom have been sent on a new mission. They were able to contact us and give us a new clue that we need your help with."

"I thought you boys were going to put the Liahona away for a while after the last mission?" replied Cheri, as she crinkled up her nose and squinted her eyes.

"We were, but Mom got suspicious and found the Liahona," replied Bubba.

"And before I could explain everything to her, she picked up the Liahona and activated the lights. Within seconds, they were gone, and I couldn't do anything to stop them," added Hero. "It's all my fault. I should have done a better job with the Liahona."

"This isn't anyone's fault, and right now we have more important things to worry about than whose fault this is. Now, let me see the clue, so we can help your Teammates get home safely," said Cheri, as she held her hand out for the paper.

Hero smiled at how Cheri was always able to make

him feel better about the situation. He quickly placed the paper with the symbols into her hand.

"All right now, what do we have here?" she asked, as she stared at the drawings on the paper. "Okay, Stick, because Tater is not here to write down the clues, will you please get a piece of paper and write down everything I say?"

"Sure, Cheri," replied Stick, as he retrieved paper and pencil from his backpack.

"Bubba, I also need the *Book of Egyptian Hieroglyphics* on my desk up front. Will you please hurry and retrieve that for me?" asked Cheri.

Bubba nodded, turned, and quickly scurried to the front of the library.

"Okay, Stick, are you ready?" asked Cheri.

Stick nodded, and Cheri quickly started translating the clue.

"Okay, let's see just what this clue has to say," Cheri started. Quietly, she studied the paper for several moments before she looked up at Hero and asked, "Now, is this a man kneeling? And this man, a few words later, standing?"

"Yep," replied Hero.

"And this picture that you have drawn like a plug, could it possibly be more like a bobbie-pin for steam curlers?" asked Cheri.

"Yes, it could be. Tater kinda hesitated when he described the picture to me," replied Hero.

Cheri nodded and continued studying the symbols for several more seconds before she noticed Bubba was back with the book from her desk. "Bubba, let me see that book, will you?"

He handed Cheri the book, and she scanned several pages. She looked up, smiled, and then looked again at the drawings on the small piece of paper before she started translating.

"All right, Stick, here we go. The first word is *Alma,* followed by the numbers *37* and *40*. The next word is *And,* followed by the word *it,* then *did*." Cheri paused, looked up at Stick, and asked, "Are you getting all this?"

"Yep, I've got it," he replied. "I'm good. Keep going."

Cheri smiled, rummaged through the small book on hieroglyphs again, then continued. "Okay, let's see here. The next set of pictures represents the words, *work* and *for,* followed by *them*. Now, this next word is…I believe it is the word, *according,* followed by the words *to, their, faith, in,* and the last word in the sentence is *God*. Are we still good?" she asked.

"Yes, still good," replied Stick.

"Cheri, I have a question," said KP.

"Sure, what?" she replied.

"The words Alma, *37* and *40*. Do you think that is referencing a scripture?" he asked.

"Most likely, or at least that is what it looks like to me," she replied smiling. "You could check by looking up the scripture while I continue translating, and see what it says."

"Cheri, why do you keep referencing that book?" questioned Bubba.

"Well, often there are pictures that represent the entire words in the hieroglyphic language. However, the pictures that you bring me are literal—meaning every picture represents one letter. I keep checking the book to make sure I have the letters translated correctly," she replied. "Do you understand?"

Bubba nodded, and Cheri quickly continued with her translation. "This next part seems to be different from the first. Rather than quoting scripture, I believe it is giving directions. *'Follow with faith through water and walls. Tunnels will appear where nothing is there at all.'* Are you sure this was everything?" she asked, as she flipped the paper over, looking for more on the back.

"Yes, that was everything Tater told us," replied Hero.

"Okay, hopefully this will help them," Cheri replied, as she handed back the paper.

"Thanks, Cheri. You've saved us again," said Bean as she quickly gave her a hug.

"Okay, Team, you know where I am if you need anymore help," Cheri replied, smiling. "Oh, and by the way, I think it was very smart, mature, and wise of all of you to discuss these adventures with an adult. I am very proud of you."

Hero smiled and quickly rushed the Team outside to Aunt Maggie's car.

"Mature and wise, huh?" laughed Bear, as he climbed inside his mom's car. "Not so wise for the guy who gets grounded for the rest of his life!"

"Bear, if you think you have it rough, why don't you think about how much trouble Hero and Bubba are going to be in when their mom gets back from this mission?" asked Bean, as she closed the car door.

"Yeah, Bear, your mom has been great so far," agreed Stick.

"Great to you," snapped Bear. "You're not the one that will be grounded, or the one who's gonna get in trouble when you get home!"

"Come on, Bear. You don't know for sure that's she gonna be mad when you get home," replied Bean. "Give her a chance; she just might surprise you."

"So, where to now, Team?" asked Aunt Maggie, as she finally climbed in the car, excited for Cheri's help.

"What were you doing, Mom?" Bear asked suspiciously.

"I needed to talk to Cheri for a moment," she replied. "I had a question about translating hieroglyphics. Now, what is the plan?"

"Usually, we call on the walkie-talkie as soon as it is safe and tell the others the translation Cheri came up with," Hero replied. "But since we can get home quickly in the car, why don't we hurry home and call them from there?"

"Home it is," Aunt Maggie replied. She turned on to Fort Street and headed back toward the Treehouse.

Chapter Eleven

As Aunt Maggie pulled into the driveway, the Team hurried out of the car and up to the Treehouse. They scrambled as fast as they could up the hanging ladder and moved quickly inside. Hero pulled the walkie-talkie from his bag, turned it on, and patiently waited for Stick to retrieve Cheri's translations. As he began to call for Tater, Aunt Maggie finally climbed inside the Treehouse.

"Hero, do you mind if I call?" she asked, holding her hand out for the walkie-talkie.

Hero shrugged his shoulders. He handed her the small black unit and paper with Cheri's translations.

"Your mom will never believe that I am here helping you," she said, as she held the unit close to her mouth and pushed the talk button. "Hey, is anybody there? We've got it."

Butch scrambled to pick up the walkie-talkie. "Well, it's taken you long enough," he replied hastily. "I was wondering if we would have any battery left by the time you called."

"We had to go to the library and find Cheri to help us translate the clue. You know we can't do it without her help," said the hard to understand voice. "And sometimes she can be really slow."

"Stick, is that you?" questioned Butch, unsure who he was talking to. "'Cause if it is, you're holding your mouth too close to the receiver. I can barely understand a word you are saying."

"Sorry," replied the unfamiliar voice.

Mrs. M. listened to the conversation, scrunching her eyebrows and puckering her lips. "Butch who are you talking to? Is that the librarian?" she asked, unsure of the voice.

Butch shrugged his shoulders and said, "I don't know. Hey, who is this?"

"This is Maggie," she replied, through the static on the walkie-talkie.

"What? Who told you about this?" yelled Butch nervously. "Why are you telling me about Cheri's translations?"

"The Team told me, Butch. They needed an adult's help to keep this mission secret," she replied, snickering. "I can't believe you really found the Liahona."

Mrs. M. held out her hand to Butch and motioned for

the walkie-talkie. He handed her the small black unit, and she quickly pushed the talk button.

"Well, if they wanted an adult, why did they come to you?" asked Mrs. M., chuckling.

"Funny, sis," replied Maggie. "I guess I was just in the right place at the right time."

"So, did they tell you everything that has happened?" asked Mrs. M.

"Yes, they did. It looks like your younger sister is here once again to clean up your mess. Boy, you have a knack for getting yourself into trouble," Maggie teased. "I've been cleaning up after you since I was a little girl."

"You're still a little girl, aren't you?" teased Mrs. M. "And I always thought it was me cleaning up your messes. It's about time you helped."

"All right, enough playing. Are you doing okay, Sis?" asked Maggie.

"I am if you got those drawings translated. Tell me you got to the library and have the information we need?" she asked intently. "We're stuck without knowing what they mean."

"I didn't, Sis. In fact, I didn't do anything," she quickly replied, hearing the stress in her sister's voice. "But don't worry; the Team has everything under control. They knew exactly what to do. They handled the translation while I stood back and watched them in action."

"They amaze me," replied Mrs. M. "I can't believe everything they've already done."

"I agree. They amaze me as well. And, I can't believe you're doing this," replied Aunt Maggie. "You're afraid of everything! What made you think you could handle an adventure in another land?"

"Well, I can tell you this for sure, I didn't plan to do this. If I had really believed or known what the Liahona could do, or what the Team was searching for with the treasure map, I would have stopped them in the beginning," Mrs. M. said firmly.

The walkie-talkie suddenly went dead.

"Maggie?" called Mrs. M. frantically. "Sis, are you there?"

Several moments passed with no sound. Mrs. M. looked over at Tater and said, "I think it has gone dead again."

"Hopefully it's because the batteries are still wet," replied Tater. He took the unit out of her hands, slid off the cover, and pulled out the batteries. He carefully dropped them into the edge of his shirt and started to dry them. Tater handed the walkie-talkie to Butch, pointed to the inside of the battery compartment and said, "Use your shirt and dry off the inside for me. Let's see if we can make this work for a minute or two more."

Without a word, Butch quickly dried off the inside while Tater worked on the batteries. When the boys were sure the unit and batteries were as dry as they could get them, Butch handed Tater the walkie-talkie. Tater swiftly slid the batteries back inside, placed the cover back over them.

"Try it now, Mrs. M.," said Tater, as he handed her the walkie-talkie.

She hurriedly turned on the unit, then located the

black talk button and called, "Sis, Hero, Bubba, anyone there?" But still, there was no answer. "I think they really are dead this time, Tater. We may really be in trouble."

"Try again, don't give up yet," insisted Squeaks, as she watched her mom turn off the walkie-talkie.

"Yeah, come on, try again," insisted Butch. "We don't ever give up this easily."

Mrs. M. smiled at their determination, then quickly turned on the walkie-talkie. She adjusted the channel and again called, "Hello, Team, is anyone there?"

Static startled Tater, Butch, and Squeaks as Mrs. M. released the talk button.

"All right, you got power!" shouted Tater. "Try to get Cheri's translation of the hieroglyphs, quickly."

"Yeah, try again before the batteries go dead," insisted Butch. "We've got to have the translation to that clue as fast as we can, or we're never going to get this mission solved."

Nervously, Mrs. M. held the walkie-talkie to her mouth, pushed the black talk button, and yelled, "Hello, Team, is anyone there?"

Suddenly, static burst through the silence, followed by Aunt Maggie's shrill voice. "Come on, can you hear us?" she frantically called.

"We got ya," Mrs. M. answered excitedly. "Now quick, do you have the translation from the hieroglyphs? We've got to hurry. Our batteries aren't going to last very long."

"Real quick, Sis, I talked to Cheri, the librarian, for a minute, and she mentioned that the pictures are a literal translation of each letter. Keep that in mind if you run across another translation, just in case we aren't able to communicate with each other," added Aunt Maggie.

"I understand. Thanks," replied Mrs. M., anxious for the translations.

Hero took the walkie-talkie from Aunt Maggie's hand, and grabbed Cheri's translation. "Okay, Tater, you know the drill," he said. "Get some paper and pencil, and write this down, quick."

As Tater heard Hero's instructions, he dropped his backpack to the ground, and unzipped the front pocket. Then he grabbed a small notebook and pencil from inside.

"Tell him I'm ready," called Tater, as he sat down on the ground to write.

"He's ready, Hero," called Mrs. M. "Go ahead, and tell us what you've got."

"Okay, Tater, start writing," said Hero, as he began to read the deciphered letters. "The first part is a scripture, but the hieroglyph letters that you gave us only quote part of the scripture. KP looked up the reference and verified the first part. So, if you have your scriptures with you, you might want to look it up; there may be more clues in it. The scripture is Alma 37:40, 'And it did work for them according to their faith in God.' The second part of the hieroglyphs indicates what you're looking for, or at least that's what Cheri thought. The pictures spell out the following words, 'Follow with faith through water and walls; tunnels will appear where nothing is there at all.'"

"Thanks, Hero. But do you have any idea what the last part of the clue might mean?" quizzed Tater, scrunching up his face as he finished writing the clue in his notebook.

"No, but we'll work on it from here and see what we can come up with. There's a good chance that this clue will lead you to another set of hieroglyphs, kinda like we did when we were on our adventure. We better get off the walkie-talkie, so you can save your batteries," added Hero.

"I agree. We'll try to check in with you as often as we can. We aren't sure of the dangers here yet, or exactly what we're dealing with; so as we find out, we'll try to let you know how we're doing," said Tater. "But whatever you do, don't try to call us. If we're in an unsafe area, you could get us into a lot of trouble."

"Only call us and report in when it is safe for you," said Hero. "We know not to call you. We were almost caught a few times because of that walkie-talkie."

"Love ya, Mom," called Bubba, worried for her safety. "Be careful, and hurry back."

Tater held the talk button down as Mom called, "Don't worry, boys. We'll get everything done before you know it. Take care of Dad, and we'll be home soon."

With that, Tater quickly turned off the walkie-talkie and placed it in the front pocket of his jeans.

"Okay, what do we do know?" asked Butch.

"We've got to, 'Follow with faith through water and walls, tunnels will appear where nothing is there at all,'" replied Squeaks, reading the clue over Tater's shoulder.

"I'm not quite sure I understand," said Mrs. M.

"Well, I think we have already completed parts of the clue," replied Butch.

"What do ya mean?" questioned Tater.

"Well, think about it. 'Follow with faith through water

and walls? Didn't we swim through the secret opening under water?" asked Butch.

"I don't think that is what our clue is referencing," replied Squeaks, deep in concentration.

"Okay, if that is not right, then what do you think the clue is referencing?" Butch asked sharply.

"Think about it," snapped Squeaks. "'Follow with faith through water and walls.' I think the clue is indicating the waterfall."

"How?" asked Tater.

"The waterfall itself is a wall of water, right?" reasoned Squeaks. "'Follow with faith through water and walls' that has to be referencing the waterfall. Besides, we located the hieroglyphs next to the waterfall."

"That makes sense," agreed Tater. "Squeaks could be on to something."

"Why is it that tunnels are always hidden in dark, creepy, scary places?" asked Mrs. M. as she moved closer to the waterfall.

"'Cause that is the safest place for secret hidden tunnels," Butch replied smiling.

"Hey, everyone, wait," called Tater. "I think we should look up the scripture that the clue references before we start searching. That way, if there is a clue in it, we might have a better chance of finding the tunnel. Butch, we do have scriptures with us, don't we?"

"I've got mine," he replied. "They're a little wet still, but even wet, they have the information we need."

Butch unzipped his backpack, located his scriptures and carefully turned to Alma 37:40. "Do you want me to read the reference?" he asked, looking up at Mrs. M.

She nodded and Butch started reading. "Alma 37:40, 'And it did work for them according to their faith in God; therefore, if they had faith to believe that God could cause that those spindles should point the way they should go, behold, it was done; therefore they had this miracle, and also many other miracles wrought by the power of God, day by day.'"

"I think the clue in that scripture is telling us is to have faith, not necessarily giving us a specific direction to go," replied Mrs. M., after listening to Butch.

"I agree," added Tater. "I think Squeaks has got the right idea; there must be a secret tunnel entrance somewhere near the waterfall."

"All right, so let's go find this secret tunnel," suggested Squeaks, ready to get moving.

"Wait a minute. Before we go, Tater, will you please read the clue again?" asked Butch.

Tater nodded and read from the small piece of paper. "'Follow with faith through water and wall; tunnels will appear where nothing is there at all.'"

"So do you think that there is a tunnel behind the waterfall?" asked Mrs. M.

"I can't imagine finding the secret tunnel would be that easy, but it could be," replied Tater, as he shrugged his shoulders.

The group swiftly moved toward the waterfall. They soon found a narrow opening in the rock that led behind the waterfall.

Butch turned to the others, placed his finger to his lips

and whispered, "I think we found something. Follow me!"

"Do you want me to go first, Butch?" offered Tater. "It could be dangerous in there."

"Ssshhh, be quiet. You never know if someone could be hiding in here, waiting to kill us," replied Butch, as he smiled and then quickly disappeared inside.

Squeaks, Tater and Mrs. M. silently squeezed through the opening behind Butch. Once inside, they were surprised to find that the tunnel was beautiful. The sun shone through the waterfall outside, casting ornate shadows all over the rock wall. Mist floated throughout the area, with occasional drops of water falling from the ceiling to the floor. The tunnel was only twenty feet long, with a solid rock wall on one side, and the waterfall, opening to the lake below, on the other.

Butch, watching the shadows from the sun and water dance around the area, maneuvered swiftly to the end of the tunnel.

"There's nothing here!" he called, as he reached the other side.

"What do we do now?" Squeaks asked, confused by the tunnel. "This has to be the right place."

"Well, doesn't the clue mention something about following with faith through water and walls?" asked Mrs. M.

"Yeah, why?" asked Tater.

"I was thinking that maybe our clue has more to do with this beautiful waterfall," she replied, as she stuck her hand into the water.

"What, though?" asked Tater.

Mrs. M. shook her head and shrugged her shoulders.

"Do you think we need to move through the water?" asked Squeaks. "Maybe if we do that, a secret opening will appear in the river below."

"Come on, Squeaks. Be serious, will ya?" said Butch sarcastically. "If we do that, we'll just end up in the river again."

"She does bring up a good point, though," interrupted Tater.

"What's that?" asked Butch, still smiling as he looked over the edge of the banks to the lake twenty feet below.

"The clue says to have faith, through water and walls. If we do that, maybe the second part of the translation will make sense."

"But where do we enter the water?" questioned Mrs. M. "According to the clue we need to move through water and walls?"

"What about over here?" called Squeaks pointing to the far end of the tunnel. "A portion of the waterfall is flowing through the rocks, causing a mini waterfall that runs down the rock wall, across the path, and then rejoins the main fall that drops into the lake below. What if this is the waterfall we are looking for and all we have to do is take a step through the water and something will happen?"

"I can tell you what will happen," replied Butch, as he reached through the water, and placed his hand against the wall. "We'll crash into the rock wall."

"I don't see any other water around here that we could walk through without having to jump into the lake," Squeaks replied, on the verge of tears.

"Yeah, but how is this an option? There's just a small

amount of water running down the side of the wall," said Butch.

Tater quickly produced the small piece of paper with the translation written on it and read it aloud, "Follow with faith through water and walls; tunnels appear where nothing is there at all."

"The beginning of the clue that references the scripture also tells us the same thing. Everything works with faith. If we don't have faith that we're in the right place, then we'll never find the secret tunnel," said Mrs. M.

"I agree. None of us is showing a lot of faith right now," said Squeaks. "What if there is a secret lever or button or something?"

"A secret lever?" asked Butch, intrigued by the idea. "I guess there is enough water here to hide a secret opening and a lever or trigger to open it, maybe."

"Yeah, like on Scooby Doo, you know, something that moves and opens the secret tunnel," replied Squeaks.

"Hey, I think you might be right!" exclaimed Tater, as he raced to where Squeaks was standing. "Maybe we don't have to walk through the wall, but only pretend like we're going to. Maybe that will trigger the opening," he reasoned, as he quickly stuck his shoe into the falling water.

"I would think that finding how to get the secret tunnel to open would be a little harder than that," chuckled Butch.

"Yeah, now all you have is a shoe full of water," added Squeaks, smiling.

"Well, kids, at least he is trying something," replied Mrs. M. She swiftly walked to the wall and started searching.

"Any idea what we're looking for?" questioned Butch, as he crawled on his hands and knees, feeling for anything that might move.

"What about a rock," replied Squeaks. "Maybe there is a small rock that lifts or something."

"I can't see any rocks," replied Mrs. M. "What about a button or something that pushes into the rock wall?"

"I can't see or feel anything on the rock that moves," answered Tater. "There has to be something else."

"Hey, everyone, wait a minute," insisted Squeaks. "What if we have to try and walk through?"

"I just tried that, remember?" asked Tater, making a face at Squeaks.

"Not hold our foot in the water, but try to walk through the water," Squeaks replied. She faced the small waterfall and quickly took a step toward the rock wall.

Suddenly, something happened. Wind began to whistle through the rocks behind the water, splashing it everywhere. Then a loud crack rang behind the falling water. An eerie breeze suddenly raced through the secret tunnel, flipping Squeaks' long, blonde tresses all around her face. Afraid to move her foot from the floor and water, Squeaks smiled as a narrow opening appeared in the wall. She gazed into the dark, frightening opening in the rocks. She was sure this was the opening to the secret tunnel they had been looking for. She looked over her shoulder at her mom and said, "Can I lead the way?"

"Ummm, no," Mrs. M. sarcastically replied. "I think someone a little bigger than you would be better to lead the way this time."

"I guess I will lead the way into the scary tunnel. Mrs. M., you can bring up the rear," suggested Tater. He pushed past Squeaks and headed into the secret opening.

"Be very careful, Tater," insisted Mrs. M. "You never know what you might find in there."

Chapter Twelve

❝Do you think we found the right secret tunnel?" asked Squeaks, as she watched a snake slither across the floor.

"Yeah, are we sure we've translated the clue correctly?" questioned Butch, not excited to see cobwebs and spiders covering the entrance to the tunnel.

"I can't imagine that we've got this wrong," Mrs. M. replied excitedly.

"I sure hope you're right," replied Squeaks, nervously peering inside the tunnel. "I'm afraid we've left Alma too long already. Who knows what wicked King Noah could have already done to him and his followers?"

"Every time I read the clue, I'm sure we have done everything that it told us to do," added Mrs. M. reassuringly.

"Well then, I guess there's no more procrastinating. Who wants to follow Tater into the creepy, tomb-looking tunnel first?" asked Butch, as a terrified look spread across his face.

Only a few feet inside the tunnel, Tater was unable to see anything. He quickly opened his backpack and removed his flashlight from the small, back pocket. He hurriedly shook the light, charging it up. He turned it on and then continued moving slowly through the narrow pathway. Moving only ten feet into the tunnel, the sides suddenly became smaller, and Tater was forced to his hands and knees. He moved cautiously, attempting to knock down the spider webs as he crawled. About five yards further into the tunnel, he called, "As far as I can see, everything's all right in here. There are a few bugs and spiders, but other than that, I think we'll be okay. Everybody, climb in and follow me. Let's see where this tunnel goes."

Slowly, Butch climbed inside the tunnel, followed by Squeaks, and then Mrs. M. They carefully followed Tater as he moved through several twists and turns, until finally, the tunnel stopped.

"Why did you stop, Tater?" asked Butch.

"I ran out of tunnel, Butch," Tater replied sarcastically, shining his light onto the tunnel wall.

"So, where do we go from here?" asked Squeaks nervously.

Tater searched the area and found a small opening above his head. "Hey, there's something up above us," he called. "What should I do?"

"We gotta keep going," answered Squeaks.

"Can you see what's in the opening, Tater?" Mrs. M. asked nervously.

"No, the opening is straight above my head about three feet and turns sharply to the right," Tater replied.

"Can you even climb up there?" questioned Mrs. M. "And if you can, does the opening look like that is how the tunnel continues?"

"Sure, I can climb up. This opening does look like the way to continue through the tunnel. But, I think I should help some of you up, unless you want me to stay in the lead," he replied.

"Yes, stay in the lead. I will help Squeaks," Mrs. M. replied. "I feel better if you boys are scouting ahead of us to keep us all safe."

Tater nodded. He stood and jumped up, grabbing the ledge above his head. He pulled with all his might, struggling, until finally, he maneuvered his way up to the next level.

"What'd ya find, Tater?" called Butch, as he waited at the bottom of the opening.

"There is a narrow hallway up here," he quietly replied. "It reminds me of pictures that I've seen of old-time castles. In fact, I wonder if we're in a castle or something."

"Can you see anyone in the tunnel?" questioned Butch, as he, too, struggled to maneuver his way into the hallway.

"Hey, boys, I could use a little help down here," interrupted Squeaks, holding her hands as high above her head as she could, still unable to reach the ledge.

"Sorry, Squeaks," said Butch. He reached down into the tunnel, grabbed hold of her hands, and pulled her tiny body up into the hallway.

"Can you make it, Mrs. M., or do you need help?" called Tater.

"I think I can pull myself up," she replied. She reached up to the ledge, took hold, and struggled to pull her body up into the hallway. Several nervous moments passed before Tater took hold of her arm and helped her, as she fought to get her leg up onto the ledge.

"Nice job, Mom," said Squeaks. "I didn't think you were going to make it there for a minute."

"Me neither. I'm glad I made it, too. I wasn't sure I was going to make it until Tater helped me. I'm not as young and mobile as I remember," replied Mrs. M., as she brushed the dirt from her pants.

"Where to now, Tater?" questioned Squeaks, ready to get out of the creepy tunnel.

"I guess we follow this spider-infested tunnel some more," he replied, shining his flashlight into the darkness, and lighting up the shimmering lines of the countless spider webs. "Come on, everybody. Follow me!"

They continued down the tunnel, following every twist and turn, unsure where it might lead them. Tater led the way for more than one hundred yards. Then Butch suddenly spotted an old torch hanging on the wall.

"Wait a minute, Tater. Look what's up on the wall. Isn't this a torch?" asked Butch, as he pulled it from the holder on the wall.

Tater turned to see an unlit torch. "Nice job, Butch. That will help light things up in here," he said sarcastically.

"Do you have any matches?" Butch asked.

"I think so," replied Tater, sure he had matches in his first aid kit. Quickly, he rummaged through his backpack, found the kit, and searched inside for the matches.

"It doesn't matter if you do. The matches aren't going to work," Squeaks said confidently, as she watched him pull the small bag from inside the kit. "They're going to be ruined from the water."

"No, they're not," replied Tater, smiling as he held up a small plastic bag. "Not only are they waterproof matches, but I also put them in a plastic bag for added security."

"Nice thinking, Tater," said Mrs. M., smiling. "I can't believe everything you have hidden in that backpack of yours. I'm sure it will come in handy several more times on this mission."

Tater grinned, quickly opening the bag. He removed a match, striking it on the rock wall. A sudden flash of light sprayed across the area as Tater lit the match and then the torch.

"Should we put it back in the holder on the wall or take it with us?" asked Butch, looking at Mrs. M.

"Definitely take it with us," she replied, smiling. "'Cause I am tired of walking in the dark. I keep stepping on things that I know I would love to avoid if possible."

Butch held the torch, walking several feet behind Tater. They had barely walked ten yards, when Tater reached an opening in the tunnel. Shining his light into the opening, he suddenly gasped in terror.

"I think not using the torch might be better in here," he suggested, turning around with a frightened look on his face.

"Why? What's the matter?" demanded Squeaks worriedly.

"I'm not sure you want to know," he replied seriously.

"Well, if she doesn't, I do," insisted Mrs. M. "What can you see that has you so upset, Tater?"

"Rats," he replied. "Thousands of them!"

"Rats?" Butch asked apprehensively, unsure he had heard Tater correctly. "What do you mean, rats?"

"I mean living, crawling, dirty, four-legged creatures, that bite you and eat everything in sight," Tater replied sharply.

"What are they doing?" questioned Mrs. M.

"I don't know," Tater replied sarcastically. "Crawling all over each other."

"Are we sure we're in the right tunnel and going the right way?" asked Squeaks, looking back over her shoulder, sure she did not want to walk through thousands of rats.

"Hey, wait a minute. You've been telling us from the beginning that this is right, and we've got to hurry up and save Alma," replied Tater. "Now you're going to say this tunnel could be wrong?"

"It's not the wrong tunnel," Butch said confidently.

"How do you know that? It could be the wrong tunnel," insisted Squeaks, as she peered through the opening of the tunnel into the room of rats.

"Well, the reason I know that it's not the wrong tunnel is because of those—look!" insisted Butch, pointing to the writing on the torch handle. "I think these are the same symbols that we saw on the wall."

"Look—the kneeling man, the jaguar, the owl—they all seem to be the same," agreed Tater. "I even see the pictures that represented the numbers for the scripture."

"I guess we are going the right way, Squeaks," said Mrs. M. "Even if there are rats in here."

"How do we get across the rats, then?" Squeaks questioned nervously. "I can't walk through them. If they touch me, I'll totally freak out."

"You may have to handle it, Squeaks," replied Tater. "Unless you can find another way across."

"Then let's find another way across, 'cause I don't think I can handle this," she replied adamantly. "There has to be another way. Can you see where the tunnel leads to?"

Tater moved to the opening of the tunnel, shone the flashlight around the room, and searched the area for any sign of where or how the tunnel continued on to the city. The room was constructed of square blocks, approximately two feet wide by two feet tall. Each stone was ornately decorated around the edges and had an Egyptian hieroglyph picture carved onto the face of the stone. Directly across the room from where they were all standing, Tater spotted an identical narrow hallway that continued on to what he hoped was an entrance to the city.

"I can only see one way out," said Tater. "If you look beyond the rats, you can see straight across the room where there is another tunnel. That has to be where we need to go."

"Let me take a look at this room, Tater," said Mrs. M. She wiggled her way past the kids to the opening of the room. She gazed around the room and gasped when she saw the huge, black, gray, and white rats. "I think you're right, Squeaks, I'm not sure that I can maneuver through that many rats either."

"What are we going to do then?" questioned Butch, as he gazed out over the room.

"I've always found that when a problem presents itself, that you can't either solve or understand, there is only one thing that you can do—you must kneel down and pray to the Lord for help. When I do, this, a solution always presents itself," replied Mrs. M. She leaned up against the tunnel wall and slid down until she was sitting.

"Okay, Mrs. M., I think you're right," replied Tater. "Would it be okay with you if I say the prayer?"

"Sure you can," replied Mrs. M. "I think that is a great idea."

Tater waited as everyone shifted to their knees. As soon as they were ready, he said a prayer. He asked for direction, focus, help to complete all obstacles placed in their paths, and clear minds to find the answers the Lord desired for them to find. He also asked for safety for everyone and ended with sincere gratitude for being allowed to go on such a special mission for the Lord.

As Tater ended the prayer, he stood up and said, "Now, I'm sure we can find a safe way to cross through all of these rats."

"So, do any of you have any ideas?" asked Squeaks, as she peered into the room and cringed at the sight of the rats.

"Well, I think crossing the room safely has something to do with faith," replied Butch, smiling.

"What makes you think that?" questioned Tater. "Why would you think getting across the rats has something to do with faith?"

"Well, this tunnel is only known by those with faith. The tunnel also helps faithful followers of Alma and Abinadi who believe the Lord's teachings. We found the tunnel through faith that the hieroglyphs were real, and faith that the Team back home could help us decipher the hieroglyphs' meanings. Everything we have done so far on this mission has had to do with faith," Butch explained.

"Okay, I agree with that," replied Tater. "But does that mean we have to have faith that these rats, which are probably starving, are not going to bite us as we cross the room?" asked Tater.

"No, I think there is another way; we just have to have the faith that we will find what it is," Butch replied sharply.

"What about the pictures on the stones?" asked Squeaks. "Do you think they could have a meaning?"

"Possibly," replied Tater. "But we don't know what they mean."

"Actually, we do know what they mean," said Mrs. M., as a mischievous smile crossed her face. "Aunt Maggie told me, before the walkie-talkie went dead, that the pictures were a literal translation. Remember?"

"I heard that, but what, exactly, does that mean, Mrs. M.?" questioned Butch.

"I hadn't thought about that earlier, but she's right, every picture represents one letter," snickered Tater. "By knowing the translation from earlier, we can look at the hieroglyphs and know which letter each picture represents."

"Like a code?" asked Squeaks, unsure what they were talking about.

"Exactly! Like a secret code," Mrs. M. replied excitedly.

"Okay, if they are hieroglyph pictures, then we should be able to decipher them, but which stone do we start with?" questioned Squeaks. "Every stone on the top row around the entire room has a picture."

"I think we should just start at the corner to our right and decipher the letters all the way around the room," replied Butch.

"Why to the right?" asked Mrs. M. "When we read a book, we read from left to right, not the other way."

"Because in ancient times, they read their text from right to left," replied Tater. "So if we start at the right, and decipher to the left, we might find the code."

Mrs. M. nodded and then replied, "You know, you kids are too smart for me. I never would have thought of that."

"So, what is the first picture, Butch?" Squeaks asked impatiently.

Butch looked at all the letters and replied, "Tater, why don't you get a paper and a pencil, and write down all the letters? There are too many to remember them all."

Tater nodded and replied, "You describe the picture, and Mrs. M. and I will decipher what the letter should be."

"What should I do?" asked Squeaks, upset to be left out.

"Why don't you help Butch describe the letters to us?" replied Mrs. M.

Squeaks grinned slightly and agreed, walking closer to Butch and the pictures carved in the rock.

"All right, let's see here. The first picture looks like a man kneeling down," started Butch.

"And the next two pictures look like vases or maybe handcuffs," Squeaks added.

"Probably more like fat, round vases," said Butch.

"The next picture looks like…," started Butch.

"Like what?" Mrs. M. questioned anxiously.

"Like a claw," replied Squeaks. "Or, I guess it could be half of a boat or half of a banana."

"That picture could represent the letter o," suggested Tater, as he scanned through the Team's earlier translation. "Okay, what is next?"

"After that is a picture I'm not quite sure how to describe," started Butch. "But maybe it is a carnival ticket or something like that."

"Followed by the all seeing eye!" shouted Squeaks.

"Wait a minute, wait a minute," protested Mrs. M. "We're still looking for the letter that the carnival ticket represents."

Several anxious seconds passed before Tater finally called, "Okay, after the all seeing eye, what's next?"

"The next picture is two squiggly lines followed by…lips," described Butch.

"Lips?" questioned Tater, looking up at Butch with a confused look on his face.

"Yeah, lips," he replied, shrugging his shoulders.

Working their way through the pictures, they soon translated all of the letters around the room.

"So, can you determine what they all are?" asked Squeaks, as Butch described the last picture.

"Let's see, we can tell you all of the letters, but we don't know what they are referencing exactly, yet," replied Mrs. M.

Tater placed the paper with the series of letters written across the page on the floor. They all studied the letters, trying to figure out the message. Several frustrating minutes passed, and they still could not figure out what the letters meant.

AccordingtotheirfaithintheLord

"The letters might be a series of words," suggested Mrs. M. "I can see the word *Lord, the,* and *faith.*"

"I can see the words *to* and *their,*" added Squeaks.

"I figured it out!" exclaimed Butch. *"According to their faith in the Lord."*

"So, what does that mean?" Squeaks asked excitedly.

"I don't know," replied Tater, shrugging his shoulders.

"You guys said earlier that the letters were a code. What if their meaning or secret is hidden inside all of these letters or words?" questioned Squeaks. "And the word has something to do with our mission?"

Tater, Butch and Mrs. M. looked at Squeaks, surprised by her idea.

"Wow! I didn't know you could be that smart," Tater said teasingly.

"Funny! So, do you think I could be right?" she asked, smiling.

"I think you have a good idea," replied Tater. "So, what words are there that could help us?"

"Well, the word *faith* is there," replied Squeaks. "*Faith* is a key word in our mission."

"You're right, but I think it is a different word," said Mrs. M., rubbing her chin as she contemplated what Squeaks said. "I think the word *faith* is just too obvious. We're missing something."

"What are all the words again," asked Tater.

"The letters around the room spell out the words, *'According to their faith in the Lord',*" replied Butch.

"So, what are we missing?" asked Tater.

"Aren't those words part of the scripture from the clue we found earlier?" asked Squeaks.

"Hey, I think your right," said Mrs. M. "Tater, get your scriptures really quick, and let's look up that scripture again. Maybe there is another clue hidden inside the scripture."

Tater pulled his backpack from his shoulder, opened the zipper, and located his scriptures. Flipping through the pages, he located the scripture from the earlier clue.

"Do you want me to read the scripture out loud?" Tater asked, looking at Mrs. M.

"Yes, please," she replied.

Tater quickly read, "Alma 37:40, 'And it did work for them according to their faith in God; therefore, if they had faith to believe that God could cause that those spindles should point the way they should go, behold, it was done;

therefore they had this miracle, and also many other miracles wrought by the power of God, day by day.'"

"Hey, did any of you notice the one word that didn't match the scripture?" asked Squeaks.

"No, everything was the same, wasn't it?" replied Tater, looking up from his scriptures with a perplexed look on his face.

"No, there was one word that was different," Squeaks answered adamantly. "Read that part about according to their faith again."

Tater scanned the scripture, found the part Squeaks referenced, and read, "'And it did for them according to their faith in God.'"

"See, the scripture is a little different than the words around the room," Squeaks replied excitedly.

"What's different, Squeaks?" asked Butch, as he shrugged his shoulders. "I'm not catching it."

"The scripture reads, 'According to their faith in God', and the pictures around the room say, 'According to their faith in the Lord'," she replied. "Come on, guys, pay attention!"

"Well, that means the same thing, doesn't it?" questioned Butch. "There's not a lot of difference."

"Yes, but the words are different," Squeaks replied, smiling. "That has to mean something. I'm sure of it."

"I think Squeaks might be on to something," replied Mrs. M. She puckered her lips, moving them back and forth. "I've been thinking about the words. What does it mean, 'According to their faith in the Lord'?"

Tater shrugged his shoulders without saying a word, unsure what alternate meaning the sentence could possibly have.

"You know what, Squeaks? I think you're probably right," replied Butch. "I bet there is something hidden inside the letters."

"What words can we find hidden in this group of letters," asked Mrs. M. "Words that are not obvious, but pertain to our mission."

"Like anagrams?" asked Tater.

"Kinda, maybe something like that—where a word is hidden inside other letters," she replied.

"I'm looking, but I can't find words that have to do with our mission," said Butch. "But then, I'm not very good at this game either."

"I can't find a word either," added Tater. "You can't spell Alma, Abinadi, King Noah, anything."

"I'm struggling to find a word as well," added Mrs. M. "I can't spell scripture, time, forest, jungle."

"I can spell something!" shouted Squeaks excitedly.

"What is it?" asked Tater.

"What about the word, *Liahona*? All the letters for the word Liahona are there" replied Squeaks. "And the word makes sense, because the Liahona works, according to our faith in the Lord. That's also what the scriptures tell us."

"Well, that would make sense as to why the words in the room spell out *Lord,* rather than *God,*" said Mrs. M.

"Why?" questioned Butch. "I don't understand."

"I think Squeaks is right. The code in the letters that

we are looking for is the word *Liahona,*" replied Mrs. M. "But without changing the word *God* to the word *Lord,* you can't spell Liahona."

"Hey, I didn't even see that word. Good job, Squeaks," replied Tater, shaking his head. "I think you just might be right."

"Yeah, maybe each stone that spells out the word *Liahona* moves or something, and gives us a bridge across the room," Butch suggested excitedly.

"Well, the stone with the 'L' is right here," said Tater, touching it. "Should I try to push it or something?"

"You could see if it moves at all," replied Butch. "Maybe if you can push it, it will release part of a bridge or something like that."

Tater crouched down on one knee, reached his hand over the ledge, and pushed against the picture as hard as he could. "Well, the stone isn't budging," he replied, shaking his head. "And I was using all my strength."

"Try to see if something is sticking out that you could push in—like a button," suggested Butch, excited to cross the room. "There has to be something there."

"The stone feels mostly flat," replied Tater, as he rubbed his hand across the picture. "The only fluctuations are minor rough spots. There's only one small area that sticks out a little, but I think it's part of the natural contour of the stone."

"Push on that," Squeaks insisted nervously. "That has to be it."

"That has to be what?" asked Tater, as he looked up at Squeaks and smiled.

"That has to be the button or switch to something, so we don't have to try and walk through the rats!" she replied, her voice shaking with excitement.

Tater again rubbed his finger across the small, rough, slightly-protruding area, and pushed as hard as he could. Surprisingly, the small area slowly slid in about one-half inch. Then quickly, the entire rock slid out approximately twelve inches from the wall.

"I told you the pictures were the key," Squeaks bragged.

"What do we do now?" asked Tater.

"We have to spell out the word *Liahona*," replied Mrs. M.

"So, do I step out on the rock and check to see if the stone with the 'I' will do the same thing?" questioned Tater.

"Yes, I think you're gonna have to go out on the stone. I bet the next letter in the word will give us the next step. Hopefully it will make a pathway to the other side," replied Butch.

"Everyone stay here until I find all the stones that work and make a pathway," suggested Tater, as he cautiously maneuvered onto the stone and struggled to reach the next letter.

The others watched as Tater slowly worked his way from stone to stone around the room. He finally reached the last letter in the word *Liahona* and the opening to the tunnel on the other side of the room. He crawled off the stone ledge and into the tunnel. Then he turned and said, "Be very careful; the stones are strong but small. If you fall, you'll probably be the rats' next meal."

"Oh, great, Tater," Squeaks whined anxiously. "Now I'm not scared at all."

Tater smiled and motioned for her to start across the stones. "Come on, get going! We still have to go save Alma and his followers."

Chapter Thirteen

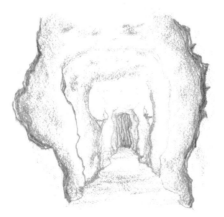

Tater, Butch, Squeaks, and Mrs. M. reached the other side of the room safely. Then Squeaks spotted a shadow on the wall, not far ahead of her. Holding her finger to her mouth, she motioned to the others to look toward the shadow. Quickly, she took Tater's flashlight, and flipped the small, red button to off. She scurried away from the edge of the room and ducked behind a large rock, frantically motioning for everyone to follow her.

"What are you doing, Squeaks?" asked Tater, as he grabbed his flashlight, annoyed she had taken it from him.

"Will you shush, please? And get down here. You're all going to be seen!" she insisted, pointing at the shadow again.

"Seen by what? There is nothing but spiders, bugs, and rats in this old, mysterious, tunnel," replied Butch, scrunching his nose at her demands.

The words had scarcely left his mouth when the group heard a man's spine-chilling voice.

"See, I told you someone was here. Now get down behind this rock and hide before we all get caught!" Squeaks insisted, motioning for everyone to hurry.

The group moved swiftly behind the rock and listened as the deep, frightening voice moved closer and closer toward their hiding spot.

"That doesn't sound like a very friendly voice," Butch whispered nervously. "I thought this was a secret tunnel."

"I wonder if it's a soldier searching for Alma's followers," said Mrs. M. "I'm sure the soldiers could have found this tunnel, especially if it begins in King Noah's city."

"Yeah, but they would never be able to figure out the secret code to get across, even if they could read the letters carved onto the stones," replied Squeaks quietly.

"Oh, no," said Tater, holding his hand over his mouth. "The stones marking the path back to the other side are still sticking out. Those soldiers won't have any problem finding the secret Waters of Mormon now!"

"How do we get them to slide back in?" questioned Squeaks, unsure what to do. "We can't reveal to King Noah's soldiers the way to Alma's secret valley."

"What do we do?" questioned Tater.

"We've got to reset them," replied Mrs. M. She hurried back to the edge of the rat room. She reached down to the protruding rock, quickly finding the rough patch on the stone, and pushed it inward. She watched for several seconds as nothing happened. Unsure what else to do, she looked back toward the others and shrugged her shoulders. Suddenly, she heard a loud, grinding noise. Turning back toward the stones, she was surprised to see the first stone on the other side of the room slowly slide back into place. "It's working," Mrs. M. announced.

"Well, they better hurry. The voices sound like they are just on the other side of the wall," Butch replied nervously.

"Get back here, Mrs. M. We've got to trust that the stones will move back into place before the voices get here. And we've got to find a way to escape as quick as we can, or we are going to be King Noah's next victims," insisted Tater.

"Does anyone have any ideas?" asked Squeaks, as she peered carefully over the rock and down the tunnel.

"I have an idea," replied Butch. "If we have truly made it somewhere into the city, then maybe this tunnel is a secret passage that Alma learned about when he was an active High Priest. Maybe this is an underground escape for the King or something."

"Hey, maybe you're right," agreed Tater. "Maybe if we continue down this tunnel, we will end up inside King Noah's temple."

"Then there has to be another way out of here," replied Mrs. M., grabbing Tater's flashlight.

"Someone is going to see us if you turn that light on, Mom," said Squeaks.

Holding the light high toward the ceiling, Mrs. M. silently examined every inch of the solid rock wall. She could find no indentations or markings—nothing that might be an opening.

Sure they would be caught at any moment, Butch, quickly jumped to his feet and helped to search for any sign of another exit. "Hey, I see something that might be a hidden door!" Butch called out, as he stood on his tip toes next to the rock they were hiding behind.

"How does it open?" questioned Tater, as he looked at the small square area where Butch stared. "There are no hooks, holes, or gadgets of any kind."

"There may not be one. Feel around for anything that moves or pushes in, like on the stones in the rat room," replied Butch. "I bet the entrance is hidden by a similar button."

Mrs. M. hurried to where Butch was standing and studied the small, square area in the rock. "You know, it looks like we need a knife or something to pry this rock open."

"Would a pocket knife work?" asked Tater, as he frantically rummaged through his backpack.

"Yeah, that might do the trick," replied Mrs. M., smiling.

Tater found the small item. He flipped open the knife and carefully handed it to Mrs. M. Grabbing the handle, she slid the knife into the small area and quickly started prying.

"Quick, everyone hide; someone is coming," warned Squeaks, grabbing at her mother's arm.

"Wait, Squeaks! The knife is stuck," replied Mrs. M., pulling her arm away from Squeaks' tight grip.

"No, now Mom. They're only a few feet away," declared Squeaks, tightly grabbing her mom's shirt and pulling with all her might.

Mrs. M. hid behind the rock, leaving the small, red pocket knife hanging precariously from the ceiling. The group watched as three soldiers, carrying long, thin spears, swiftly moved through the tunnel to the room filled with rats. A tall, thin soldier looked out over the small rat infested room. Not finding what he was looking for, he turned to the other soldiers and said, "Well, if any of Alma's followers tried to come this way, they surely died at the mouths of these rats."

"Let's keep searching then, Captain" replied another soldier.

Suddenly, the small army knife fell from the ceiling. Falling toward the rock, it was sure to give away their hiding place. Instinctively, Tater reached up and amazingly caught the knife out of the air. He pulled his arm safely behind the rock, praying that the soldiers had not seen him.

The third soldier, sensing someone was nearby, started searching the area again. But the tall, thin soldier, annoyed to be waiting for him, called, "Come on already. I told you no one is there! Now, let's go!"

Apprehensively, the third soldier moved away from the opening to the room and the rock where the kids and Mrs. M. were hiding. He still suspected someone was there, but gave up his search and quickly moved to catch up with the other soldiers.

"Whew! That was close!" exclaimed Butch.

"We've got to get out of here quick, kids," Mrs. M. insisted, as she took the knife from Tater and again tried to pry open the small, square in the rock.

"I agree," replied Butch, as he climbed up on the rock

and tried to help. "I have a bad feeling about those soldiers. That last one seemed to know that we were here."

"Yeah, he was kinda making me nervous the way he kept looking around," agreed Squeaks. "I'm gonna keep watch in case the soldiers start to come back."

"Good idea, Squeaks!" said her mom, as she continued to work on the opening.

"There has to be another way to open that, I'm sure of it!" said Butch, as he rubbed his hand across the rock.

"I couldn't find anything," replied Mrs. M., still digging at the rock with the knife.

"There is no way this rock is going to open with a small Swiss army knife," replied Butch.

"We've got to hurry. I can hear those soldiers again," interrupted Squeaks.

"Are they coming back?" asked Tater nervously.

As Mrs. M. inserted the short knife blade into the crack in the rock again, almost at once, a small brown piece of leather slipped out. She immediately began tugging on the piece of leather. When nothing happened, Tater climbed onto the rock next to her and helped her pull. Almost instantly, there was a groaning, followed by a scraping noise. Then the small, square opening began to move downward.

"We've got to hurry, guys. I really think the soldiers are close," Squeaks said frantically. "I can hear their voices again."

Mrs. M. and Tater continued to pull on the small leather strap. Slowly, a small, folded, rope ladder, attached above the rock, fell out of the opening.

"The hidden secret passage is up here!" exclaimed Butch, excited to have a way to get out of the creepy, spider-infested tunnel.

"It may be too late," announced Squeaks. "I can see the soldiers; they are only fifteen yards down the tunnel. The one soldier is returning to check the area again. He believes that someone is hiding up here. The other two soldiers are waiting for him at the tunnel's opening."

"Then we better get out of here quick," insisted Tater. He grabbed Squeaks' shirt, lifting her up next to the ladder. "This is the same kind of ladder we use back at the Treehouse. Hurry as fast as you can, and wait for the rest of us at the top."

Squeaks nodded and started climbing up the ladder. She reached the top, but was afraid to look around her dark surroundings. She turned and steadied the ladder, staring down at the others who were hurrying to get up to safety. Squeaks watched as Butch scaled the ladder in seconds, followed fairly quickly by Tater. But Mrs. M. meticulously crawled up every single step. She had to be sure she had a solid foot on the step before she maneuvered to the next one.

"Come on, Mom. You've got to hurry," insisted Squeaks. "That soldier has to be really close by now."

"I'm trying, Squeaks," she snapped, as she reached the opening and climbed inside.

Without a word, Tater and Butch grabbed the ladder and pulled it safely up into the opening. Then they grasped the small, leather band, pulling the rock as quickly as they could back into place, before the soldier found them. Tater quickly found his flashlight, flipped it on and shined its light around the area.

"I wonder where we are, now," said Squeaks.

"I don't care. All I know is that we weren't found by those soldiers and taken to King Noah," Butch answered, relieved.

"Well, where do we go from here?" asked Mrs. M.

"There's a pathway against this wall that I think we should follow," replied Tater. "I think it leads to an opening up ahead."

"Why do you think there is an opening, Tater?" asked Butch.

"I can see a faint light not too far in the distance," Tater replied, pointing. "I hope that it might get us safely into the city, or at least give us a place to start. Everyone, follow me."

The group agreed and moved silently behind Tater as he led the way. They soon reached the light Tater had seen marking another small, square opening that was covered by a stone door.

"What is it with all the rock doors?" questioned Squeaks. "They are too hard to open."

"I think we can push this one open," answered Tater, as he inspected the opening.

"Do you think it's safe to push open the stone?" asked Butch. "There could be soldiers outside."

"We're gonna have to take that chance, Butch. We can't stay in here all day," replied Mrs. M. "We really have no way of knowing if the soldiers heard the rock opening close. If they did, they could be working on getting it open. Tater, why don't you see if you can get through that opening and check to see if the area is safe," suggested Mrs. M. "If it is, signal us so that we can all follow you."

Tater nodded and cautiously pushed open the small, but heavy, stone door as far as he could. Warm air burst through the tiny opening, and the sky glowed a vibrant orange as its light splashed through the opening and into the tunnel. Squeaks held her hands over her eyes, shielding them from the sun's rays, as she waited for them to adjust to the brightness.

"Eee, eee, eee!"

"Kah, kah!"

"Eee, eee!"

"What was that, Tater?" shrieked Mrs. M. She held her hand over her chest, trying to calm her rapidly-beating heart.

"Something in the trees," replied Tater. "I'm not sure if it's a monkey or a bird. I've got to open the door a little more."

Mrs. M. nodded, and Tater pushed again on the heavy stone door, opening it wide enough to squeeze his body through. He then walked out into a forest.

"Can you see anyone?" called Butch, nervously peering through the door. "Are there soldiers nearby?"

"No, no one," Tater quietly replied. "I think we're safe. I think this secret passage has brought us to the edge of the forest, near the city. Everyone, come out here, and let's get this door closed before anyone finds the secret tunnel."

Quickly, Butch, Squeaks, and Mrs. M. moved out into the forest next to Tater. Just then, two animals leaped out of the trees into the warm sun's rays. Their faces were dark and framed with light-gray fur. They had long, white tails and looked like they were wearing dark jackets.

"Look at those," Mrs. M. said excitedly, pointing to the monkeys. "Hero would have loved to see monkeys this close."

"Yeah, they're beautiful," replied Squeaks.

"They look like they're wearing trench coats with that dark fur on their bodies," added Butch.

"I sure wish Hero could see them. He'd be able to tell us what kind they are," said Tater, smiling.

"They keep looking at us," said Squeaks, watching every move they made. "Watch them, they just keep swinging back and forth over our heads."

"Ooo, ooo!"

"Aaahh, aahh!" screeched the monkeys again, swinging directly toward Tater.

"Watch out, Tater," squealed Squeaks, as she ducked for cover. "They're coming toward us."

"Eee, eee!"

"Ooo, ooo!"

The monkeys squawked loudly. Then suddenly, they jumped straight toward Tater.

"Here they come!" screamed Butch. "I think they're going to attack."

Squeaks watched as the larger of the two monkeys jumped on Tater's shoulder and calmly ate a banana. The second monkey climbed onto a branch just above Tater's head and stared at them. Calling and chattering loudly, the monkey in the tree seemed annoyed that the other monkey was sitting on Tater's shoulder. Angrily, it continued calling for several moments. Then, using its long tail, it swung down to the other monkey and knocked the banana out of its hands. The monkey on Tater's shoulder seemed angry. He jumped at the monkey in the tree, and like siblings, they started squawking at each other.

"They're kinda fun to watch," said Butch, breaking the silence.

"Kinda scary too," added Squeaks.

"I think they're just playing around," said Mrs. M. "I bet they're just excited to see humans in the forest."

"The one on my shoulder acted as though he had seen and interacted with humans before," replied Tater, as they all watched the monkeys climb the large, beautiful, leafy tree. They were amazed at the agility of the monkeys as they swung from branch to branch, using both their tails and hands.

"This is so cool," said Squeaks, as she smiled at the monkeys.

"I bet if those monkeys have been around humans, the city has to be close by," said Mrs. M. "We better be careful."

"You're right. If the city is close, then there could be soldiers or guards nearby," agreed Butch.

"What's our plan from here?" asked Squeaks.

"Well, we know we've got to find the city. And according to what you said earlier, Alma wants us to save his people, right?" questioned Tater.

"Yeah, that's true. He asked that we get them out of the city before King Noah's guards find them. But we can't just walk into the city dressed like this. We'll be caught as spies or something like that, and King Noah will have us killed immediately," replied Butch, nervously looking around the area.

"What do you suggest, Butch?" asked Mrs. M.

"We've got to find some clothes or something else to wear, so that we can blend in with everyone else," he replied.

"Any idea which way the city is?" questioned Squeaks.

Suddenly, the monkeys were once again swinging in the trees above their heads. One of the monkeys jumped onto Tater and again perched itself on Tater's shoulder.

"I think that monkey likes you, Tater," said Butch, laughing. "You have a new friend."

"What do I do?" asked Tater.

"You could always try taking it off," replied Squeaks.

"And upset it?" exclaimed Tater. "No thanks! I don't want it squawking at me."

The monkey, sensing Tater's nervousness, climbed down off his shoulder and onto the ground next to him. Then it reached up, taking Tater's hand.

"His paw feels like a tiny, hairy hand," exclaimed Tater—his eyes as wide as golf balls.

"What is the monkey doing?" asked Butch.

"I think it is leading you somewhere, Tater," replied Mrs. M.

"What should I do?" asked Tater, as he slowly walked with the animal.

"Keep walking," replied Mrs. M. "Maybe it is leading us toward the city."

As the monkey walked Tater deeper into the trees, they followed cautiously several feet behind. They walked for several minutes. The hot air suddenly smelled sweet, and the bright afternoon sun gave the outline of the nearby trees a fiery glow.

The forest suddenly sounded alive. Birds of every kind squawked and sang wildly. Frogs croaked constantly, and dragonflies whizzed around, snapping at insects on the trees. Geckos and other small animals scurried all over the forest floor.

"This has got to be paradise," Squeaks said softly. "Everything here is beautiful."

"Aaahhh, aaahhh!" screamed Mrs. M. "There is a snake in the tree! Watch out!"

Butch looked up just in time to see a small, emerald-green, boa disappearing into the thick leaves of the tree. "Don't worry, Mrs. M, that snake isn't going to hurt you."

"But whatever made this could," said Tater, as he passed several deep gashes in the trunk of a nearby tree.

"A jaguar or a leopard?" questioned Butch.

"Probably," Tater replied calmly.

"A jaguar or leopard?" Squeaks squealed, nervously looking around the area.

"I think that is the least of our worries," replied Tater, scanning the surrounding area.

"Why? What's the matter?" asked Mrs. M., scanning the area.

"We're surrounded," Tater whispered nervously.

"Surrounded?" echoed Mrs. M., starting to panic. "Where? I can't see anything."

Only a moment passed before the monkey, that had been leading them toward the city, released Tater's hand and scurried into the leaves and bushes of the forest. Moments later, three young soldiers appeared from behind the trees and yelled into the small clearing where the monkey had led them. The soldiers were dressed in baggy, cream-colored shirts with brown, animal-skin skirts tied around their waists. Their hair was dark brown, but they had fairly light skin and similar facial features to the Team. Unsure what the soldiers were doing, and afraid to move an inch, they stood motionless as the young, spear-carrying soldiers approached.

"Who are you?" demanded one of the soldiers, in a deep, gruff voice.

Sure the soldiers would not be able to understand them, Mrs. M. stepped forward and started drawing a picture of the city in the dirt with her hands.

"Can you not speak?" asked the soldier, irritated by her silence.

Mrs. M. turned back to Tater and said, "Will it annoy the soldiers if I answer in a different language?"

"Maybe the Lord has given us the gift of tongues," he whispered. "We can understand everything they are saying."

"Speak to me, not each other!" screamed the soldier. "Are you spies? Have you been sent here to destroy our city?"

"No, we're not spies," replied Mrs. M., unsure if the soldiers would understand or believe her.

"Who are you then?" the soldier asked gruffly, pointing his spear toward her.

"We are friends of Alma," Squeaks replied, moving closer toward her mom.

"Alma?" asked another soldier. "Alma the high priest?"

"Alma, the man who used to be a high priest," replied Tater. "Currently, he is being sought by King Noah."

"Being sought? He has been captured," announced the soldier. "King Noah has declared that Alma has only a day to deny his God or die the same death as Abinadi."

Squeaks gasped as she raised her hand to cover her mouth, horrified by the story the soldier was telling them.

"Has Abinadi already been killed?" asked Mrs. M.

"I will ask the questions here. Are you followers of Alma?" the soldier sternly demanded.

"Yes, we are," Butch declared boldly. "We believe that what Abinadi and Alma say are the words of God."

"Do all of you believe this?" asked the soldier, pointing his spear at the group.

"I do," replied Tater.

"So do I," Squeaks replied, matter-of-factly.

"And you?" questioned the soldier, holding the spear toward Mrs. M.

"Every word they've said," she calmly replied, though somewhat afraid their answers might cost them their lives.

Chapter Fourteen

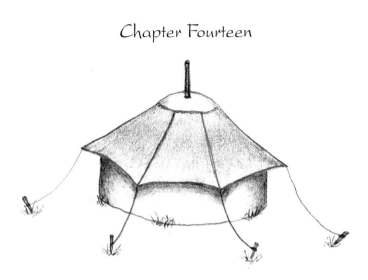

Unsure what the soldiers were going to do with them, the group waited patiently as they whispered amongst themselves for several, long, nerve-racking moments.

"What are they talking about?" asked Squeaks nervously. "How we should die?"

"I don't know," replied Tater, shrugging his shoulders. "Maybe!"

"Do you think they are King Noah's soldiers?" asked Butch.

"They could be," replied Mrs. M. "We have to be careful not to give them too much information until we know for sure."

"What do you mean?" asked Squeaks.

"She means that they could be trying to trick us and get us to lead them to where Alma's people are hiding," replied Butch.

"But we don't know where Alma's people are; that's who we are trying to find," replied Squeaks. "That's why we're on this mission."

"I know that, but they don't know that!" Butch exclaimed loudly.

"Quiet, prisoners!" one of the soldiers yelled angrily. He walked over to the group and firmly took hold of Butch's arm, roughly pulling him toward the trees of the forest.

"Where are we going?" Mrs. M. asked calmly, as the soldiers surrounded the group and forced them to follow the soldier with Butch.

"Quiet! No more questions!" yelled the soldier. "Be quiet and walk, all of you."

The group quietly followed the soldiers into the forest. They walked for nearly fifteen minutes, watching as the foliage around them grew thicker and thicker. The soldier holding Butch's arm finally released him. He took his machete from his waistband and struck wildly at the thick trees and bushes in the forest, making a pathway for the group.

Nervously, Squeaks whispered, "What should we do? We've got to get away from these soldiers before they take us to King Noah. We could be on our way toward the city right now."

"Isn't that where we're trying to go?" asked Butch.

"Yeah, but I didn't really want to end up in King

Noah's prison," Squeaks bluntly replied. "If we're all in prison, none of us will be able to help Alma."

"So, what do you suggest?" questioned Butch.

"We've got to get away from these soldiers and try to find the city on our own," Squeaks said.

"No, we follow them," Tater replied firmly. "There is no way we could hide from them or outrun them in this forest. They have lived here all their lives, and we wouldn't even know where to go. Besides, I really don't want to be killed. Anyway, I think these soldiers might be able to help us."

"But what if they take us to King Noah?" Butch whispered over his shoulder. "You know, Squeaks could be right."

"Then we'll have to formulate a plan to escape," Mrs. M. replied. "But I think Tater is right. These soldiers don't seem to be bad."

The soldier leading the group abruptly stopped, turned to the group and asked, "Are you really followers of Alma? Do you honestly believe and follow the teachings that Abinadi taught?"

"Yes, we have traveled a very long distance from another land to help Alma," Tater replied boldly.

"Do you know that supporters or followers of either Abinadi or Alma are killed?" asked the soldier. "Just for telling me that you support Alma and Abinadi, I have every right to kill you—by order of the king."

"If we have to be killed then we will," replied Mrs. M. "But, none of us will deny the words of the Lord."

"Killed?" Squeaks repeated fearfully.

"Yes, killed," replied the soldier, ignoring Mrs. M.'s comments.

"There have been a lot of times in history when doing the right thing has not always been easy," answered Mrs. M., as she squeezed Squeaks' hand tightly.

"Well, dying isn't easy," Butch said anxiously. "And I would like to see my parents again. But you are right, Mrs. M."

"Does that mean your faith wavers?" asked the soldier, pointing his spear at Butch.

"No, my faith does not wavier. I wouldn't be on this mission if I didn't have the faith to be here," Butch angrily answered. "And I will never deny the words of a prophet or the teachings of the Lord."

"Mission?" questioned the soldier. "What do you mean a mission?"

"Yes, we are on a mission for the Lord," replied Mrs. M. "We have been sent here by the Lord to help Alma."

The soldiers looked at each other for several seconds. Then the soldier in charge motioned for the other two to move closer for a private conversation.

"Don't move, or I will kill you," warned a soldier with long, pale-brown hair.

The group nodded and huddled together, as the soldiers whispered in private for several moments.

"What do you think they are talking about?" whispered Butch.

"Maybe they believe us, and they are discussing whether they should let us go or not," replied Mrs. M., trying to be positive.

"Or maybe they are determining whether they should kill us or take us to King Noah to be killed," replied Squeaks.

"How do we know this is not a trick?" asked Nahom.

"I feel as though the Lord has brought them to us," replied the soldier in charge.

"What about you, Ramin. What do you think?" asked the soldier.

"Well, Seth, I think they are telling the truth. I feel as you do; I think the Lord has sent them to us. Why else would your monkeys have led them to us? They must have a good feeling about them," replied Ramin.

"I hadn't thought about that, but you are right," agreed Seth.

"I still don't like this," argued Ramin suspiciously.

"Then keep a close eye on them, Nahom," suggested Seth. "'Cause, I have a good feeling about them."

Nahom nodded. Seth turned to the nervously-waiting group and asked, "The mission that you spoke of, does that bring you from a far away place?"

"Yes," replied Butch.

"Is that why you wear the odd clothes that you do?" asked Seth.

"Yes," answered Butch. "This is how the people of our time dress."

"Well, you will never make it past King Noah's soldiers dressed like that," he said. He took hold of Tater's shirt, rubbing the material. "We don't have anything like this is our land. My name is Seth, this is Ramin," he said, pointing to the soldier on his left. "And this is Nahom," he said, pointing to the soldier on his right. "We are also followers of Alma."

"You're not going to take us to King Noah?" Squeaks excitedly asked.

"Not unless you'd like us to," Seth replied, smiling. "We would like to take you to our secret camp, if that is okay with you."

"Yes, thanks," said Squeaks, with a grin on her face. "That way we can get started looking for Alma and helping his people."

"Can you please tell me, what are your names?" asked Ramin.

"This is Squeaks," answered Mrs. M. "And I am either Mom or Mrs. M."

"I'm Tater."

"And my name is Butch."

"It is nice to meet more followers of the Lord," replied Seth. "Now, follow me to camp, but be very careful. We are not far from the city, and King Noah's soldiers are searching everywhere for us."

"Are you soldiers?" asked Squeaks.

"Yes, we are soldiers for King Noah. However, after hearing the words of Alma, we have had a change of heart.

We want to follow the teachings of the Lord," replied Ramin.

"Have you been able to keep Alma's followers safe?" asked Mrs. M.

"So far," replied Nahom. "That is, if you four are who you say you are."

"We are," Tater replied reassuringly.

"Are all of Alma's followers in the camp?" asked Mrs. M.

"No, we are still waiting for more to join us before we leave," replied Ramin.

"Why haven't they joined you yet?" asked Tater, following closely behind the soldiers.

"Because their every move is being closely watched in the city, and the forest is being searched continually. If they did somehow get passed the soldiers in the city, they would likely be seen by the soldiers searching in the forest. And if they are followed here, all of our lives would be in danger," Nahom explained. "All of us must be very careful. Besides warning soldiers in the area, there are numerous traps that have been set by King Noah's men to catch who he calls 'traitors'."

"How are we going to help them escape, so that we can do as Alma has requested and return home before it is too late?" Squeaks asked fretfully.

"I'm sure the Lord will show us the way," Tater replied positively. "He has already led us to some of his followers. I'm sure he will help us save the rest."

"Have you spoken with Alma?" asked Nahom, with a shocked look on his face.

"I think it is our fault that he was captured," answered Tater.

"What?" yelled Nahom. "It is because of you that a messenger of the Lord was captured? See, I told you, Seth, they are only here to capture Alma's followers. We have revealed ourselves as soldiers of King Noah and that we are followers of Alma. We are doomed for sure."

"Yes, unfortunately, some responsibility lies on my shoulders for Alma's capture," replied Squeaks, with a sad look on her face. "But we do not have anything to do with King Noah. It will not be because of us if you are discovered."

"Relax, Nahom. Take a breath. They must have a good explanation as to why they had anything to do with Alma's capture," insisted Ramin.

"I do! I accidentally fell into the river," started Squeaks. "And as my friends searched for me, they were followed by King Noah's soldiers. While I waited for my friends in the water, the soldiers found Alma and arrested him."

"See, I told you, Seth. They are not here to help us. They are here to lead King Noah's soldiers to us," insisted Nahom.

"No, we are not here to lead King Noah's soldiers to you. It was an accident," insisted Squeaks.

"How were you able to talk to Alma if he was arrested?" asked Seth.

"The soldiers held him upside down, sticking his head in the water and trying to get him to talk. While they were holding him, he saw me hiding in the water. He told me he was expecting us, and he told me what he needed us to do," replied Squeaks.

"What else did he say?" asked Ramin.

"Alma told me that we needed to help his followers get to safety. Then he told me how to get to safety and to follow the promptings of the Lord," Squeaks replied softly.

"He told you where the hidden Waters of Mormon are?" Seth asked excitedly

"I don't know if they were the hidden Waters of Mormon, but they were very secret. We found a hidden passage from the river to the hidden waters, which led us to you," answered Butch.

"We were going to the secret Waters of Mormon before Alma was arrested. He was on his way here to our secret camp to lead us there," Nahom said angrily. "It is because of you that we are not already safe."

"I'm sorry," Squeaks answered softly, as a tear rolled down her cheek. "I really didn't mean to lead the soldiers to Alma."

"No need to worry about that now. We have more important things to think about," interrupted Tater. "Like how we are going to rescue Alma, and how we are going to get the rest of Alma's followers to safety."

"I agree," said Ramin. He pulled back the leaves of a large tree, revealing a small, hidden village.

"Are we safe here?" asked Mrs. M., as she cautiously climbed through the leaves of the trees and headed toward the village.

"Yes, you will be safe here," answered Seth, as he hurried toward a small tent near the center of the village.

"Father, Father, are you in here?" Seth excitedly yelled. He threw the tent flap back to reveal the interior of the tent.

"Quiet, Seth. You are going to lead the entire army right to our camp!" a deep, strong voice answered.

Mrs. M., Squeaks, and the boys watched as a stout man, approximately five foot ten, appeared in the doorway. He had dark-brown hair, dark eyes, and very well defined muscles on his arms and legs.

"Now, who do you have with you?" asked the man, with a suspicious look on his face.

"Nahom, Ramin, and I found them wandering in the forest. They say they are followers of Alma. They are here to help free his people and get us to the Waters of Mormon safely," Seth replied, excited at his find.

"And you believe these people, Son?" his father asked suspiciously.

"Yes, Father. In fact, they have already been to the hidden Waters of Mormon and were in the river when Alma was caught. They talked to him," Seth replied.

"You have spoken with Alma?" asked the man, looking directly at Mrs. M.

"I didn't," Mrs. M. replied. "My daughter, Squeaks, did."

"And what did he tell you, child?" questioned the man, unsure whether or not to believe her.

"He told me how to get through the river to safety. He told me the Lord told him we would come to help. He also told me that we needed to get his followers to safety before King Noah's soldiers found them," Squeaks confidently replied.

"I apologize for all the questions, but you have to

understand how careful we need to be," stated the man. "Now, can you tell me exactly what I would have to do to get to the hidden Waters of Mormon?"

"From the river?" Squeaks asked confidently.

"Yes, from the river," replied the man.

"Well, under the water on the river bottom are three large rocks, which, by the way, are guarded by all sorts of scary fish. But, between the rocks is a secret entrance. If you travel through the entrance, it leads down a long, dark tunnel. At the end of the tunnel is a small lake, with a beautiful waterfall surrounded by trees, making the entire area hidden," Squeaks replied.

The man's face softened and he nodded, turning abruptly and moving back inside the tent. Seth, unsure what to do, followed his father inside.

"So, what do you think, Father?" he asked.

"I think they are exactly who you say they are," he replied.

"Can you help me get them into the city safely?" Seth asked, hopeful for his father's help.

"Bring them in, and I will see what can be done," his father replied.

Seth appeared outside the tent. He looked out at the group as a huge smile spread crossed his face. My father has agreed to help us," he announced. "Please follow me inside. He wishes to talk to you."

They group nervously entered the room. Surprisingly, the tent was filled with many comforts. Covering the dirt on the floor was a beautiful hand-sewn rug. Several blankets were neatly folded in the corner of the tent, and at least six small pillows were scattered over the rug on the floor. A large bowl of fruit was sitting on a small table, and several small, wicker baskets were neatly stacked together by the blankets.

"Do not be afraid," said the man, as he pointed to the pillows. "Please sit down; we have much to talk about."

"Why do you believe them, Helam?" Nahom asked. "It is their fault that Alma was captured. We could be free of King Noah and be safe, if Alma had not been captured."

"Nahom, you know that only the Lord's will is done," replied Helam. "What if there is someone in prison that the Lord needs Alma to talk to before we depart this city?"

"Your name, it is Helam?" Mrs. M. quietly interrupted.

"Yes, it is," he replied.

"You are the first of Alma's followers to be baptized?" Mrs. M. inquisitively asked.

"I can only hope so, but that is up to the Lord," he replied. "I was going to be baptized today. We were all planning to go to the hidden Waters of Mormon. But, with Alma's capture, I will have to wait. How did you know I was to be baptized?"

"In our time, we have the records of the prophets, all complied together as a book. That book tells us about the things that happened in your day. We hope to learn from the mistakes of your day, and we try not to make the same mistakes in our day," she replied.

"Your day?" Helam questioned.

"We have been sent here by the Lord from another time to help Alma and his followers. When we have set right what has gone wrong, the Lord will send us home,"

Mrs. M. replied. "However, we only have a small amount of time to complete our mission."

"Then we will help you to complete your mission, so that you may return home as quickly as possible," said Helam, as he motioned for Seth to move closer.

Seth quickly moved toward his father, kneeling at his side. "Yes, Father?"

"Take Nahom and Ramin, go into the city as soldiers of King Noah, and help our new friends reach Alma," insisted Helam. "Before you leave, find them suitable clothes to wear, so they will not appear as visitors while they are in the city. Help them to speak with Alma, or at least relay their message to him. Then, if possible, help those followers who are still waiting to escape, to leave the city. Then hurry back."

Seth nodded. He quietly turned, motioned for his friends to follow, and quickly left the tent.

"These are good boys and great soldiers. Trust them to keep you safe, and do as they ask," counseled Helam. "My prayers will be with you for a safe journey. Now hurry."

The group jumped to their feet and hurried out the tent door to the waiting soldiers. Seth had tied leather bands around his arm and leg, indicating his seniority with King Noah's soldiers. All three men had put on different color robes.

"My mother, Caina, has found suitable clothes for you," said Seth. He handed dresses to the girls, and shirts, pants, and robes to the boys. "Change your clothes, and leave all of your belongings here."

"What about my backpack?" asked Tater, hesitant to leave it.

"We have nothing like that here. If you take it with you, others will recognize that you don't belong here," answered Ramin.

"Yes, but both men and women carry knapsacks here. They are made of leather and are tied with a drawstring at the top. Would that work for you?" questioned Helam.

Yes, that way I can take the things with us that I will need to help Alma escape," replied Tater, relieved not to leave the contents of his backpack.

Helam motioned to Seth, and he quickly disappeared into his family's tent. Only moments passed before he returned with two brown and black leather bags. Seth handed one to Tater and one to Butch.

"Thank you, Seth," said Tater. He dumped the contents of his backpack on the ground and started to fill the knapsack.

"The knapsack isn't going to be big enough for everything, so take only what you think you might need. Leave the rest in your backpack here at camp," suggested Mrs. M.

"Is it safe?" asked Butch, not wanting to lose anything.

"Everything you leave will be safe here. My father will see to it," answered Seth. "Now, hurry and change," he ordered impatiently. "We must get moving."

The girls followed Caina to a tent, not far away, while the boys moved back inside Helam's tent to change. Once they were finished, everyone hurried outside. Then Seth and the other soldiers set out with the group toward the city of King Noah.

Chapter Fifteen

The group silently maneuvered through the thick bushes and trees of the forest, struggling with every step, for nearly a mile. Mrs. M., unable to move another inch, sat down on a fallen log and worked to regain her breath.

"Everyone wait, please," she called, panting for breath. "I can't keep up with your pace. Please give me just a minute."

"Hold it, Seth," called Tater, standing back by Mrs. M. "We need just a minute."

Wiping the sweat from her head, Mrs. M. leaned back on the log, enjoying the slight breeze in the air. She hoped the rest might help to cool her down. Wishing she had a little water to drink, she scanned the area, searching for any sign of water.

"Aaaahhhhh, aaaahhhhh, a dragon!" she screamed at the top of her lungs. She struggled to get away and fell off the log, startled by the animal.

"Are you okay, Mom?" asked Squeaks, as she hurried to her mom's side.

"What happened? What's the matter, Mrs. M.?" called Butch, frightened by her screams.

"Quiet! Quiet now! We're close to the city," insisted Ramin. "If you scream like that, soldiers will come to see what is wrong."

"Yeah, I don't want other soldiers to come searching," added Nahom. "It's only an old lizard. Now, be quiet."

"Sorry, guys," replied Mrs. M., as Butch helped her to her feet. "I was just surprised to see a very large, dragon-looking lizard an inch from my face."

"We better keep moving," suggested Seth. "I don't feel safe just sitting here."

Mrs. M. nodded as she brushed the dirt from her pants. The group continued working their way through the area. Mrs. M. smiled as she glanced back at the huge lizard, still sunning himself on a rock next to a fallen tree.

The group pushed through the forest, finally reaching an enormous willow tree. Its branches reached all the way to the ground and were covered in large, beautiful, green leaves. Seth cautiously maneuvered through the branches until the group stepped into a clearing. The group was excited as the opening revealed a series of beautiful buildings and temples.

"Is this the city of King Noah?" asked Squeaks, as a grin spread across her face.

"Yes, this is where the city begins," Nahom replied abruptly. "Now, don't act like you have never been to the city before."

"Yes, that is right," agreed Seth. "People will get suspicious if you act like visitors."

"This is actually the outer most edge of the city," added Ramin. "There are not a lot of people, and everyone knows each other."

The group walked down a small city street, nearly one hundred yards, until the buildings began to be more frequent.

"Are the buildings that we are passing temples?" questioned Tater, as he admired their beauty.

"No, these buildings are actually homes," replied Nahom.

"Wow! They're beautiful," said Mrs. M., gazing at the lush beauty they were surrounded by. "I can't believe they are just homes. I bet the temples are even more dramatic."

"You're acting like you don't belong in the city. Now please, do as I have asked. Act normally, and don't point or draw attention to yourselves or cause a commotion. You're going to get us caught and killed if you don't stop," Nahom said angrily.

"Sorry," replied Mrs. M. "I've just never seen anything like this before."

"Act like you have, or you will never get the chance to again," replied Nahom, looking around the area to make sure they were not being watched.

The group walked through the city, amazed at the beauty of the area, but unable to really admire all of the details. They passed a few scattered houses made of wood, but the rest of the homes they saw were built of stone and bricks. Beautiful gardens with flowers and trees decorated every home. As they moved further into the city, the gardens grew scarce and buildings became more abundant. Buildings and temples were constructed of stone and carved with beautiful pictures and symbols.

"What do all these symbols mean?" asked Squeaks, pointing toward a building.

"Please don't point. Just describe the building, and we'll tell you what the building is used for," Nahom insisted angrily.

"On the buildings owned by King Noah, each picture carved in the stone describes what is done in that building," answered Ramin. "For instance, the building you pointed at is where taxes are collected. So, carved in the stone is King Noah's tax system, telling that one fifth of everything you own must be given to him."

"And that building?" questioned Butch, nodding toward the building on his right.

"That is the weaponry," replied Nahom.

"Weaponry?" questioned Squeaks. "Like guns?"

"No, not guns, Squeaks," replied Mrs. M., smiling. "Weaponry in Book of Mormon times are things like spears, bows, machetes or knives."

"Oh, I didn't think about that," Squeaks replied, smiling as she shrugged her shoulders.

"Yes, Mrs. M., you are right. Can you see the arrow,

spear, and armor engravings on the front of the building?" asked Tater, nodding his head in the direction of the building.

"Wow," replied Squeaks. "That is really cool."

"I wish I could read Egyptian," said Mrs. M. "I would love to know what everything means."

"Well, some of the writing is good, but some of the writing is bad," replied Seth. "You're lucky you can't read all of it."

The group continued deeper into the city. They walked on roads that were paved with small rocks, carefully laid to form a nearly-flat surface. They tried to walk casually with each other, talking and laughing as though the group belonged in the city, marveling at all the sites. They walked passed what looked like a saloon filled with people laughing and eating, a man playing a silly-looking instrument, and then through the market. In addition to food of all kinds, they saw jewelry, clothes, pottery, farming tools, weaponry made of stone, metal and bone, fishing equipment, and even canoes.

As Tater walked passed one of the shops, he noticed large bowls filled with grains and dried fruits, and he suddenly remembered how hungry he was. He looked longingly at the food, hoping dinner time would come shortly. Seth noticed Tater's face and stopped at a vendor, asking the small, elderly lady for something he did not understand. As he paid her for the item, Seth turned and handed everyone a piece of his purchase.

"Eat," he suggested, as he tore off a piece and placed it in his mouth.

"What is this?" asked Squeaks, as she hesitantly took a bite.

"Some of the best bread you will ever eat in your life," Seth replied. He tore another small piece from his slice and placed it in his mouth. "This is called Spelt, or the bread of kings."

"Thank you, Seth," said Mrs. M., taking the bread from his hand and eating. "This is very good."

Starving after their breakfast hours ago, they all gladly ate, wishing they had more to fill their hungry stomachs. The group continued further into the city until they reached another series of shops and vendors that filled a large square. People, horses, carts, and more shops were everywhere.

"Honey cake! Bread! Eggs!" sellers called, hoping for business from the group.

"Don't listen to that crazy Abinadi!" yelled a man standing on a box, giving a speech to the crowd. "We can make our own choices."

"What are they talking about, Mom?" Squeaks whispered, surprised by the man's comments.

"There are people who don't believe Alma or Abinadi. That man evidently doesn't believe in the Lord's word, and he is trying to persuade others to believe as he does," she replied.

"The nice part is, we all have the freedom to make our own choices," added Seth.

Just beyond the square, at the inner most part of the city, they reached the most elegant and ornate building they had seen so far. Large stones, over fifty feet tall, marked the entrance and beautiful stone walkways led to the door.

"This is King Noah's palace," said Seth. "It is marked by several carvings, like the bird, the snake, the jaguar, and the cat, but each has its own meanings."

"I can see them all," replied Mrs. M., staring at the carved pictures. "Is this where he is holding Alma prisoner?"

"No, if you look to the north, just beyond that grove of trees, there is a building. You must cross a bridge, about thirty feet in length, to get to the prison. The prison is surrounded by a man-made moat that is about one-hundred feet deep. The moat is filled with approximately twenty-five feet of water and every dangerous water animal known to man. That is where Abinadi is being held, and most likely where the king is also holding Alma," replied Nahom.

"How do we find out?" Squeaks asked impatiently, worried about the prophet's safety.

"There are only two ways that I can think of," replied Ramin. "Either be captured and thrown into jail with them or...," he paused, looking over to Seth.

"Or what," insisted Tater.

"Or I can ask to be a prison soldier and work at the prison," Seth replied.

"That sounds easy," said Butch. "Why don't you do that? Who do you have to ask?"

"Easy?" gasped Seth. "Do you find it easy to whip your prophet?"

"Whip? What do you mean?" Mrs. M. asked anxiously. "Why would you have to whip the prophet?"

"As a rule, King Noah expects that every soldier treat all the prisoners with disrespect. The prisoners are regularly beaten and whipped by the soldiers. I'm just not sure if I can do it," he replied.

"I agree," said Mrs. M. "I would never ask you to disrespect a prophet of the Lord. We will find another way to locate Alma."

"I know of another way," Nahom said quietly. "But it is very risky."

"How? What other way?" demanded Seth. "I don't know of any other way."

"Alma once told me there is a secret entrance through the high priest's throne room inside King Noah's temple. The tunnel travels under the water, making it very dangerous. But it leads to an underground opening by a large rock, with stairs that lead up inside the prison on the island," replied Nahom.

"Are you sure?" Tater asked excitedly.

"I have never seen the tunnel myself, but that is what Alma told me," Nahom replied. "I'm sure he told me, just in case something like his capture ever took place."

"Do you really think we could use the tunnel to rescue Alma?" Squeaks asked anxiously.

"If the tunnel is really there, then that is very possible," replied Seth, deep in thought. "I'm just surprised that I didn't know about the secret tunnel."

"If one of you will tell me how to get into the High Priests' throne room, I will try to find the entrance," said Butch, as he stared at the king's temple. "I'm fairly small; I know I could sneak inside and find the entrance."

"If you are caught, you will most likely pay with your life," replied Ramin. "We cannot let you go into the temple alone. King Noah does not allow peasants into his temple."

"We'll have to make a plan," suggested Seth, as he turned and headed back toward the market. "Follow me. We look suspicious standing here staring at the temple."

The group hesitantly followed Seth fifty yards back into the marketplace, listening to the vendors call out their wares in hope of a sale. Seth found a safe place to sit down, with a clear view of the temple, and waited as the others sat down around him.

"Okay, what is the plan?" questioned Ramin. "You know as well as I do that without an invitation or an escort, no one is allowed in King Noah's temple—especially into the High Priests' throne room."

"There has to be a way to get inside," insisted Tater. "I think that is our best option."

"I agree, that is our best option," repeated Mrs. M. "What about me? Would they expect anything bad from a middle-aged woman if I entered the temple?"

Silently, Seth shook his head, holding his hand over his mouth for several moments before he responded. "Mrs. M., I'm sorry, you are the last person I would allow to try. You would be spotted immediately, I'm sure of it."

"I agree, Seth," said Nahom. "I think it would be better for me and one of the boys to try to get inside."

"Why not me?" asked Squeaks, obviously disappointed. "No one would think I was a threat."

"For one, you are too small," said Tater.

"And two, you are a girl. Girls are not allowed into the

High Priests' throne room—only invited women or maidens," added Seth.

"And three, I would never let you go alone," Mrs. M. said sternly. "A little girl by herself in an unknown land...I don't think so!"

"But Mom, I think that I can find the entrance and not be seen," argued Squeaks. "As the smallest one here, I could easily move through the area."

"Not a chance," her mom replied firmly. "That's not an option."

Squeaks, disappointed and sure her mom wouldn't change her mind, took a deep breath, shrugged her shoulders, turned and walked into the market. "Since you're not going to let me help, I'm gonna take a look around the market and see what they have for sale," she said angrily, trying to annoy her mom.

"Stay close," replied Mrs. M., smirking. "And even if you give me attitude, I will still not allow you to go inside King Noah's temple alone."

The group watched as she heatedly marched off into the distance, slowly looking around at the wares in the market.

"Back to business," started Seth. "We only have a few hours before the High Priests will leave the room for the day. We will not have another opportunity to enter the temple today."

"Would it make more sense to try and find the secret entrance after dark?" asked Butch. "When no one is there?"

"I don't think so," replied Nahom. "King Noah is very suspicious of everything. He has more than thirty soldiers who guard the temple at night. I think we would certainly be caught."

"I could go in and report my findings in the search for Alma to the High Priests," suggested Seth.

"Would that work?" asked Ramin.

"Maybe," replied Seth. "I could say that I was unable to locate the commander, and wanted to report to the priests my findings, so that they could inform the King. Maybe you could go with me, Tater, and inconspicuously scan over the area while I talk to them."

"That could work," replied Mrs. M. "Risky, but possible."

"How would we explain who I am?" asked Tater. "I'm sure they would ask."

"You are a new soldier in training," replied Ramin. "That way, they wouldn't question why you were looking around the room."

"It's a long shot," replied Nahom. "But I think it might work."

"If we find the secret entrance, what then?" asked Tater. "It's not like we would be able to enter the secret entrance right then."

"You could return right before the high priests leave the room," suggested Butch.

"No, I think that might be suspicious," replied Nahom.

"I don't think we'll be able to sneak in later - the patrolling soldiers would likely catch us," replied Ramin nervously.

"I think Butch might have the best idea. We might

have to try and sneak inside the room, just as all the high priests leave for the day," said Tater. "Especially if I spot the secret entrance."

Seth nodded his head and replied, "Yes, I think you're right. Our only option will be to sneak inside the room just as everyone is leaving for the day. That way, we can search without anyone knowing."

"Well, we better hurry," insisted Ramin. "You never know for sure how long the High Priests are actually going to work."

"All right," started Seth, taking charge. "Tater and I will leave right now to report to the High Priests. While we're inside, we'll try to locate the secret entrance. Then we'll wait outside. Just as the high priests are leaving, I will try to sidetrack the priests while Tater sneaks back inside the room. After they are gone, I will knock on the door lightly three times, and Tater, you can let me in. After we're both inside the room, if we didn't spot the opening, we'll search for it. When we find it, we'll search the tunnel for the entrance to the prison that Alma talked about."

"What do you want us to do?" asked Nahom.

"Wait here for us to signal that we've found an entrance. After you see the signal, walk over toward the prison. Stay far enough away that you do not to bring attention to the group. Watch for any sign of us from there," replied Seth. "We're going to need some help to get the prisoners out without being caught."

"Why don't you take them out the secret tunnel?" asked Tater.

"Because we'll have to return through the High

Priests' room and then out the temple. We would be seen for sure by the night guards," replied Seth.

"Can anyone see Squeaks?" interrupted Mrs. M. "I can't locate her anywhere in the market."

"I just saw her a minute ago," replied Tater, looking over at the vendors.

"So did I," said Ramin. "She was looking at the jewelry."

The group frantically scanned the market, but found no sign of Squeaks anywhere.

"You don't think she was caught, do you?" Mrs. M. nervously asked.

"No, not in the market," Nahom replied optimistically. "She's got to be here somewhere. I'm sure she is just shopping."

"What about Butch?" questioned Seth, looking around the group. "Where did he go?"

"He's right...," started Tater, as he looked to where Butch had been standing.

"Where did he go?" asked Mrs. M. "What is going on around here?"

"You don't think he would have tried our plan by himself do you?" Seth asked nervously.

"I don't think so," replied Tater.

The group looked toward King Noah's temple, hoping not to see any sign of the two. Then Nahom spotted Butch moving cautiously toward the main entrance.

"Look," he shrieked angrily, pointing toward the temple. "Isn't that both Butch and Squeaks?"

"Oh, it better not be," Mrs. M. replied angrily, as she

looked to where Nahom was pointing. "Those two are both gonna be in serious trouble."

"It is Squeaks and Butch!" answered Tater. "What in the world are they doing?"

"Trying to get killed," said Nahom. "Or tip off the King that the Lord has sent people to help us."

"Should I call them back?" asked Tater. He placed his hand up to his mouth, ready to scream their names.

"Wait, no, no, don't call them," insisted Seth. "If you do that, we'll have all the soldiers in the city after us."

Unable to say or do anything, the group watched as Butch and Squeaks cautiously maneuvered up to the temple. They pulled the huge door open, rounded the corner and then suddenly vanished inside.

"What now? What should I do now?" shrieked Tater. "If they get caught, they will be killed!"

"Let's go on with the same plan," insisted Seth. "If they happen to find the entrance then we'll meet them there and all of us escape at the same time."

"And if they are caught, then they'll be put into prison, and we'll be able to free them with Alma," added Tater.

"I think you're right, guys," replied Mrs. M., as she looked at them nervously. "Just please get them out of there safely. I don't want then to be caught or killed."

"Don't worry, Mrs. M. We'll get those two back safely," Seth said reassuringly. "We've just got to find them before the King does."

"Yeah, Mrs. M. Everything will be all right," agreed Tater. "We'll get them back."

"Nahom, Ramin, after we signal you, please take Mrs. M. over toward the prison and follow the rest of the plan." asked Seth. He patted his friends on the shoulders and headed for King Noah's temple. "Hopefully, we will see you very soon."

"Wish us luck," Tater called, smiling.

"You know we do," replied Ramin. "We'll be waiting for you."

Chapter Sixteen

"Where should we go, Butch?" asked Squeaks as she quietly hid behind a stone statue.

"I don't know. I guess we better just start checking all the rooms," replied Butch, nervously looking around the area.

"You know we're gonna be in major trouble, right?" said Squeaks.

"I know, but I couldn't sit there anymore," replied Butch. "I wanted to start getting something done!"

Butch scanned the great room, which seemed to be the main hall of the temple. Directly in the center was a large stone pool with a beautiful stone statue right in the middle of the water. The room was filled with large paintings and several large statues scattered around the room.

Butch searched the area for any sign of people, but saw no one. With the great room empty, Butch motioned for Squeaks to follow. They cautiously moved from behind a stone statue near the main door, deeper into the temple. As the two walked through the grand hall, Butch spotted two small hallways, one at both ends of the room.

"In the books that I have read, the family lived and the business took place in the same temple. So, I bet one of those hallways leads to business-type rooms and the other hallway leads to personal bedrooms," said Butch, pointing.

"So then, which one do we take?" asked Squeaks.

"You choose, Squeaks. Either way, we have a fifty-fifty chance of finding where the high priests' room is," replied Butch. "But hurry. We've got to get out of here before someone comes."

"Okay, let's try the one on the left," suggested Squeaks, as she started walking that way.

Carefully, they moved through the room toward the hallway. Butch kept an eye on the area. He moved into the lead, keeping Squeaks a few feet behind him for safety. As he peered down the hallway, he noticed several rooms with their doors propped wide open. The hallway was beautifully decorated with fine linens on the windows, hand painted murals on the walls, and vases of all sizes and shapes placed in several locations throughout the area.

"What do you think? Is this the right hallway?" asked Squeaks impatiently.

"I can't tell for sure. I think this might be the house side of the temple," replied Butch. "I can hear singing and voices, but I'm not sure they are men's voices."

"Should we try the other hallway?" asked Squeaks.

"I think so," replied Butch. He moved tentatively toward the hallway on the other side of the room.

"Why are you moving so slowly?" questioned Squeaks, anxious to find the secret tunnel.

"I have a bad feeling about all of this," he quietly whispered. "None of this moving around in an unknown temple, with the possibility of guards and King Noah being anywhere, feels safe."

Squeaks, sensing the tension in Butch's voice, silently followed him from statue to statue, careful to stay hidden, in case anyone entered the room. When they were nearly to the opening in the hallway, three men unexpectedly walked into the grand room, surprising the two teammates.

"Uuhhh," Squeaks softly said, trying to move behind the statue before she was seen.

"What'd ya say?" questioned the closest soldier.

"I didn't say anything," replied another soldier.

"I thought I heard something, sorry," answered the soldier, looking suspiciously around the room.

The soldiers continued through the grand room until they reached the front entrance. Then they swiftly disappeared outside.

"That was close, Squeaks," Butch snapped. "You've gotta watch and be careful, no matter what."

"I didn't mean it," she replied, as tears welled up in her eyes.

"I know," Butch replied. "But you've got to be careful, or we're gonna both be in a lot of trouble."

Butch moved from behind the statue. He glanced down the hallway and saw six rooms with the doors propped open. He could see no silk draperies, no statues and nothing decorating the hallway.

"This must be the right hallway," Butch said excitedly.

"Which room do we try first?" asked Squeaks, looking down the hallway.

"We've got to get out of this main room before someone spots us," insisted Butch. "So let's just start with the first room and move our way down from there."

"We're gonna have to move fast," said Squeaks. "I can't see anything we can hide behind down the hallway.

"Are you ready?" Butch questioned as he took hold of Squeaks' hand. "Come on then, we better hurry."

Butch raced toward the first doorway, nervous that at any moment soldiers might walk out. As they reached the opening, Butch laid his body against the stone wall and cautiously peered inside the room. As he scanned the area, he noticed what resembled a court room. There was a galley of benches where he thought an audience would sit, and a table on the right and left sides of the room. There was a raised platform for the judge, and three small benches for the jury or high priests in the front of the room.

"Can you see anything?" Squeaks asked anxiously, as she watched the hallway leading to the grand room for anyone to enter.

"No, this must not be the High Priests' chambers," replied Butch. "Are you ready to go to the next room?"

Squeaks nodded. Butch again took her small hand

and headed deeper into the hallway toward the next open door. As they neared the door, several loud obnoxious voices echoed through the stone walls.

"I guess there are people in this room," whispered Squeaks. "What now?"

Butch shrugged his shoulders and held his index finger to his mouth, signaling for Squeaks to be quiet. He laid his body flat against the stone wall and cautiously peered through the door. Inside, he could see at least thirty men, and about ten or so women. The women were serving the men drinks and food, while the men yelled and argued with each other.

"This has to be the right room," Butch said excitedly, as he turned and looked at Squeaks. "All the men are debating, and no one is coming to any conclusions."

"So what now?" asked Squeaks. She was glad they found the right room, but sure at any moment they would be found by soldiers entering the hallway.

"We've got to get inside," Butch replied, quickly looking back into the room.

"Any ideas how, without being seen?" Squeaks asked sarcastically.

Silently contemplating for several moments, Butch surprised Squeaks when he replied, "I know what we can do! All we have to do is dress up like those women and bring in trays of food, like we're here to serve the High Priests more food."

"Do you think that will work?" she asked. "And where are we going to find something to dress in and trays of food?"

"I'll bet there is a kitchen in here somewhere. Maybe we can find something in there," Butch replied. He swiftly moved passed the opened door and further down the hallway.

"Hey, wait for me," Squeaks whispered quietly, as she hurried past the opened door.

Butch and Squeaks moved swiftly through the hallway, being careful not to make a noise. As they reached the next room, Butch nervously peered inside. To his surprise, he saw several soldiers sitting inside. He turned to Squeaks, motioning for her to be quiet and pointed inside.

Squeaks, anxious to see what he was pointing at, curiously looked inside the room. "That's the soldier that took Alma," she nervously whispered, pointing toward one of the men.

"We've got to keep going," Butch insisted. He maneuvered as fast as he could past the door with Squeaks right behind him.

Reaching the last door down the hallway, Butch anxiously looked inside, hoping it would be a kitchen. Relieved when he spotted fruits and vegetables of all kinds on the counter, he turned to Squeaks and softly said, "All right, we're in luck."

He moved cautiously inside the kitchen, searching for any sign of people. Unable to see anyone, he hurried to the table of food. After grabbing a handful of berries and throwing them inside his mouth, he turned to Squeaks and said, "Now, all we have to do is find something we can wear to conceal who we really are."

Squeaks, starving, hurried to the table and picked up

three carrots. "This food looks so good. I'm so hungry," she said and took a bite of a carrot.

"Hey, look what I found," said Butch, holding up several cloths.

"What are they?" questioned Squeaks through a mouthful of food.

"I'm not sure, but I think they're big enough that we could use them to veil our heads and faces," he replied. He threw the material over his head, pulled it tight under his chin and posed for Squeaks.

"That's scary," Squeaks teased, laughing at Butch's expression. "Now, what do we use over our clothes?"

"There has to be something in here," replied Butch, hastily scanning the kitchen.

"What about an apron?" questioned Squeaks. "Do you think that would work?

"Probably, why?" asked Butch. "Did you find one?"

"Yeah, they're kinda big, but I think these might work," Squeaks replied, holding up the brightly colored material.

"Are there any colors that are not so vibrant?" he asked, as he took one of the aprons from Squeaks' hand.

"No, you've got a choice of neon yellow, red, magenta or bright green," she replied, chuckling.

"Which color isn't going to be as noticeable?" asked Butch, as he shook his head.

Squeaks chuckled and rummaged through the aprons for several moments. She chose green and quickly handed it to Butch. Then she ate several grapes from the table as she watched Butch tie on the apron. Smiling, she helped him throw the material over his head.

"Oh, this is perfect. The material is long and hangs down your back, covering your hairy legs," Squeaks giggled.

"Good, let's get going then," replied Butch. He grabbed a tray of fruit and headed for the door. "I sure hope no one sees me like this. Promise never to tell anyone."

"This is going to be a great story," replied Squeaks, almost laughing out loud.

"Oh, great!" exclaimed Butch as he turned and walked out the kitchen door.

Squeaks tied on her apron and threw a veil over her head. She grabbed a tray of food and hurried to keep up with Butch.

"What do we do now?" she nervously asked, as Butch continued down the hallway.

"When we reach the High Priests' room, walk in confidently. Act as though you belong here. Take a tray of food and carry it around the room, offering something to everyone that you see. Continue maneuvering around like you are waiting on someone who needs food. But the entire time, search for the secret opening Nahom talked about. If we find the opening, then let's find a place to set the trays down. If possible, try to disappear into the opening without being seen," he replied. "Otherwise, we'll wait until it's safe to enter the secret opening."

"What do we do if we can't find the secret tunnel?" asked Squeaks, moving quickly to keep up.

"Then we keep looking," Butch replied, annoyed by all the questions.

As he reached the door, to what he hoped was the

high priests' room, Butch took a deep breath. He pulled the cloth tightly over his face and confidently walked inside. Following only seconds behind was Squeaks, trying to act as confidently as Butch. Unnoticed by anyone in the room, the two wandered around and offered fruit and vegetable to the people inside, being careful not to attract any attention to themselves. As they walked around, they searched for any sign of a secret entrance.

"Do you see anything, Butch?" whispered Squeaks, as she passed him walking around the room. "I haven't seen anything yet."

"I haven't either," he softly replied, careful no one could hear him. "But we haven't searched the area where the high priests sit. I wonder if something is hidden behind the seats or pulpit up there."

"So, do we wait until they leave, or what?" asked Squeaks, looking up at the group of men.

"No, I have an idea," replied Butch. "You start on the left, and I will start on the right. Offer the men food, look behind the pulpit for any openings, and then quickly move away Okay?"

Squeaks nodded nervously. Then the two started to maneuver toward the high priests' area. Half way across the room, Butch headed to the right and Squeaks moved to the left. They offered food to everyone while looking down toward the ground, being careful never to make eye contact with anyone. As they reached either side of the room, they both took three steps up onto the high priests' platform. Then they slowly moved toward each other, offering the high priests food as they walked by, searching the area.

"I have an idea!" shouted one of the high priests. Standing as he yelled, and throwing his arms into the air, he accidentally knocked Squeaks' tray of food out of her hand. Food sprayed all over the floor.

The high priest momentarily looked at the mess on the floor as Squeaks fell to her knees and quickly starting picking up the food. Without a word, he turned back to the people in the room and said, "Let's break for dinner and return tomorrow to argue and fight over these issues. We've worked nearly three hours, and I'm tired. Besides, with this food mess all over, I can't think."

"I agree!" shouted another high priest. "Let's resume tomorrow."

Silpah, the High Priest in charge, stood up from his position of power. He looked around the room and replied, "I agree. I don't think we will be seeing King Noah today. Without his input, we'll never settle on these issues."

Suddenly, a cheer rose in the room, frightening Squeaks as she continued to clean the mess on the floor. She looked up just as the high priest, Silpah, looked down at her. She quickly turned her head away and continued to clean. As everyone stood and started to leave the room, Silpah walked toward Squeaks. Her heart raced as he moved closer and closer. Butch watched in horror from the other side of the room, frantic that Silpah would soon be standing over her. Then Silpah simply stood silently, watching Squeaks clean for several nerve-racking minutes.

"Why is a child in the High Priest' room?" he asked softly, trying not to frighten her.

"My sister helps in the kitchen, and she is very sick today. I didn't want her to get into trouble, so I filled in for her," Squeaks softly replied, hoping he would accept her explanation.

Quiet for only a moment, he sharply replied, "Make sure you hurry and get this mess cleaned up, or she will be in serious trouble tomorrow. When you are finished, close and lock the door behind you. And tell your sister that I never want to see a child in here again. Do you understand me?"

"Yes, Sir. I'm sorry," she softly replied, relieved he had believed her.

"You," Silpah called, pointing toward Butch. "You help this girl clean up this mess."

Afraid to say a word, Butch nodded. He set his try on a table, tightened the grip of the cloth over his face, and hurried toward Silpah and Squeaks.

Silpah watched as Butch hurried to help Squeaks with the mess. Then, without a word, he turned and quickly headed for the door and the other high priests. "When you are finished cleaning, make sure this door is closed and locked."

"Yes, Sir," Squeaks nervously called, looking over the pulpit toward the door.

She watched as Silpah turned and exited the room with the other high priests, disappearing down the hallway.

"Nice going, Squeaks," said Butch. He looked around the room, making sure no one else was still inside. "I can't believe you dropped a plate of food and cleared out the entire room!"

"I didn't do it on purpose," she replied, as a tear trickled down her face. "That screaming high priest knocked the tray out of my hands."

"No, I'm not mad. This worked out perfectly. Now we can search the room, and we won't be bothered by anyone."

Squeaks smiled slightly and quickly picked up several more pieces of fruit. "I can't see an opening anywhere, and I've been looking all over this room," she said, as she finally picked up the last grape.

"I know it's here somewhere," replied Butch. "It has to be. A secret tunnel is Alma's only chance."

"I bet it's hidden in a very obvious place. All we have to do is find the statue that moves, or the book that you pull out of the bookcase, or something like that," said Squeaks, quickly scanning the room.

"You know, I bet you're right," agreed Butch, standing and looking around the room again. "The only problem is, there are no statues or books in this room."

"There has to be something, somewhere," insisted Squeaks, as she stood up and again scanned the area. "And, I bet I can find whatever triggers the secret door before you do."

Squeaks hurried to the side of the room. She ran her hands across the wall, feeling for anything that did not seem right. She meticulously checked every square inch of the walls, completely circling the area. As she reached the high priest' platform, she rubbed her hands on her chin, deep in thought.

"Someone's coming," whispered Butch, startling Squeaks.

She sprinted to the platform, and dove onto the floor next to Butch, just as the door to the high priests' room squeaked opened.

"Can you see who it is?" she whispered, as she nervously crawled under the pulpit where the high priests spoke.

"No, I can't," he faintly replied.

"What if it's soldiers coming to arrest us?" Squeaks whimpered. "I don't want to go to Book of Mormon jail."

"Book of Mormon jail?" Butch asked, almost laughing out loud, as he crawled under the pulpit next to Squeaks.

"Don't make fun of me. I'm scared, Butch. What do we do?" Squeaks asked anxiously, as she heard the men moving around in the room.

"Sssushhh," Butch whispered, holding his finger to his mouth. He pulled his feet in tighter under the table, afraid the men might see him.

※

"Why did the high priests leave this door open?" asked a deep, frightening voice.

"Why is there food in here? They know better than to leave a tray of food. King Noah will be very upset to hear this," said another man's voice.

"The work day is not over, Commander. Maybe they plan to return," replied the first deep voice.

"Let's go find out," replied the commander, softly chuckling. "I know the high priests, and I'm sure they are done for the day."

⁂

Butch and Squeaks listened as the door was pulled firmly shut, followed by an eerie silence.

"We don't have a lot of time," Squeaks said softly, unsure how long the men would be gone.

"I know," replied Butch. "When they return, if we haven't found the entrance, we're gonna be caught for sure."

"Where else do we look?" asked Squeaks. "I don't know where else a secret door could be."

"Well we haven't checked the floor yet," replied Butch, as he stared at the stone under his feet. "Maybe there is a hidden opening in the floor somewhere."

Squeaks looked down, took a deep breath and replied, "I guess we better hurry. Who knows how long the soldiers or high priests will be before they return." She leaned forward, grabbing the table leg for leverage. She was surprised when the leg slid forward, but the table didn't move. "Huh, that's funny."

"What?" asked Butch, as he looked over at his friend.

"The leg of the table moves funny—watch," she replied, as she again slid the leg of the table forward.

"Maybe one of these tables or chairs marks the secret entrance," suggested Butch, as he leaned toward Squeaks.

Shocked as the floor underneath her feet gave way, she suddenly disappeared into darkness.

"Squeaks? Squeaks, where are you?" called Butch frantically, as he moved toward the opening in the floor searching for her. "Squeaks?"

Nervously, he looked inside the opening, afraid she could be hurt. "Squeaks, are you okay?" he called, when he saw her lying in a heap on the floor, fifteen feet below.

Squeaks moaned in pain as she rolled away from the ladder and laid flat on her back. Holding her head, she looked up at Butch and said, "Everything hurts!"

"Is anything broken?" he asked, worried for her safety.

"I don't think so," she softly replied.

"I'm coming!" he called, as he quickly slid down the ladder.

Chapter Seventeen

Seth and Tater walked confidently to the main entrance of King Noah's temple. Seth opened the enormous main door, and Tater hustled inside. As they looked around the area, Tater was surprised by the beauty of the room and was shocked at the modern décor and design of the area.

"This temple is a lot like our modern-day offices," said Tater, staring at his surroundings.

"Modern-day offices?" questioned Seth, looking at Tater with a confused look on his face. "What does modern-day mean?"

"I guess this building is 'modern-day' for the year one hundred and forty-eight, isn't it?" asked Tater, smiling.

"I don't know anything different," replied Seth, looking around the temple. What year do you come from, if this year is not your modern-day?" he asked.

"We have been sent by the Lord from a year way in the future," replied Tater, concerned that Seth would be frightened by the year two thousand six A.D.

"Commander, is that you?" called Seth, surprised to see tall, muscular silhouette in the distance.

"Yes, Seth, it is me. Why are you here at King Noah's temple? Have you found something? Have you found any of those traitors who are following Alma," he asked, looking suspiciously at Tater.

"No, not yet, Sir," Seth replied, quickly trying to think of a reason to be inside King Noah's temple.

"Commander," said Tater, reaching his hand out toward the soldier. "My name is Tater."

The commander looked at Tater's hand, unsure why he was holding it out and asked, "Who are you?"

"I am from a land far away. I have traveled to your great city to meet the man who keeps King Noah's city safe. My king sent me to find you, in hopes you could give me information that will help to keep my city and king safe," replied Tater, trying to look serious.

"I found this man as I was searching the forest for traitors," added Seth. "When he told me who he was, I brought him here to find you, Sir."

The commander looked suspiciously at Tater for a long minute, without saying a word. He slowly circled the two boys, not sure whether to believe anything Tater was saying. Finally, he turned to Seth and asked, "Where did you find this boy?"

"Near the river, Sir. He was following the shore line, hoping to find our city," Seth nervously replied.

"And you say you are here to meet me?" the commander doubtfully questioned.

"Yes, Sir. The stories of how you keep King Noah safe have traveled all the way to my land. I am only a captain over our soldiers, but I have been promised a higher position if you will teach me how to be such a great soldier and leader like yourself," replied Tater, hoping to trick the commander.

The commander remained quiet for several moments before he finally said, "Well, now is a good time to start learning. Follow me." He turned and headed for the temple door.

"Where are we going, Sir," asked Seth. Unsure where they were headed.

"We're on our way to find the high priests," replied Aiath, another soldier with the commander.

"Why?" questioned Seth. "Aren't they currently in session?"

"No. No one is there. Something is wrong in the high priests' chambers, and we're on our way to find them," replied Aiath.

"What are we going to do when we find them?" Tater asked innocently.

"We'll take them back to the temple and let them explain to us why the room is open," the Commander replied angrily.

"Why couldn't you have closed the door for them?" asked Tater, searching for more information.

"Because, there are several things in that room that could lead to the destruction of King Noah, I do not allow anyone, high priest or not, to ignore my rules!" shouted the commander.

The Commander, Aiath, Seth and Tater traveled in silence toward the market, searching for any of King Noah's high priests.

"Who are we looking for, Commander, so I can help search?" asked Seth, finally breaking the silence.

"We are looking for the high priest in charge - Silpah," he replied gruffly. "Closing the court room is his responsibility. He can answer as to why it is still open."

"What is in the room that is so important?" asked Tater casually.

"As I said before, there are secrets in the high priests' room that keep King Noah, his family, and even the high priests themselves safe," the commander replied, agitated by Tater's question.

"There he is, Sir," called Aiath, pointing toward a vendor in the marketplace selling bread.

"Where?" asked the commander angrily. "I can't see him."

"Over by the bread vendor," replied Seth.

The Commander turned and spotted the high priest, Silpah. Grunting to himself as he saw him, the commander marched angrily toward the man. "Let's get to the bottom of this," he called. "Follow me, men."

Seth, Tater and Aiath hurriedly followed the Commander, as he nearly ran toward the high priest.

Finally reaching the man, the commander quickly grabbed Silpah's shoulder and swiftly spun him around. Then he, placed his head in the High Priest's face and screamed, "You know the rules in King Noah's temple! Why did you leave your court room open and unlocked?"

Shocked by the soldier yelling at him, Silpah was unable to speak for several moments. He stepped back from the commander, cleared his voice and swallowed hard, trying to figure out what he was talking about.

"Well?" screamed the commander.

"Well, Commander," Silpah calmly started, suddenly remembering he had left the room unlocked. "The kitchen help left a food mess inside, and I didn't want to wait for them to clean it."

"There was no one in there a few minutes ago, but the room was open and unlocked!" the commander yelled angrily. Several people in the marketplace stopped and watched the commotion.

"Then I'm sure they were still cleaning the room," Silpah replied confidently. He turned and started to walk away.

Not wanting to be embarrassed in front of Tater, the commander looked over his shoulder at the young boy, whom he thought was an impressionable soldier. He turned back toward Silpah and yelled, "Silpah, you will be escorted by me and my men back to the temple right now, so that you can either take care of the room yourself or, if you so choose speak to King Noah, explain to him why you have ignored his orders."

Silpah looked at the commander and could see by the

look on his face that he was serious. Frustrated, he shook his head, squeezed his lips together and smartly replied, "I will be more than happy to go back to the temple with you. However, when you find that everything has been taken care of, I will expect an apology from you. You may be the commander of King Noah's army, but I am the head of King Noah's high priests, and I deserve respect."

With that, Silpah dropped the bread he was holding onto the table in the market, turned and headed back toward the temple. The Commander, Aiath, Seth and Tater followed behind him.

"Men, now you will see how I demand the respect of the people in this city," said the commander, smiling as he started to follow Silpah back toward the temple. "When he finds that the door is still open, he will be begging me not to take him to King Noah."

"You are a true leader, Commander," replied Tater. "I am impressed already."

"Nice, Tater," whispered Seth. "You know exactly how to work the commander."

Tater's smile completely crossed his face as he moved quickly to keep up with the men's fast pace. The men moving at a rapid pace, soon entered the temple. They hurried across the main hall, past the waterfall and beautiful statues, straight toward the high priests' court room, located in the hallway on the right.

Silpah's mouth dropped open as he neared the doorway and found it wide open. Looking inside, hoping to see the kitchen help still inside cleaning up, he was shocked to find the room exactly as the commander had said it was.

Silpah moved slowed inside the room and quickly spotted a tray of food still lying on the table next to pulpit.

"I told you, Silpah," the commander shouted victoriously. "There is a reason that King Noah requires his rules be followed exactly. You know this could cost you your life?"

"I am sorry, Commander," Silpah replied meekly. "The kitchen workers seemed so trustworthy."

"Who were they?" demanded the Commander angrily. "Could they have been spies sent to kill our king?"

"The girl was merely a child. I don't think she could kill anyone," Silpah replied in a soft voice.

"And the other one?" questioned Aiath.

"I never saw her up close," Silpah replied.

"Who were they? Were they citizens from our city?" questioned Seth, trying to act angry.

"When I asked the young girl who she was, she told me that her sister worked as kitchen help and was ill. She was filling in for her so that her sister didn't lose her job. I had never seen her before."

"What? You let someone stay in here that you didn't even know?" screamed the commander. He frantically searched the room for any sign of the intruder.

Silpah looked at the ground, unsure of what to say.

"Well, don't just stand there!" exclaimed Tater, hurrying to follow the commander. "Get in here, and see if you can find whoever you left unattended."

The commander stopped only for a moment, watching Tater order around the high priest. Then he turned toward the plate of food on the table and picked it up.

Holding it in one hand, he turned to Silpah, who was walking toward his seat on the pulpit, and asked, "Aren't these the trays used only to feed King Noah's family?"

Silpah looked up from the ground, gazed at the trays and replied, "I didn't notice before. But yes, they don't belong in here."

The commander dropped the tray of food, turned to Aiath and said, "Check the kitchen. Look for any sign of an intruder. Move swiftly, as the king's life might be in danger. Seth, you and your friend search the main room and hallway. Return as fast as you can, and help me check this room. There are many secret passageways in this room, and a number of them lead straight to the king and his family. We cannot afford any more mistakes."

Aiath nodded, turned quickly and disappeared down the hallway. Seth and Tater also moved rapidly out the door and toward the main room, pretending to do exactly as the commander ordered.

"You know who everyone is looking for, don't you?" muttered Seth.

"Yes, I'm afraid I do," Tater replied softly.

"If the commander finds them, they could really be in a lot of trouble," warned Seth. "Their lives could be in danger."

"I'm aware of that. I don't know why those two would have sneaked in here without us," replied Tater, shaking his head in frustration.

"I think they must have found the secret tunnel," said Seth. "Otherwise, I'm sure someone would have found them by now."

"I think so, too," agreed Tater. "I just hope that both of them are alive and safe."

"Let's get back to the high priests' room before the commander discovers them," suggested Seth. "He could surely kill them if we are not there."

Tater anxiously nodded, and the two ran down the long hallway toward the high priests' room. Pushing the half-closed door open, Tater spotted the commander still searching the platform. He breathed a cautious sigh of relief.

Staring at the spilled plate of food on the floor, the commander asked, "Silpah, why is this food all over the floor?"

"That tray of food was spilled. That is why I allowed the two girls to stay and clean up the mess after all of the high priests left," he replied, looking at the mess on the floor.

"Do you think they found one of the secret tunnels you spoke of?" asked Tater. He pretended to scan the room, hoping to pry more information from the commander.

"I'm sure they have," the commander replied angrily. "I can only hope that the tunnel they found doesn't lead straight to King Noah."

"Do you know where the tunnels are located?" asked Tater, trying to act genuinely concerned. "Could we possibly start searching the tunnels and catch them before they get to the king?"

"I do know where the tunnels are. However, I do not know you well enough to reveal them to you," the commander replied suspiciously.

"I will leave if you do not trust me," replied Tater, sensing the commander's distrust.

"Hey, I think I have found something," called Seth,

down on his knees. "There is an opening in the floor over here."

Everyone hurried to where Seth was kneeling and saw a square opening with a ladder leading into the darkness below.

"Is this one of the secret tunnels?" asked Seth, excitedly looking up at the commander.

"Yes, this is the main tunnel. There are passageways that lead to every part of the city, including: King Noah's private quarters, the soldier's training temple, the prison, as well as a few other areas in the city," replied Silpah.

"Do you think Alma told his followers about the secret tunnels, and that is who tricked Silpah, commander?" asked Aiath, finally returning from the kitchen. "Would Alma have known about the secret passageway?"

"All of the high priests know about the secret tunnels," answered Silpah. "We have used them, on occasion, to escape when the citizens were upset and once when we thought the city was under attack."

"With the entrance opened, this has to be the tunnel that they found, right?" asked Tater.

"I don't know, but I intend to find out," replied the commander. He pushed past Seth, then climbed through the opening, and down the ladder.

"May I come as well?" asked Tater. Careful not to enter the opening, without an invitation from the commander.

The commander paused for a second and looked up at Tater. Then he smiled and replied, "We would love to have you come and help us find these traitors."

Hurriedly, the group climbed through the opening and down the ladder to the bottom of the dark tunnel. Once they had all reached the bottom, the commander, obviously familiar with the tunnel, took a torch from the wall and lit the end. Without a word, he led the group through the twists and turns of the dark, foreboding tunnel.

Sure this was where they would need to go to free Alma, Tater tried to memorize every turn the group made. With each new turn, Tater became worried that he could not remember everything. He noticed the floor was paved in small stones. As the group reached a fork in the tunnel, the stones on the ground either stayed the same color or changed, depending on which direction he turned.

"I get it," Tater thought to himself. "Each area of this tunnel is coded by the color of the stones. Very clever."

"Commander," Tater called. "How do you remember your way through this secret tunnel? I think I would be completely lost by now if you weren't here to lead the way."

"That is why I let you join us, Tater," replied the commander.

"What is?" Tater questioned.

"This tunnel is the main tunnel and the most confusing. Only a few men know how to travel through it safely," he chuckled.

"What happens to those who don't know how to travel through here?" questioned Tater, nervous for his friends.

"That is where we are going right now," the commander replied. "Strategically placed throughout the tunnels are several traps. If you happen to fall into a trap, they all lead to one place."

"Where is that?" asked Seth.

"Underneath the moat that surrounds the prison," the commander replied, still laughing.

"Do they drown if they land under the moat?" Tater nervously asked.

"No, but they will wish they had, after I take them to King Noah," he replied.

"King Noah!" shrieked Silpah, startling everyone. "Those intruders will wish they had drowned after I get through with them!"

Suddenly, the sound of water echoed all through the cave, surrounding the group. The tunnel widened to the size of a small classroom. It had five puddles of water— one in every corner of the room, and one directly in the middle of the room. Water seeped through the rock walls of the cave, playing a beautiful song as it fell into every puddle and hit the small pebble walkway on the ground. Just ahead of the torch, in the dim light it cast into the cave, the group saw two small figures.

"Did we catch them, Commander?" questioned Seth, trying to act excited.

"It looks like it to me," he replied, as a huge grin slowly spread across his face. "King Noah is going to be pleased that his traps have worked so well."

The commander moved quickly toward the figures, sure he had caught two of Alma's followers. Placing the torch he was carrying into a holder attached to the wall, he quickly turned to the figures and watched them struggling to get out of the water.

"I would quit moving if I were you," the commander

said calmly, as he followed the small pebble pathway around to face the two intruders.

A tear trickled down Squeaks' face as she watched the mighty commander slowly march around the puddle. He kicked the bottom of his spear with every step, as he made his way toward them. Frantically, she struggled harder to release her leg, from the trap they were caught in under the water.

"I told you to quit moving," barked the commander angrily. "Have you ever heard of the attacking Piranha? They are attracted to wild movement and thrashing around. If you keep moving, I guarantee you will not have feet to walk on in a few minutes. If that happens, the pain will be so intense, I'm sure it will be worse than the punishment King Noah has in store for you! Now tell me who you are!"

"We're kids from the village," replied Butch.

The commander, surprised by the high-pitched voice, turned to face the two figures. "His mouth dropped open as he saw their two faces. "Children? You really are children," he said, looking toward Silpah.

"I told you they were fairly young," Silpah replied, shrugging his shoulders.

"How did children find their way into the secret tunnels of King Noah?" asked Seth, as he followed the light-brown pebbles on the walkway toward the commander.

"That is what I would like to know," said the commander, looking at the Silpah.

Silpah, unsure of what to say, shrugged his shoulders. He smiled at the commander and replied, "They looked a lot older with their heads and faces covered." He turned to the children and asked, "How did you know of the secret tunnels?"

"We didn't," replied Squeaks. "We were cleaning up the food mess and I bumped the table leg that opened the secret passage," she tearfully replied, still struggling to free herself from the water.

"He said to hold still!" yelled Tater.

The commander patted Tater on the shoulder and said, "Let them wiggle around. They will soon know the pain of sneaking into the temple of King Noah. Every wrong turn leads to a puddle, and every puddle has a trap. There is no way they could make it through the tunnels unless they were told how to."

"So, with these two caught, we know they are not followers of Alma, right?" asked Seth.

The commander thought for a moment and asked, "Who are you children, and why are you here in the King's secret tunnel?"

"We were playing. We didn't mean to do anything wrong," Squeaks replied tearfully.

"What should we do with them, Silpah?" asked the commander.

"They disobeyed my direct orders to clean up the high priests' room and close the door. They were messing around where no children should ever be, and they got me into a lot of trouble," Silpah replied angrily. "I think they should be lashed and thrown into jail."

"That's a little harsh for their crimes, isn't it?" questioned the commander. He reached into the puddle of water, and flipped a small lever under a rock, releasing the kids' feet and freeing them from the trap.

"What would you suggest?" asked Silpah, as he watched the kids quickly climb out of the water and onto the rock path.

"Should we just let them go?" asked Tater, hoping the two men would listen to him.

"Let them go!" Silpah snapped furiously. "They must be taught a lesson, and freedom is not the answer."

"We will not decide for ourselves. They must go before King Noah," insisted Seth, acting like a soldier.

"I agree, Seth. We do not rule over this city. I wouldn't want King Noah to hear of us deciding their fate," chuckled the commander. "Seth, Tater, bind their arms, and let's get them up to the temple as quickly as possible."

With the two prisoners bound, the group quickly retraced their steps back to the high priests' room. Once they had climbed out of the tunnel, Silpah fixed the bent leg of the table and the secret opening inside the room quickly disappeared.

The commander, Seth and Tater marched Butch and Squeaks down the hallway, across the main room to the east hallway, and into King Noah's chambers.

"King, I am sorry to interrupt you, Sir. I have found these two children wandering around your temple, and I need to know what you would like me to do with them," said the Commander.

"Where were they?" asked King Noah.

"In your secret tunnels under the high priests' room," replied the commander.

"Which one?" asked King Noah, obviously agitated by the children.

"They were in the main tunnel that leads all over the city," replied the commander. "They could have gotten anywhere in the city."

"How did they get in there? I thought those tunnels had secret entrances only known by a few men," he said. "Did one of my high priests show them the way inside?"

"I asked Silpah, and he claims that none of your high priests know these children, King," replied the commander. "I believe they were playing around when the secret entrance was found and, like most children, wandered into something that they shouldn't have."

"How? I thought these entrances were hidden?" screamed King Noah, frustrated they were inside his temple. "They had to have found out about them from someone."

Silence filled the room for several moments while the commander struggled to find an answer to the King's question.

"We found them on our own," interrupted Butch, afraid King Noah might connect them with Alma.

"Yeah, our friends dared us to sneak into the high priests' chambers. We did, and we were able to trick the high priests into believing we were kitchen help. The men left for the day. After they left, we were playing when we accidentally found the secret hidden entrance," added Squeaks. "Curious to see what and where the entrance led to, we entered the tunnel. That is when we were caught in the traps under the water."

"So the traps worked?" asked King Noah, looking at the commander elatedly.

"Just like I said they would," he replied proudly.

"So, what else did you see while you were down in my secret tunnel?" questioned King Noah, as he stared into Butch's eyes.

"We were only there for a few minutes before we got caught, and then your commander found us. We didn't have time to see much," replied Butch.

"All I could see was a lot of dark," added Squeaks. "The tunnel was very hard to see in."

King Noah walked toward his throne and gracefully turned toward the kids. He took a loud, deep breath and said, "I do not allow peasants into my temple. I especially don't allow kids, on a dare, to come running, hiding, and playing games in my temple. And I surely will not tolerate your childish prank sneaking in here. Who are your parents? I will hold them responsible for your actions!" King Noah yelled angrily.

"We have none here," replied Butch, in a shaky voice.

"Where are they?" he asked.

"We don't have any idea," answered Squeaks.

King Noah paused a moment before he shouted, "Then as an example to other children and orphans in the city, you will be thrown into my prison, where you will spend the next fifteen years as my personal slaves. After that, you will work in the wheat fields for the rest of your miserable lives, trying to repay your debts to society.

"Commander, take these children away. I do not wish for them to be in my sight any longer." King Noah waved his hand and robe in the air, turned, and sat down in his throne.

The commander, sensing King Noah's anger, roughly grabbed the rope tied to both of the kids' wrists and forcefully pulled Butch and Squeaks to their feet. With Seth, Tater and Aiath behind him, he marched Butch and Squeaks out of King Noah's private chambers, down the hallway, through the main room, down the stairs and through the courtyard, toward the small prison across the bridge.

"You children should have known better than to play anywhere near the king or his temple," said the commander, frustrated by King Noah's sentence. "I am sorry to have to carry out his sentence, but King Noah is not a king that tolerates this kind of behavior. I hoped he would give you a lighter sentence, but…"

"Did he really mean it when he said we would have to be slaves?" interrupted Squeaks, in a whiny voice.

"Yes," the commander replied abruptly. "In fact, with the mood he was in, you are lucky that he spared your lives. Most of the prisoners he keeps alive only for a few days before they are killed."

"Killed?" questioned Butch. "For playing in his temple?"

"Killed for less than that," replied the commander. He reached the suspension bridge and cautiously took hold of the rope.

"If the king has a secret tunnel that leads to the prison, how do we find it so that we can escape?" asked Squeaks, hoping the commander would take mercy on them and tell them the way out of the prison.

The commander turned and looked over his shoulder at Squeaks, softly smiling and replied, "You should have explored the tunnel you found a little faster. Then you might have the answer to your question. You know that King Noah would not spare my life if I gave away his secrets."

"Don't you think it is wrong for King Noah to arrest us, or give us such a severe sentence?" asked Squeaks, still searching for sympathy from the commander.

"It does not matter what I think. He is my king, and I am bound to do what he commands me to do," the commander replied sharply, as the group finally reached the other side of the suspension bridge.

"Do you believe anything that Alma or Abinadi have spoken about," questioned Squeaks, closely watching the commander's face.

Shocked, he looked over at Squeaks and replied, "If you are followers of those men, it does not matter to me. I must do as I am commanded by King Noah."

"You know we could help save you from his unjust ways," added Butch, sensing that the commander did believe their words.

"Who said King Noah's ways are unjust?" asked the commander. "A God that you can neither see nor talk to? I should have known that you children are Alma's followers."

"Commander, you seem like a good man with fairness in your heart. You have to know that King Noah is not a good king," added Butch.

"You children have sealed your fate," the commander replied angrily. "You know that no matter what I believe,

I have a job to do, and I will not wavier."

With that, the commander twisted the lock, pulled open the door, and motioned for the two to walk inside. As soon as they entered the dark hut, the commander slammed the door behind them and quickly turned the lock.

Chapter Eighteen

❝Commander, who were those kids talking about? Who are the men that they spoke of?" asked Tater, acting as though he did not know who Abinadi or Alma were.

The commander, still angry, looked over at Tater and gruffly replied, "Two traitors to the king who have been punished and sentenced to death."

Tater nodded, feeling the tension in the commander's voice. He quietly followed him across the bridge. "Did that girl make you angry, Sir," he asked cautiously.

The commander took a deep breath. Letting it out slowly, he paused for a moment and replied, "No, I just hate to see young people throw their lives away. Those children could be good citizens to King Noah someday."

"It was a simple mistake. Would King Noah reconsider his punishment?" asked Seth.

The commander shook his head and laughed, "You know King Noah better than that, Seth" he replied. "I have never seen him reconsider a punishment—never."

"Sir, would it be all right if we left you now? I must check in with my father before he gets worried," asked Seth, anxious to start on a plan to save Alma, Squeaks and Butch.

"And your new friend, is he going with you?" asked the commander.

"Yes, I'm sure my family will give him a place to stay for a few days until he returns to his city," replied Seth, as he nodded his head.

"Very well, soldiers. Tater, I hope that you have learned a few things about being a good leader by watching me today," the commander said proudly.

"Yes, Sir. Thank you for spending time with me and allowing me to learn," replied Tater. "May I spend more time with you tomorrow?"

"We still have followers of Abinadi and Alma to find. So Seth, when you start your search again tomorrow, bring Tater with you," replied the commander. "Report to the temple at noon, and we will see who, if anyone, has been caught by then."

"See you in the morning, Sir," responded Seth. He took hold of Tater's arm, pulling him toward the outskirts of the city.

Seth and Tater watched the commander disappear into the city market place, as they slowly walked along the edge of the city. Waiting until the commander was far enough away not to hear them, Seth exclaimed, "Tater, you are the biggest kiss-up. I've never seen the commander be that nice to anyone before."

Tater smiled and said, "You never know what being nice might do for you!"

"We better find Mrs. M., Nahom and Ramin and tell them what's going on," insisted Seth. "They're bound to be worried by now."

"Where did you tell them to meet us?" asked Tater, almost jogging to keep up with Seth.

"Up there," replied Seth, pointing toward the forest. "Right outside the market place, in the thick grove of trees next to the temple. There they could keep the prison in their view without being seen by anyone."

The boys hurried to where the others were waiting, anxious to tell them everything that had happened.

"We saw you walking with soldiers and leading Squeaks and Butch to the prison. What happened?" asked Mrs. M., with a worried look on her face.

"Squeaks and Butch found the secret entrance in the high priests' room. Instead of waiting for us to help them, they climbed inside and started searching the tunnel alone," replied Tater.

"And what happened?" pressed Mrs. M., frightened to hear his response.

"Well, they were not aware that King Noah has several traps placed throughout the tunnel, and they were caught in one. The commander was easily able to find them," added Seth.

"Yeah, and when the commander found them caught

in a trap, he took them to King Noah," said Tater. "I was kinda scared."

"What happened next?" asked Ramin, anxious to hear the story.

"What do you think?" Seth retorted. "King Noah was not happy with them. He quizzed them about who they were and why they were playing in his secret tunnels."

"What else did he do?" asked Nahom.

"You saw the wicked King Noah?" interrupted Mrs. M., shocked by what she heard.

"Not only did I see him, but I listened to him speak. I was amazed at his callousness when he sentenced Butch and Squeaks to be his personal slaves for the next fifteen years, and then to work in the fields for the remainder of their days!" replied Tater.

"What?" asked Mrs. M. "Personal slaves?"

"Yep!" answered Tater.

"That's not good," she anxiously replied. "What do we do now?"

"Well, don't worry. We're going to break them out tonight," replied Seth, trying to calm the frightened look on Mrs. M.'s face. "And we're gonna have to hurry and make a plan. After all, we only have so many hours in the night, and we need to be prepared."

"What's your plan, Seth?" asked Nahom. "I can tell by the look on you're face you've got something in mind."

Seth cautiously looked around the market, making sure no one was watching them. He could see no soldiers anywhere, and the vendors were busily closing down their stores for the night. He motioned for everyone to sit down close to the willow tree. Then he quietly began to reveal his plan.

"I think that enough of the commander's soldiers saw Tater and I with him tonight, that I might be able to tell them we are here to do some work for him, bring him something or get something for him. If they believe me, then we should be able to get past the guards and get everyone inside the high priests' room.

"In addition, while we were with the commander, we found the entrance to King Noah's secret tunnel. After we climbed inside the tunnel, I attempted to memorize the path the commander took when we were looking for Squeaks and Butch. Although I'm not positive of every move we made, I think I can work my way back through the tunnel to where he said the entrance to the prison was located."

"I memorized the path as well," interrupted Tater. "There was a rock pattern on the floor, and I tried to memorize every step we took!"

"Nice job, Tater!" exclaimed Mrs. M. "Way to be paying attention."

Seth patted Tater on the shoulder and said, "If we all act like we are supposed to be going in to the temple, the soldiers shouldn't ask us too many questions."

"What about me?" Mrs. M. asked worriedly. "Won't they ask why a woman is with you?"

"Yeah, Seth. What are we going to tell the guards if they ask why a woman is with us?" questioned Nahom.

Seth placed his hand over his mouth, closed his eyes and contemplated what they were going to do. After several moments of nervous silence, Seth finally responded,

"Okay, I have an idea. Actually having Mrs. M. with us might work out better."

"Well, let's hear it all ready," teased Ramin.

"Why don't we pretend that King Noah has asked for Mrs. M., and the commander told us to bring her to him? The guards would never question that."

"Hey, good idea," replied Nahom. "I think you are right, the guards would never question a woman going to see King Noah."

"Wait a minute! I don't want to go see King Noah!" Mrs. M. exclaimed nervously.

"No, not actually see him," replied Tater, smiling. "Just pretend so that we can get past the guards."

Mrs. M. took a deep breath as she shook her head. Then she replied, "Wow, I was worried for a minute. I thought you really wanted to take me to see King Noah."

"So, does everyone understand the plan?" asked Seth, ready to get moving.

Everyone nodded, and Seth quickly started walking toward the temple. "Mrs. M., will you please stand in the middle? Tater, come up front with me. Nahom and Ramin, please stand behind Mrs. M. If we stand this way, I think it will look like we are escorting her inside."

Everyone moved into position, and the group headed straight for the temple's main entrance. Nearing the door, six soldiers suddenly appeared. Dropping their spears so the group could not pass, a soldier asked, "Who are you, and what business do you have in the temple tonight?"

"I am Seth, one of the commander's head soldiers. He has ordered that we bring this woman, who is a follower of Alma, to King Noah immediately," answered Seth, stepping toward to the door.

"Halt! I have not been told of this," replied the guard.

"Then you go ask the king yourself," Seth replied confidently. "That is, if you would like to be thrown in to prison for interrupting him."

The soldier remained silent for a moment, glaring at Seth. He lifted his spear away from the door and replied, "If the king is expecting a delivery of Alma's followers, then you better get moving, I don't want to be the one that holds up King Noah's orders."

The soldier moved from in front of the door and pushed it open for Seth and the group to enter. Seth nodded as he confidently walked passed the guard and quickly entered the main hall of the temple. The soldier watched as Seth quickly led the group toward King Noah's personal hallway. Finally reaching it, Seth heard the temple door close. Cautiously, Seth looked over his shoulder and was relieved when he saw that the soldiers were no longer inside. He motioned for the group to move away from the family hallway and follow him toward the high priest hallway.

The group moved swiftly to the corridor. Seth cautiously peered around the door, checking for any sign of guards or soldiers. With none in sight, he carefully moved down the hallway to the high priests' room. Guardedly, he pushed the door open, causing a loud and frightening 'creeaaakk' sounding through the corridor.

"Quiet, Seth, we're going to get caught," warned Nahom. He pushed the door and hurried through the opening into the room.

"Why wasn't the door locked?" asked Ramin, as he entered the room. "This door is always supposed to be locked."

"Well, because after the commander found Squeaks and Butch, he asked Tater and I to pull the door closed. I did, but he never mentioned locking it, so I didn't," Seth replied, smiling. "That way we wouldn't have any trouble getting back in here."

"So, boys, show us where the opening to the secret tunnel is," insisted Mrs. M., looking around the dimly-lit room. "We've got to find the prison as quickly as we can."

Tater hustled to the stage and pointed underneath the high priests' desks. "The opening is here," he softly called. He reached down and moved the table leg, revealing the opening to the secret entrance.

Mrs. M. was the first to reach the opening. Without pausing, she maneuvered, feet first, into the opening and climbed down the ladder to the bottom of the tunnel.

"Hurry up, guys. We've got people to rescue," she anxiously called.

"Mrs. M., be careful," insisted Tater. "There could be soldiers or guards in the tunnel. You never know what might be down there."

Seth, Tater, Nahom and Ramin hurried to catch Mrs. M. Once they all had reached the bottom of the ladder, Tater took the lead.

"Now, when we were down here earlier, every time we came to a bend in the tunnel, the commander always reached up and took hold of the wall," started Tater.

"He was probably checking to see if he was going the

right way," replied Nahom, shrugging his shoulders, unsure what Tater was thinking.

"No, that's not what I mean," replied Tater, carefully looking around the area. "The commander seemed sure that he knew where the intruders would be when we were in the tunnel. In fact, he headed straight for the ponds where Squeaks and Butch were stuck. At first, I thought the colored pebbles on the ground led the way, but I'm wondering if the commander could see markings in the rock walls."

"Why?" questioned Ramin.

"He always seemed to be reaching up to the walls. I thought maybe there was something that directed him which way to go," replied Tater, as he tried to remember everything that happened earlier. "Either that, or he was flipping a switch or pushing buttons that disarmed traps, or something like that."

"I believe that their might be traps around that we need to watch out for down here. But, how are we going to find our way through these dark tunnels, following colored pebbles that we can't even see?" questioned Nahom, unable to see much in the dark.

Tater pulled his leather knapsack from his shoulder, located the leather ties on the front pocket, and untied it. Reaching inside, he rummaged around for several seconds before he finally pulled out a small black object. Holding it up for everyone to see, in the faint light cast from the high priests' room above, he said, "I think this might help us."

He turned it on, instantly splashing light throughout the tunnel, startling Seth, Nahom and Ramin.

"What is that?" asked Seth, frightened by the light. He moved quickly to stay out of its path.

"There is nothing to be worried about," replied Mrs. M., trying to calm the young soldiers fears. "In our day, this is called a flashlight."

"Flashlight?" asked Seth. He reached out, placing his hand in the beam of light. "Can it hurt you?"

"No," she replied reassuringly.

"Why it is called a flashlight?" asked Seth.

"When you turn the switch on," Tater replied, "It flashes light in the area where you point it."

"Is this trickery?" Nahom asked nervously.

"No, this is science developed in our day," replied Mrs. M. "The people of our time have developed what are called batteries and light bulbs. It is energy stored in a small container. When you put the energy inside this flashlight with a bulb and turn it on, the light flashes around the area. Do you understand?"

"Are you sure that this light, or energy, won't hurt me?" asked Ramin, nervously backing away from the flashlight.

"No, this light can't hurt you," Mrs. M. replied reassuringly "All it does is light the way for us. I promise. So, Tater, do you know the direction to start?" asked Mrs. M., anxious to get moving.

"You bet I do. Especially now that I can see," replied Tater. He quickly pointed his flashlight at the small, colored stones on the ground.

"I think I should go first, Tater," insisted Seth. He grabbed Tater's shoulder, holding him back. "If there is a trap, I think it would be better if I'm in the lead."

"Yes, Tater, we know a lot of the tricks and traps that King Noah uses, and we can watch for them," added Nahom, nodding. "We've helped build a lot of his traps in the forest."

"Come on, I can do it," replied Tater, pulling his shoulder away from Seth. "Besides, I know how to watch for modern-day traps, which I'm sure are more treacherous than anything you can think of."

"Don't get arrogant, Tater. If you do, something bad is bound to happen," Mrs. M. replied nervously.

"Can any of you have faith in me?" asked Tater, annoyed by everyone's comments.

"I can," answered Ramin, calling from the rear of the group.

Tater, looked back at Ramin and smiled. Then he briskly started moving through the tunnel, with the group quietly following. The tunnel twisted right, then left. Then they headed deeper, and the path suddenly became steep. The group cautiously followed Tater as he confidently maneuvered through the tunnel, following the colored stones on the ground. When Tater reached another fork in the tunnel, he always reached up and placed his hands on the rock, similar to what he watched the commander do earlier. The group carefully maneuvered to the bottom of a steep grade, and suddenly Tater stopped.

"What is it, Tater?" asked Seth. "Can you see someone?"

Suddenly unsure where they were, Tater looked at Seth with a confused look on his face. "Can you remember which way we went from here? I don't remember this turn," Tater said.

"After all the twists and turns, I really have no idea. I wasn't paying that close of attention," replied Seth worriedly. "Why?"

"Are we lost?" interrupted Nahom.

"No, not lost, just momentarily delayed," replied Mrs. M. "Take your time, Tater. Look both ways, and see if anything sparks your memory."

Tater looked up, smiled slightly at Mrs. M. and replied, "I'm just a little confused. I was following the stones on the ground like the commander did earlier. However, if you look at the colored stones on the ground, the brown and pink pebbles go both directions from here."

Mrs. M. walked to where Tater was standing and optimistically replied, "Okay, there has to be a clue here somewhere. Everyone look around, and see what you can find."

"What am I looking for exactly?" asked Ramin.

"Maybe an arrow pointing the way, or hieroglyphs that tell us what to do—something like that," replied Mrs. M., running her hands across the cool stone in the tunnel.

"I can't see anything," Seth replied nervously. "If we get lost in this tunnel, Alma, Squeaks, and Butch are doomed for sure."

"Relax, Seth," said Nahom. "We'll figure it out. Be positive."

"Hey, I found something," Ramin called excitedly. "There is a picture over here."

"What does it say?" asked Mrs. M. excitedly.

"I can't see it very well. Tater, will you please shine your light over here?" Ramin asked, anxious to look at the picture.

Tater pointed the light at the tunnel wall, and Ramin studied the picture carved into the rock.

"Well, what does it say?" Tater asked impatiently.

"Something about a room," Ramin replied evasively. "I'm not exactly sure."

"A room?" asked Seth. "What else does it say?"

"Something about a door that takes you to a room of illusions," replied Ramin, with a concerned looked.

"I don't know anything about a room of illusions," said Nahom. "What does that mean?"

"I don't know," replied Seth. "I've never heard anything about a room of illusions. And we didn't travel to a room of illusions with the commander today."

"Then let's push the switch and see what happens, the writing could be trying to trick us," said Tater. He reached up to the wall, seeing a small round stone, and pushed it squarely into the tunnel wall.

"No, Tater, wait!" screamed Mrs. M.

The tunnel made a loud, frightening creak, and rumbled for several seconds. Then nothing—everything was silent.

"What'd ya do, Tater?" questioned Mrs. M. nervously.

"All I did was push the rock. I was hoping the rock was hiding the secret room we are looking for. I think that is what the commander did when he led us through here in search of Squeaks and Butch earlier," Tater replied.

"Yes, but I don't remember the cave ever making a noise and rumbling," said Seth.

Without warning, the floor suddenly disappeared from beneath the groups' feet, and abruptly, everyone fell into the darkness below, screaming as they headed toward the unknown.

"Aaaahhhhhh!" screamed Mrs. M., as the group fell twenty feet into a room below. "Aaaaahhhhhh! Someone help me."

"Uuuhhh!" shrieked Nahom, as he hit the ground—hard.

"Oh," groaned Tater. He lifted his head slightly from the ground and held up his flashlight so he could see. "Where are we?"

"I have no idea," moaned Ramin as he tried to slowly move. "What did you do, Tater?"

"I don't remember doing this with the commander earlier today, Tater," Seth complained sarcastically. He slowly picked up his aching body from the floor, brushing the dirt from his clothes. "So, where are we?"

"I can't tell in the dark," replied Mrs. M., whimpering in pain. "Do you think this is one of King Noah's traps?"

"It has to be," replied Nahom. "Why else would we have fallen into a secret room?"

"We'll all be killed if King Noah finds us in here," said Seth, coughing several times to clear the dust and dirt from his mouth.

"Don't move, Seth!" screamed Mrs. M. "Hold still."

Seth brushed the dirt from his eyes. Then he quickly opened them and tried to look around the area. Unable to see anything, he rubbed his eyes again and waited for them to focus.

Mrs. M. quickly moved to Seth's side and frantically grabbed his elbow to pull him away from the edge.

"Oh my, where are we?" asked Ramin, with a quiver in his voice.

"We are in one of King Noah's death chambers," replied Nahom, looking over Seth's shoulder.

"A what?" Tater exclaimed nervously.

"A death chamber," answered Seth, his eyes now focusing on the room.

"What is a death chamber?" whimpered Mrs. M., staring over the ledge. "And how do you know that is what we're in?"

"I have heard about these rooms, but I have never seen one before. I wasn't sure they really existed," answered Nahom. "Stories have been told of these rooms since I was a child."

"Well, now we know that they do exist," Tater grumbled in a frustrated tone. "This room is crazy. There's a ten foot wide ledge that we landed on. It appears that the remainder of the room is dug an additional twenty feet deep, and is filled with poisonous snakes and spears. If we fall over the edge we will be killed instantly. There is no way to cross the room to the other side and get safely through the door over there."

"Well, in a death chamber, escape is granted only to those who can solve the secret of the room," responded Seth, still looking around the area. "That is why the only way out of here is the doorway on the other side of the room, across the pit of snakes and spears."

"So, how we get to that door?" asked Mrs. M., trying to be rational. "Somehow there must be a way to cross the room and get to that door."

"That's the secret," replied Seth, with a smirk on his face. "If we figure out the secret, then we will be able to cross safely and escape King Noah's death chamber."

Suddenly, the wall behind the group slowly started to rumble.

"Now what's happening?" asked Tater. He looked over his shoulder at the wall, watching as it started to inch toward them.

"That's not good," announced Seth. He ran toward the wall, pushing with all his might, trying to stop it from moving forward.

"That isn't going to work, Seth," declared Nahom. "We've got to figure out the secret to crossing the room before the wall pushes us into the pit of snakes and spears below."

"How do we do that?" screamed Ramin. He raced to the wall, helping Seth push, hoping to keep it from moving any further.

"I'm not sure," Nahom replied angrily. "I've only heard about death chambers. No one has ever told me how to get out of one."

"Tater, do you have any ideas?" asked Mrs. M., as she worriedly watched the wall move closer. "Have you read any books about death chambers?"

Tater moved away from the wall and looked into the pit below. He held his head in his hands and frantically replied, "Uuhhh, Mrs. M., nothing is coming to me!"

"What do we do, Seth?" screamed Ramin.

Seth stepped away from the wall and stopped pushing. He calmly walked to the edge and replied, "Well, we could just jump in and save the wall the trouble of pushing us over."

"Seth!" screamed Ramin, not amused by his joke. "This is not a time to be sarcastic. Real solutions would be good right about now."

"Oh, I've got it!" yelled Nahom. "This room is an exact replica of King Noah's private chambers. His way of making this trap a joke."

"So, what good is that going to do us?" yelled Tater, as the wall continued slowly inching closer and closer to the edge.

"In his private chambers," started Nahom, "King Noah has mirrors set all around the room. He loves the art of illusion, but mostly he loves mirrors so he can continually admire himself."

"Uummm, Nahom, we don't have time to hear all about his private chambers," persisted Seth, as the wall moved within a foot of the edge. "Is there a point to this story?"

"Sorry," replied Nahom, looking over his shoulder at the wall. "Okay, if I remember the story correctly, the mirrors down the left side of the room cast a shadow back toward King's Noah's throne, making the area look as though it is covered in snakes. However, I believe it is actually an illusion. If you stand right in front of what looks like the mirror, you won't be able to see your reflection because there really is no mirror there."

"So, what do we do?" screamed Mrs. M. frantically, sure at any moment the moving wall would push her into the snake pit below. "We don't have a lot of time."

"Let me find the mirror," replied Nahom, hurrying around to the right and then the left side of the room. "Quick, everyone follow me."

Knowing Nahom's idea was their only hope for survival, the group quickly followed him around the room. They watched as he looked out at the pit and back at the wall, over and over again.

"Come on, Nahom. We're out of time," insisted Seth. "Make a decision."

Several anxious moments passed until he finally turned to everyone and asked, "Do you trust me?"

"Yes! We trust you, Nahom," Mrs. M. replied anxiously. "Now what do we do?"

"Everyone, follow me!" he screamed. He jumped from the ledge out into the middle of the open room, straight for the pit of snakes below.

As the wall reached within three inches of the ledge, everyone jumped, following Nahom. Sure they would die in the pit of snakes below, they were surprised when they hit what felt like a floor.

Tater opened his eyes, looked around at the floor, and tapped his foot on the solid ground. He was confused as to why the ground looked to be twenty feet below him, and he was not covered with snakes and stuck by sharp spears.

"What is this?" asked Tater, unsure what had happened.

"I told you," replied Nahom proudly. "This is a room of illusions. It looked like we should have fallen straight to the spears below, and in most of the room, we would have. But, over here is a solid glass floor, three or four feet wide that runs all the way across the room. The glass and mirrors in the room cause an illusion that we will fall off the ledge, to the poisonous snakes and spears below, but, nothing is what is seems. This is the secret of the room. If you figure it out, you will be saved."

"Nice going, Nahom," said Tater, as he knocked his knuckles on the glass below his feet.

"Where to from here?" asked Mrs. M. nervously. "I don't like this. I've got to get to more solid ground."

"Follow me," replied Nahom. He led the way across the room, carefully making sure that there was a hard surface beneath his feet. Then he jumped onto the ledge on the other side of the room.

"Whew!" said Mrs. M., as the group finally reached the other side. "I can't believe we made it! Good job, Nahom. I thought we were gonners for sure."

"Come on, guys. We're running out of time," said Tater, moving rapidly toward the door. "We've got to save the others."

"Be careful, Tater. There could be more traps," called Seth, as Tater rounded the corner and disappeared into the tunnel.

Only seconds had passed when the group heard Tater scream at the top of his lungs.

"You're not funny, Tater," called Ramin. "I don't need any more excitement today."

"Helllpppp me, helllppp!" Tater called.

"Come on, everyone. We better hurry so he doesn't get hurt in another trap," insisted Nahom, as he followed Tater's voice.

"Where'd he go?" asked Mrs. M. The group rounded

the corner, but Tater was nowhere in sight. "Tater, where are you? This isn't funny, and your flashlight rolling around on the ground doesn't trick me!"

"He has to be here somewhere," replied Ramin. "He couldn't just disappear, could he?"

"Where is he? I thought he was kidding," said Nahom, trying to find any sign of Tater in the tunnel. "I didn't really think he needed help."

"I think he has fallen into another trap," replied Seth.

"How do you know that?" asked Mrs. M., as she continued to call Tater's name.

"With his flashlight on the floor and Tater suddenly gone, I think he has fallen into the same kind of trap that Squeaks and Butch did," replied Seth.

"Why?" asked Mrs. M. She was almost hysterical as she continued hurrying through the tunnel in search of Tater.

"There are several traps throughout King Noah's network of tunnels that lead to a series of ponds. The traps that are set throughout the tunnel drop you into a basket that forces you to stand, sit, or lie in the pond," replied Seth. "So, please let me take the lead, so you don't end up in one of those baskets as well."

Mrs. M. paused momentarily, then said, "Yeah, go ahead, but hurry. I can't go home without all three of these kids. If one of them gets hurt, their parents will never forgive me!" insisted Mrs. M., almost running now to keep up with Seth's fast pace. "Are the water traps dangerous?"

"Well, kinda. The ponds are filled with poisonous snakes and piranha," Seth said worriedly.

"You mean, if Tater just fell into one of those traps, he could be eaten by piranha?" asked Nahom. "Are we all at risk of falling into one of King Noah's traps?"

"Yes, if we're not careful," replied Seth. He watched the colored stones on the ground, being careful to follow the right colors.

Chapter Nineteen

Aunt Maggie nervously paced around the living room. She was sure at any minute Bubba's dad would come walking through the door wondering where Mrs. M. was and why she was not home.

"They haven't called in so long, do you think they're okay?" asked Bean, as she watched Aunt Maggie pacing.

"I'm sure they are fine," Aunt Maggie replied, as a worried grin spread across her face.

"Then why haven't they called?" asked Hero. "I was sure they would need more help by now."

"Well, Hero, I told your mom how to read some of the hieroglyphs," replied Aunt Maggie, trying to consol him. "And they probably haven't needed us to help them yet."

"What do you mean you told her how to read the hieroglyphs?" asked Bubba. "How could they possibly read Egyptian hieroglyphs?"

"Well, when we were at the library, Cheri told me that the hieroglyph pictures could be translated literally," answered Aunt Maggie.

"Literally, as in each picture always represents the same letter?" questioned Bean, not sure she understood.

"Not every time, but in the clue that Cheri translated at the library, the pictures all represented the same letters. She thought that maybe it would help the others on their mission to know that literal translation of the pictures might be possible."

"So, if I understand what you are saying, they may be able to translate any further clues they've found without our help. Their mission could be complete anytime, and they could surprise us any minute and walk in the door?" asked Bear, excited at the possibility.

"Possibly," replied Aunt Maggie.

An uneasy quiet fell across the room as the Team contemplated what Aunt Maggie had told them. Then suddenly, the front door creaked as it opened.

"Mom? Mom, Tater, Squeaks, Butch, is that you?" called Bubba, excitedly running toward the door.

"No, it's just me, Bubba," Dad replied cheerfully, as he walked in the door humming a song.

"Oh, hi Dad," Bubba called disappointedly, turning around and walking back toward the living room.

"Don't sound so excited to see me," Dad replied, as

he threw his keys on the hall table and walked toward the kitchen.

"Maggie, what are you doing here?" he asked, when he saw her sitting on the couch.

"Just came by to see my sister," she replied nervously.

"So, where is she?" asked Dad, as he reached the kitchen with no sign of Mom anywhere.

"Running some errands," replied Hero, as he whispered under his breath. "Errands for the Lord, that is."

"Where is she running errands?" asked Dad, scrunching his nose and eyes as he looked around at the Team. "Something doesn't feel right around here. Do any of you want to tell me what is going on?"

"Nothing really, Dad," replied Bubba, as he pushed past him and headed toward the refrigerator for something to eat.

"Okay, hold it," insisted Dad. "Everyone, and that includes you Maggie, come in the kitchen. Someone's gonna tell me what is going on around here."

"Nothing, really. We're just waiting for my mom's sister to get home," answered Bear.

"Why all the worried looks, and why aren't you in the Treehouse? Usually you would all be up there, and I would have to come ask you where she was. Now, someone better answer me. Has something happened that you're all too worried to tell me?" asked Dad. He walked around the counter, pulled out a chair from underneath the kitchen table, and sat down. "I'm waiting, Team. What's going on?"

"We are all waiting in the house in case she calls," replied Bubba. "We didn't want to miss her."

"Why?" Dad asked suspiciously.

"'Cause she kinda left in a hurry, and we're a little worried," replied KP.

"Okay, why?" pressed Dad, as a concerned look spread across his face.

"'Cause she took Tater, Butch, and Squeaks, and we can't leave until she gets back," replied Bear, smiling. "We've got our own errands to run, and we didn't want to leave part of our Team to do them."

"Okay, now we're getting somewhere," said Dad. "Now tell me, where did she take them, and why?"

"We don't know where she took them, that is why we're worried. We have no idea when they will be back for sure," replied Bean.

"All right, now I'm confused again," said Dad. "Aunt Maggie, do you want to take a stab at explaining what in the world is going on around here?"

Aunt Maggie walked from the kitchen door to the table. She pulled out a chair, took a deep breath as she sat down, and said, "I think the jig is up, Team. We've got to tell him."

"But, Aunt Maggie," started Bubba. "You promised."

"Mom!" Bear exclaimed angrily. "I knew you would let us down."

"Now you really have my curiosity going," said Dad. "What did you promise not to tell me, Aunt Maggie?"

"Well," she began.

"Well, nothing," interrupted Hero. "We can't tell you what she is doing because it is a secret."

"Why can't I know the secret?" asked Dad, his curiosity peaked.

"Because if we tell you, then it will no longer be a secret," answered Stick, smiling. "That's why we can't tell you."

"Does the secret have something to do with me?" Dad asked excitedly.

"It might," Hero replied evasively.

"Aunt Maggie, can you tell me if the secret has something to do with me," Dad asked, still smiling.

Aunt Maggie looked around at the Teammates' faces and replied, "I think there is a definite possibility of that. You are going to be shocked when you hear what the secret is."

"All right, I love secrets," said Dad, as he stood from the table and headed for the refrigerator. "I'll play along, but I think we ought to do a surprise for Mom. Let's start dinner, so when she gets home, we won't have to wait to eat."

"Great idea, Dad. What should we fix?" asked Bubba, quickly moving into the kitchen to help.

"Does the surprise include food?" asked Dad, trying to get the Team to accidentally tell him what was happening.

"No, no food is involved," started Stick. "Just…"

"Just what?" questioned Dad, sure Stick would tell him.

"Hey, wait a minute, Dad!" exclaimed Hero. "No trying to trick us into telling you!"

"Oh, sorry," he replied, giggling. "I'm just playing. I have another idea," Dad started.

"What's that?" replied Bean.

"Why don't we try to call Mom on the walkie-talkie? Then we'll know for sure how long she's going to be."

"Daaaddd, stop!" said Bubba. "It's a secret. You'll learn what's going on soon enough."

Dad nodded, puckered up his lips and said, "Okay, okay, Team. Why don't all of you surprise me and find something great for dinner, start cooking, and I'll be back in a little bit," suggested Dad. He motioned for Aunt Maggie to follow him into the living room.

"Where ya going?" asked Bubba.

"Oh, I thought while we all waited for your mother to get home, I would entertain our guest, Aunt Maggie, in the living room," he replied.

"Are you sure you're not going to try to get the secret out of her?" Bear asked suspiciously. "'Cause you know that she's smarter than that, and she's not going to tell you."

"No, I'm not going to pry the secret out of her," Dad replied, smiling. "I'm just going to see how your dad is doing and what is happening at your house. Is that okay?"

Bear looked at his mom sternly and replied, "That's okay, but nothing else, Mom!"

※

"Tater, Tater?" called Mrs. M. "Where are you?"

"Don't worry—we'll find him," said Seth reassuringly. "And I bet I know just where he is."

"How do you know?" asked Mrs. M., fear evident in her face.

"'Cause I bet that the trap that Tater has fallen into leads to the same place where Butch and Squeaks were found," Seth confidently replied.

"Do you know where that is for sure?" asked Ramin.

"Not for sure, but I think we're close," answered Seth, looking over his shoulder and smiling at the group.

"Is it all right if I keep calling for him?" asked Mrs. M.

"Sure, just don't call too loudly," said Nahom. "I don't want any soldiers to hear us."

The group wound their way further into the mysterious secret tunnels. Seth successfully found every hidden trap and disarmed each one, keeping the group safe as they continued searching for Tater and the prison. Traveling through the quiet and mysterious tunnel, the group was shocked when Mrs. M. suddenly screamed, startling everyone.

"What, what's the matter?" called Ramin, baffled by her scream.

"A spider! I think there's a spider in my hair. I can feel it moving around!" Mrs. M. screamed, flailing her arms in the air.

Ramin smiled. "A spider? You're screaming about a spider?"

"Yes," Mrs. M. cried. "Someone, please help me. I hate spiders."

Nahom cleared his throat, attempting not to laugh at her, and quickly walked to where she was standing.

Grabbing her arms so that she would not accidentally hit him, he quickly scanned her long, brown hair for any sign of a spider.

"Well, I think you're all right. I can't see a spider anywhere in your hair," Nahom said, finally laughing out loud.

"Are you sure you can't see anything?" Mrs. M. asked, afraid of all creepy crawly bugs.

"No, nothing, I promise. I really can't see anything," answered Nahom.

Cautiously, Mrs. M. ran her hands through her hair, afraid at any moment she might feel something slimy. As she reached the bottom strands, she breathed a cautious sigh of relief.

"See, I told you I couldn't see anything," said Nahom.

"I really don't like spiders," replied Mrs. M., in a quivering voice.

"Come on, we've got to get moving," insisted Seth. "No more interruptions. We're going to run out of time to rescue everyone. We're going to end up caught and in the same prison. Then what will happen to Alma and the rest of us?"

Still nervous about the spider web she had walked through, Mrs. M. slowly followed the others, continuing to rub her hands through her hair as they walked.

"I can hear someone. Everybody, be quiet," whispered Seth, as he quickly turned off Tater's flash light.

"Can you see anything?" asked Ramin.

"Ssshhh," replied Seth, as he cautiously hid in the shadows of the tunnel and maneuvered closer to the noise.

"Is it Tater?" asked Mrs. M. hopefully.

Seth turned, held his finger to his lips, and whispered, "Sssshhh." Scanning the area for the noise, he suddenly saw a dark shadow in the distance.

"Someone is just ahead of us," he softly whispered.

"Who is it?" asked Nahom.

"I'm not sure," replied Seth. "I can only see shadows."

"Do you think it's Tater?" Mrs. M. asked hopefully.

"Let's go find out," replied Seth. "Mrs. M., Ramin, stay here. Nahom and I are going to pretend to be soldiers guarding the tunnel. If it is Tater, we'll motion for you that everything is safe."

Seth did not wait for a response. He stood up straight, puffed out his chest, and walked directly for the shadow.

"Hey, who is in this tunnel? You don't belong here," he called, trying to intimidate the shadow.

Nahom pulled a small machete-type sword from the waistband of his robe and held it up for the shadow to see.

"Who are you?" Nahom called, trying to look official.

Mysteriously, the shadow remained with its back to Seth and Nahom, acting as though he could not hear them.

"Answer me," Seth screamed angrily.

Slowly, the shadow started to turn, until Seth could see his face.

"Tater, is that you?" Seth asked, straining to see.

"Seth?" replied the soft voice.

"Tater, it is you! We thought you might be a guard or something," called Nahom. "Why didn't you answer?"

"I was afraid. I was sure you were King Noah's soldiers here to arrest me," Tater replied meekly.

"Well, what happened to you?" asked Seth, as he

motioned to Mrs. M. and Ramin that it was safe.

"I don't know," Tater replied, scratching his head. "One minute I was hurrying through the tunnel, and the next I was sliding down slippery rocks straight into these pools of water, where we found Squeaks and Butch earlier."

"Are you all right, Tater," asked Mrs. M. She grabbed his hand, trying to pull him out of the water trap.

"Yeah, I'm all right," he replied. "I just don't dare move. If there really are piranha in these pools of water, like the commander said earlier, I don't want them to think my legs are a meal."

"How do we get you out?" questioned Nahom, looking around for a way to open the trap.

"There is a lever, remember, Seth?" said Tater, pointing to the floor. "It's next to the floor by the wall. I watched the commander lift the lever earlier, and the trap opened."

"Yeah, I remember," replied Seth. He moved to the wall and located the small wooden lever. "Here ya go." Seth flipped the lever up, and the trap quickly snapped open.

Ramin reached down and took a hold of Tater's hand. He pulled him from the waist-deep water and lifted him to safety. Tater kicked the small wooden lid to the trap closed and muttered, "I can't believe I fell into a trap! I should have known there would be one right outside the room of illusions."

"Oh, don't worry about it," replied Nahom. "We all make mistakes sometimes. That's why Alma is teaching us about repentance, right?"

"Yep, that's what Alma has been saying," agreed Ramin.

"Yes, you're all right," added Mrs. M., smiling.

Tater took a deep breath. He tried to squeeze the water out of his robe and replied, "Yeah, you're right. I'm just disappointed that I didn't pay better attention."

"So, where to now?" asked Nahom, anxious to keep moving.

"This is as far as we went with the commander earlier today. But, when we were talking, he said the prison wasn't much further," answered Seth. "In fact, I think we're underneath the moat right now. That is where the water in these puddles is coming from."

"Then let's get moving," suggested Mrs. M. "I don't want to keep Squeaks, Butch, Alma, or Abinadi in prison any longer than they have to be."

The group continued through the tunnel, hopeful they were close to the prison.

"Be careful, Seth. You never know when you might run into another trap," called Tater, moving slowly through the dark, damp tunnel.

"I can see a door up ahead," Seth called excitedly. "I'm sure it's the secret prison door."

"Can you open it?" asked Ramin.

"No, it's locked," replied Tater, as he pulled on the round, brass handle.

"What do we do? How to we get inside?" asked Nahom.

"There has to be a lever, like for the traps, or maybe a key," suggested Mrs. M. "Everybody, look."

"Hey, I found something!" yelled Tater. "It's not a key or a lever, but it's a code."

"What is it?" asked Seth.

"A series of pictures, carved into little boxes," Tater replied. "They're like the pictures on the boxes in the rat room, Mrs. M."

"What word do you think will work?" she asked, moving closer to Tater.

"Something that has to do with King Noah," replied Tater. "This is one of his codes."

"What things does King Noah like?" asked Mrs. M., looking at Seth, Nahom, and Ramin.

"I'm not sure what you mean," replied Seth.

"We need to find a word that King Noah would use as a code to open this door," Mrs. M. explained.

"He likes to have prisoners," replied Nahom.

"He likes money," added Ramin.

"Do either of those words work, Tater?" asked Mrs. M.

"I don't think so. What else does he like?" asked Tater.

"He likes food and parties," said Seth.

"He likes the robes he wears when he sentences people," said Nahom.

"None of those words work," replied Tater. "Can you think of any other word he might use for a code?"

"What about the types of money?" suggested Mrs. M.

"Like gold, silver, Ziff," asked Seth.

"Nope, those words don't work either," replied Tater.

"I have it!" yelled Ramin. "He loves collecting taxes."

Tater smiled and pushed the letters that spelled out

the word taxes. To his surprise, the lock on the door snapped open.

"Hey, we did it!" exclaimed Tater. He pulled the handle on the door and swung it open, revealing a small, wooden, spiral staircase leading up to the prison. "Let's go save everyone."

Tater stuck his head inside the room and shined his light on the stairs. The area was small, leaving little room to move. Everything was damp and smelled wet and moldy. Sure Squeaks and Butch were at the top of the stairs, Tater walked inside and started to climb the stairs.

"Wait, slow down, Tater!" called Seth. "Guards could be by the prisoners. You don't want to get caught. Let me go first."

Tater nodded, stepped off of the stairs, and waited for Seth, Ramin and Nahom to pass him. Cautiously, the group worked their way up the narrow, spiral staircase to a small trap door, located just above their heads.

"How do we get the door open?" asked Ramin.

"It doesn't look like it is secured by anything," replied Seth, as he examined the door.

"So just push?" he asked, placing pressure on the door.

"There could be something above holding it down. But yes, carefully push and see if it will open," replied Seth.

Ramin grinned as he looked at Seth and nervously pushed on the door. Several seconds passed while he continued to push with more and more pressure, but the door did not budge. Looking at Seth, he shrugged his shoulders and said, "I can't get it to move. Should we knock?"

"No!" exclaimed Seth. "If there are guards in the prison, they will hear that for sure. If we can get the door to open, we might be able to sneak up on them."

"Okay, then you're going to have to squeeze up here with me and help me push," replied Ramin, motioning for Seth to help.

The two boys pushed with all their might, but nothing happened. About to give up, Seth took a breath and said, "One more time, together. One, two, three, push."

Suddenly, the door flew open, exposing the inside of the prison. Cautiously, Seth stuck his head through the opening and quickly searched the room for any sign of guards.

Alma glanced over at Seth and calmly said, "Boy, it sure took you long enough to get here."

"We had to deal with a few of King Noah's traps on the way," he replied, smiling. He pulled himself inside the room. "So are we safe? Are there any guards?"

"None inside, but there are few outside," replied Alma. He stood up, walked over to Seth, and gratefully threw his arms around Seth's shoulders. "Thank you."

"I couldn't have found you alone," replied Seth, as he helped Ramin and Nahom into the prison.

"Thank you, too, boys," said Alma.

"We had some helpers sent by the Lord as well," added Ramin, pulling Mrs. M. into the room.

"I have met two of them," replied Alma. "Isn't it mysterious how the Lord helps us?"

"No, not mysterious," replied Ramin. "It's miraculous. When you pray for His help, He hears and answers your prayers."

"You have listened well," Alma said proudly.

"Squeaks, Butch, are you here?" Mrs. M. asked softly, as she worked her way around the small room.

"They are asleep next to Abinadi," said Alma, pointing to a small, dark corner.

Mrs. M. nervously walked to the corner, excited to be in the company of two Book of Mormon prophets. She found Squeaks and shook her hand. "Squeaks, honey. Wake up. We've got to get to safety before the guards return."

Squeaks opened her eyes, saw her mother, and screamed. She jumped to her feet and rubbed her eyes. She blinked them several times and looked at her mom again.

"It's me Squeaks, Mom," Mrs. M. said reassuringly.

"There's a…," cried Squeaks, pointing at her mom.

"There's a what?" asked Ramin. "And be quiet. You're going to get us all captured."

"There's an enormous spider," replied Squeaks, pointing again at her mom.

Ramin looked at Mrs. M., and his eyes bulged at the size of the spider on her shoulder. He quickly moved closer and softly said, "The spider on your shoulder is poisonous. Hold very still. And whatever you do, don't move."

Mrs. M. whimpered, closed her eyes and tried not to move a muscle. The group watched as Ramin rubbed his hands together, clapped them loudly once, and quickly swung with all his might. The golf-ball-sized spider flew across the room, smacking hard into the wooden slats on the wall.

"Did you get it?" asked Mrs. M., afraid to open her eyes.

"Yep, it's gone," comforted Ramin, as he softly placed his hand on her shoulder.

Mrs. M. breathed a deep sigh of relief. Then she again ran her hands through her hair, feeling for any more creepy, crawly things. Finally she looked up at Squeaks and said, "Are you okay?"

"Yes, Mom. I'm sorry. I never should have left you in the market. I just wanted to save Alma," she cried, dropping her head into her hands.

"Well, there is no reason to cry now," insisted Tater, as he hurriedly woke Butch.

"Tater's right, Squeaks," said Nahom, as he peered through the small holes in the wall of the prison. "Now we've got to get out of here before guards check on you."

"Abinadi, we've got to get going," called Alma. "These faithful followers of the Lord have come to save us."

Abinadi opened his eyes and looked up at the group. Blinking several times to keep the tears out of his eyes, he replied, "I'm sorry, Alma. The Lord has a different plan for me."

"What do you mean?" asked Squeaks worriedly, as she took a hold of his hand.

"Child, you know that I cannot go with you," Abinadi replied calmly.

"But we have traveled all this way to save you," she insisted.

"Have you traveled here to save me? Or are you doing the work the Lord has sent you here to do?" asked

Abinadi, as he squeezed Squeaks' hand. "The Lord has revealed to me that you have the records from our time."

"I know, Abinadi, but in those records, you are killed," warned Squeaks. "Please, come with us. We have the ability to save you," she begged.

"You know that we cannot change the records. I must stay here and do as the Lord desires," Abinadi replied peacefully.

"Abinadi is right," said Alma, as he walked toward him. "Although I do not know the records you speak of, the Lord's will and desires are far more important than ours."

"But," started Squeaks.

"No, Squeaks," interrupted Mrs. M. "We are only here to set straight what has gone wrong, not to change history in the Book of Mormon."

"Now, all of you must hurry," insisted Abinadi. "You must get to safety and continue spreading the words of the Lord."

"I am sorry to leave you, my friend," said Alma, as he took a hold of Abinadi's hand, squeezing it tightly.

"Stay strong, and remember that repentance is a change of heart. Keep your sight squarely on the things of the Lord. Be faithful, and above all else, be repentant. Know that He will lead and guide you safely home."

"We've got to get going," insisted Seth. "The light of day is going to come, and we have a long way to go."

"Lead the way," replied Alma, as he hurried to follow Seth through the trap door toward the tunnel below the prison.

✺

"Soldiers are coming; I can hear them," insisted Squeaks, as they group reached the bottom of the stairs.

"What are we going to do?" Nahom asked worriedly. "If they find us in the tunnel, they're going to take us directly to King Noah."

"We're going to quickly get back inside the prison and wait for the soldiers to leave. Then, when they have, we're going to get everyone out of here safely," Mrs. M. said calmly, as she hurried back inside the prison.

Everyone followed Mrs. M.'s lead back through the prison door. Alma slowly closed it, being careful not to make any noise as he pulled the door shut. Alma watched through the small barred window in the door, listening as the soldiers' voices grew louder and louder. Suddenly, they were standing right outside the hidden prison door of King Noah's tunnel.

"I don't know why the commander is making us guard this secret door tonight. It's not like anyone knows how to get down here," one of the soldiers said angrily.

"Maybe just to give us something to do through the night," replied the other soldier, chuckling. "You know the commander never sleeps."

All of a sudden, one of the soldiers noticed eyes watching him through the small opening in the door.

"Alma, is that you?" asked the soldier, walking closer to the door and peering inside.

"Yes," Alma replied, holding the handle on the door at the base of the stairs, making sure it was closed tightly.

"How did you know about the trap door down the spiral staircase to the hidden tunnels, and what are you doing down here?" asked the tall soldier shocked to see him. "You know there is no way for you to get out."

"He knows about the door because he was a high priest. Either he is trying to escape or he is waiting for someone to rescue him," said the other soldier, peering in at Alma.

"I guess with you here now, it doesn't really matter what I was doing," replied Alma.

"If I were you, I would head back up to the prison. You won't be finding a rescue here tonight," added the first soldier. "Not with us guarding the entrance."

"What do we do now?" whispered Tater, as he cautiously peered out the small window in the prison door. He watched the soldiers laugh as they walked a few feet away. "Looks like the soldiers plan on spending the night."

"We'll have to wait until they leave and then escape," Seth replied calmly.

"Move away from the window, Tater," motioned Alma. "If they see you, they will know that something is wrong."

"We don't have a lot of time, remember?" Tater said quietly. "King Noah plans on meeting with Abinadi and Alma in the morning."

"Then we'll have to escape before morning," said Butch. He grabbed Tater's shoulder and tried to help calm his nervousness.

"How are we going to do that if they are standing watch down here all night?" Tater asked angrily.

"Why don't we climb the stairs back to the hut and see if we can find a way to escape from up there?" suggested Butch, as he started up the first step. "We know that these soldiers will be staying by this door all night."

"That's a good idea," replied Alma, following Butch's lead. "We need to get away from here before the soldiers hear all our voices."

"How will we ever find a way to escape from up there?" Tater asked pessimistically.

"The Lord will provide a way, if that is His will," Alma replied softly, motioning for everyone to follow.

Seth, Nahom, Tater, Butch, Squeaks, and Mrs. M. followed Alma up the long flight of winding stairs to the hut above. Once they had reached the small prison room, Tater quickly closed the small trap door, and scanned the area for any other way to escape. Then he noticed that the prison was unlike any of the other buildings in the city; it was made very inexpensively. The walls were made of wooden slat tightly tied together, with most of the cracks or crevasses filled in with clay from the outside. Straw was spread all over the bamboo-covered floor. There were only two openings in the room - the main door in front of the hut, and one small ten-inch-square opening on the back side of the hut.

"Is anyone going to be waiting in King Noah's temple or across the moat?" asked Squeaks.

"No," replied Seth. "Why?"

"I was worried if you had someone that was waiting

for us to escape back through the temple, they might get caught," she replied, relieved to hear no one was waiting.

"Can we get back to how we're going to get out of here?" asked Tater, annoyed by Squeaks' comments.

"I have an idea for you," replied one of the men in the prison.

"What is it, Sir?" replied Butch. The man looked at the boys for several seconds before he replied, "I have been held captive in this prison for more than three years now. As men have been thrown into prison and then taken away, we have all worked on an escape route," he said. "If you will take me with you, I will show you our escape plan."

"And what have you found?" questioned Alma.

"Even with the secret tunnel, that only the King and high priests are supposed to know about, there is only one way that we have ever found," the man replied.

"And what is it?" Tater asked impatiently.

Again the man looked at each of the kids in the group and asked, "Are you spies for King Noah?"

"NO! We're not spies for King Noah," replied Nahom. "We are here to rescue Alma."

"Then why do you wear his soldiers' clothes?" the man questioned.

"They are not spies, Aaron," replied Alma. "I will stake my life on it. They are followers of the Lord, here to help me escape."

Aaron took a deep breath. He pushed himself to his feet and moved to a corner in the room. Brushing the straw into a pile, he carefully pulled a small piece of bamboo from the floor. Reaching inside the opening, he pulled out a long piece of rope.

"What good is rope going to do us?" Tater asked angrily.

"There are two of you kids that I think are small enough to slip out the opening in the back of the prison," he replied, pointing to the small window.

"What good is that going to do?" asked Seth. "The ravine down to the moat is more than one hundred feet. They would be killed if they tried to escape through it."

"That is what the rope is for, boy," replied Aaron, holding it up for everyone to see.

"We tie one side around your ankles and the other we'll hold while you swing yourself back and forth over to the ledge. Once you reach the ledge, run back over the bridge and let us all out," Aaron replied matter of factly. "That is the only other option that we have for escape."

"Do you really think that will work?" asked Mrs. M.

"Sure it will," replied Aaron. "I've been devising this plan for a while now. It has to work."

"Where did you get this rope from?" asked Nahom, as he grabbed an end and inspected the fibers. "I have never seen another rope like this."

"I made it," answered Aaron, pulling the rope out of Nahom's hand.

"Out of what, Aaron?" asked Mrs. M.

Aaron looked at the group. He wound up his rope and replied, "If you don't want to try my escape plan, that is fine. I will wait for another small prisoner to be thrown in here."

"They didn't say they weren't willing to try it," Alma

replied softly. "They just want to know that they are going to be safe."

Aaron looked down at his rope again and quietly replied, "I made it out of my hair."

"You're hair?" squealed Tater. "How will that hold anything?"

"Feel it. I guarantee you will not be able to break it," Aaron replied defensively. "This rope is stronger than any other I have ever seen."

Everyone huddled around Aaron's rope. They each held it and tested its strength.

"Do you think this will work, Mrs. M.?" asked Butch. "A bunch of hair twisted together?"

"Actually, I think Aaron is a genius," replied Mrs. M. "Hair is very strong. When it is wound and wrapped together tightly like this, I don't know what it would take to break it."

"So which one of us is going to try and wiggle out of the opening?" asked Squeaks, looking at Butch. "You know I am afraid of heights."

"Then I guess that I will try," Butch replied, smiling. "But if I can't get out, then you will have to!"

Squeaks watched as Alma, Aaron and Mrs. M. tied the rope as tightly as they could around Butch's ankles. Once the rope was tight, they lifted him to the opening, and Butch tried to wiggle through.

"Ouch, wait a minute!" he screamed, trying to get his arms through the opening. "Okay, I'm ready to try again."

Alma and Aaron pushed with all their might, but Butch could not get through. His hips just could not maneuver through the opening.

"I can't do it," Butch called. "I'm too big."

"Take a deep breath, and then let out all of the air," said Seth. "See if that will help."

Butch did as Seth suggested, and again the men tried to push Butch through the opening.

"Wait, wait, I'm just too big," said Butch.

Squeaks took a deep breath and softly said, "Pull him back in. I'm a lot smaller, I'm sure that I can get through."

"Are you sure you want to try, Squeaks?" Mrs. M. asked nervously. "I'm afraid this will be a little scary."

"Yes. Get Butch down before the guards hear him and come in to see what is going on," Squeaks replied. She motioned for them to pull him back.

Alma and Aaron carefully lifted Butch back to the ground and untied the rope from his ankles. Moving quickly to Squeaks, they retied the rope and lifted her up to the small window.

"Be careful, Squeaks," said Tater, fearful for his friend.

Squeaks grabbed hold of the opening, wiggled her arms and head through, and then asked, "Now, what am I supposed to do?"

"Swing your arms back and forth over your head, try to get your body swinging. We'll try to watch from here. When you get close enough, we'll release the rope so that you can drop on the ledge across the ravine," replied Aaron. "After you are safely on the ledge, untie the rope. Carefully cross the bridge, open the door, and release us."

"What if the door doesn't open?" asked Squeaks, nervously listening to the plan.

"It locks from the outside. I have seen it a hundred times for over three years," replied Aaron. "Now you've got to hurry. The sun is getting close to rising, and the guards will come to check on the prisoners when that happens."

Frightened by the nearly one hundred feet below her, Squeaks swallowed hard as the two men lowered her toward the moat below. Afraid to move a muscle, she hung upside down for three full minutes before Tater called, "Squeaks, you've got to swing your body back and forth, like a pendulum."

"I can't. I'm afraid to move," she nervously called.

"You've got to," insisted Aaron. "My plan won't work if you don't try to swing yourself. We can't do all the work from inside here."

"Come on, Squeaks," whispered Mrs. M. "I know you can do it."

Squeaks took a deep breath. She looked over at the ledge, nearly thirty feet away. Finally, she started to swing her arms and body back and forth as hard as she could, attempting to get her body to swing. After several minutes, Squeaks was swinging like the second hand on her dad's old grandfather clock.

"I need more rope," she called, as quietly as she could. "I'm not close enough to the ledge."

Alma and Aaron slowly released a few more feet of rope, as Squeaks continued to swing herself back and forth.

Still not close enough to be released, she again called, "Let out some more rope."

Alma and Aaron released as much rope as they could,

barely able to hold on to the rope they had left.

"That's it," replied Alma. "Can she reach the ledge with the rope she has now?"

The group watched the best they could through the small cracks in the bamboo and the small opening.

"She needs a little more. She's not quite there," called Mrs. M. nervously watching her daughter swing.

"There isn't any more," replied Alma.

"What do we do now?" asked Tater. "If she can't reach the ledge, then we're never going to get out of this prison."

"What if we wait for her to swing toward the ledge again, and when she does, you release the rope?" asked Butch, peering through the bamboo. "Her momentum should carry her to the ledge."

"What if she doesn't make it?" Mrs. M. asked apprehensively.

"She'll make it, I'm sure of it," replied Tater. "Alma, you and Aaron have to let go right when I tell you to."

Mrs. M., nervous for her daughter, held her breath and watched. The rope slowly swung away from the ledge until Squeaks was headed for the ledge again. As Squeaks got closer and closer, Mrs. M. could no longer watch. She closed her eyes tightly and prayed for help from Heavenly Father.

"Get ready," called Tater. "One, two, now, let go! Let go!" he demanded.

Alma and Aaron released the rope and watched as the end flew out the small opening.

"Did she make it?" called Butch. "I can't see. Did she make it?"

No one said a word. Then Tater finally replied, "She almost made it."

Worried about her daughter, Mrs. M. opened her eyes and exclaimed, "What, what do you mean she almost made it?"

"Well," started Tater. "She's not quite on the edge, but she at least has a hold of it."

Mrs. M. scanned the side of the ledge and located Squeaks holding on to the top, trying to pull herself up.

"Come on, you can do it," Mrs. M. called, trying to encourage her daughter.

"Quiet, shush! You're going to get her caught," insisted Aaron. "Be quiet."

The group watched as Squeaks finally maneuvered her small body up onto the ledge. She untied the rope around her ankles. Giving the group two thumbs up, she sneaked back toward the bridge that led to the prison. Hiding in the trees and bushes as she moved, she suddenly noticed movement in the forest behind her. "What is that?" she thought to herself.

Unable to see anything, she shook off the nervous feeling as her imagination, and she continued closer toward the bridge. When she was only a few feet away, a deep, fierce growl bellowed from behind her. The hair on the back of her neck stood on end, and she was afraid to move an inch.

Sure a tiger, jaguar, or bobcat of some kind was behind her, she started running. As she scampered toward the bridge, she purposely jumped on a sleeping soldier, causing him to moan in pain. He sat up just in time to be face to face with the tiger that was chasing her. Catching the tiger's attention, it stopped chasing Squeaks and roared uncontrollably at the soldier.

Squeaks' hands were shaking as she gripped the rope handle of the suspension bridge and hurried across as fast as she could.

Another growl shook the forest behind her and a terrified scream echoed through the area from the now wide-awake soldier.

Squeaks clasped the prison door, turned the lock, and pulled with all her might.

"Are you all right?" cried Mrs. M., as a tear fell from her face.

"I'm fine, Mom," she replied, panting from lack of breath. "But we've got to hurry before those soldiers chase off the tiger and come after us."

"Tiger?" asked Alma. "We don't have many tigers around here."

"Well, we do now," replied Seth, pointing toward the forest. "Come on, Squeaks is right. We've got to hurry before the soldiers either chase off that tiger or kill it, and then come after us."

Chapter Twenty

❝Seth, you and Nahom make sure everyone is out of the prison before you cross the bridge," instructed Alma. "I'm going to cross the bridge first and head into the city, I want to see if I can find any followers that want to leave the city under the cover of darkness with us."

"Yes, Alma," replied Seth. "But remember, the last time you were going to gather some followers, you were found and arrested by soldiers."

"I will be more careful this time," Alma replied, as he placed a comforting hand on Seth's shoulder. "I promise."

Turning to Abinadi, still standing at the prison door, Alma softly said, "I am sorry to leave you, my friend. I will never forget what you have taught me, and I will do always as the Lord commands."

Abinadi nodded slightly and replied, "You will be a great leader for the Lord. Now get moving, before you are seen."

With that, the group, now including several of King Noah's freed prisoners, quickly moved across the suspension bridge toward the fierce and terrifying growls of the tiger, which was still attacking the soldiers. As Alma and the group safely crossed the bridge, they were sure the tiger had been sent by the Lord to help them in their escape. One by one, everyone maneuvered past the soldiers and fierce growls of the tiger. Excited to find freedom, they followed Alma as he led them along the edge of town, toward the forest and the secret Waters of Mormon.

"The prisoners are escaping, Aiath," screamed Meles, pointing toward the prison and suspension bridge.

"There's nothing I can do about it at the moment," Aiath replied angrily, as he swung his spear at the tiger. "I'm trying to protect myself from the large, fierce teeth growling at me."

"The commander is going to be very angry," replied Meles, as he jabbed his spear toward the large tiger, as it's paw swung for him.

"Angry will not be the word for it," agreed Aiath, stabbing his spear toward the tiger. "Can you see who is escaping?"

"All of the prisoners are escaping," replied Meles. "Including…,"

"Including whom?" questioned Aiath, still jabbing his spear at the tiger.

"Including the soldier, Seth," he quietly replied, unsure if he was seeing correctly.

"Seth? Are you sure?" questioned Aiath. "Seth was helping the commander capture Alma's followers earlier today."

Meles turned again and squinted through the darkness, trying to see if Seth was helping the prisoners to escape. As he turned his back to the tiger, he was knocked to the ground by its large swinging paw.

"Ooouuccchhh!" Meles screamed, as he was forcefully slammed into the ground.

"Are you okay?" cried Aiath, scared by the strength of the tiger.

"I think so," replied Meles, as he picked himself up off the ground and tried to hold up his spear.

"So, did you see for sure? Is Seth helping the traitor, Alma?" asked Aiath.

"I'm sure it is. Look, before he is gone. Make sure that I am not imagining things!" exclaimed Meles.

Tired of fighting with the tiger, but afraid to take his attention away from it, Aiath quickly threw the sharp edge of his spear toward the giant cat's foot. With a direct hit, the tiger squealed in pain. It growled and flashed its giant teeth at Aiath and Meles. Then it suddenly, took off running, back into the cover of darkness in the forest.

Aiath sighed with relief, as he watched the wounded tiger fiercely growl in pain as it disappeared into the darkness. Sure the mighty cat was gone, Aiath hurriedly spun around to see where Meles was pointing. Following the direction of Meles' finger, Aiath could only see the back of the soldier's head.

"Are you positive, Meles?" asked Aiath, with uncertainty. "All I can see is the back of a soldier's head."

"Yes, Aiath. I'm sure it was Seth. I saw his face," insisted Meles.

"Well, we can't accuse him of helping Alma, unless we catch him," said Aiath. "Especially where I couldn't see for sure if it really was him."

"What should we do, Aiath?" Meles asked. "Should we follow the escaping prisoners and Seth, or should we go inform the commander?"

"Let's follow them," Aiath replied, in a sneaky voice. "If we catch them, the commander will reward us. If we don't, we will at least be able to tell him about Seth."

Meles nodded, and the two soldiers cautiously started following the group, being careful to stay out of sight.

Mrs. M., Tater, Butch, Squeaks, Seth, Ramin, and Nahom crossed the bridge and headed out of the city as fast as they could. Tater, unsure where to go, motioned for Nahom to take the lead. The group moved as quickly as they dared through the guarded streets of the city.

Suddenly, an uneasy feeling swept through Seth. He was sure they were being followed, but, he was unable to see anyone. Motioning for Nahom to keep going Seth moved into the shadows of the buildings and watched. He saw two familiar figures emerging from the darkness.

"Oh, no, Aiath and Meles," he thought to himself. "If they continue to follow us, we'll lead them straight to all of Alma's followers."

Seth devised a plan and hurried to catch up with the rest of the group.

"Whatever you do, don't turn around. But, we've got two men following us," Seth said quietly.

"What?" asked Mrs. M., looking, over her shoulder.

"Don't turn around," demanded Seth. "Just trust me when I say that we are being followed."

"What are we going to do?" asked Tater nervously. "We can't return to Alma if we are being followed."

"I have an idea. As we round the corner of the building up here, I'm gonna break off from the group and see if I can get the soldiers to follow me," Seth suggested.

"Not a chance, Seth," replied Nahom. "Your father will never forgive me if I allow something to happen to you."

"There is no other option," replied Seth. "If I don't, then we put everyone who has chosen to repent and follow the Lord at risk."

"There has to be another way," insisted Butch. "I don't like the idea of leaving you."

"There is no other way," Seth insisted. "Besides, if they have seen me, then it won't be long before the commander knows. If I can keep them busy for awhile, then Alma will have a better chance of having the time he needs to disappear into the forest."

"I can't go on any longer," Squeaks complained, interrupting the stressful conversation. She fell to the ground crying. "I've done as much as I can. I can't go on."

Tater and Mrs. M. quickly ran back to Squeaks. They picked her up off the ground and carried her back toward Seth. "We need to find a place to hide," said Mrs. M. "We've got to take a break for a minute."

"Okay, my plan can still work," Seth said. "Just around this building is a dried up well. It has been used several times by the followers of Alma to avoid capture. As soon as we round the corner, all of you climb inside and remain quiet. I will continue on through the city and try to get the soldiers to follow me. As soon as I can, I will return and let you know that it is safe to continue on our journey to meet up with Alma. Ramin and Nahom, the others will need your protection should they be found. I really need you to stay with them. Does everyone agree with that?"

Apprehensively, Ramin and Nahom agreed. The group rounded the corner of the building, finding the well right where Seth said it would be. Seth gently set Squeaks into the water bucket and quickly lowered her to the bottom. Tater, Butch, Ramin, Nahom, and Mrs. M. climbed down the ladder hidden against the wall on the inside of the well.

Squeaks hit the bottom and fell out of the bucket. Seth quickly reeled it back to the top. Then he held his crossed fingers up for everyone to see, quickly waved at the group and disappeared out of sight.

"I sure hope he knows what he is doing," Nahom whispered under his breath. "If he gets caught, King Noah will surely kill him."

"Why didn't he just come down here with us?" asked Squeaks.

"He's afraid that if the soldiers don't see him, they will know that we have hidden close by. Then hundreds of soldiers will search the area until they find all of us. And I can tell you, as stiff a punishment that the two of you received today, that would be nothing in comparison to what King Noah would do to you now."

"Sssshhhh," said Butch, quietly pointing up toward

the early morning sky. "I can see shadows. I think the soldiers are up there."

The group watched as the shadows moved around the well. Finally, the shadows turned to silhouettes of the young soldiers. They paused for a few moments at the well and scanned the area. One of the men pointed and said something, but the group was unable to hear what he was saying. Hopeful that the men would not see them, they all stayed in the shadows of the well. They held their breath, afraid to make any slight noise. And they prayed they would not be found. Moments later, the two men disappeared from the opening at the top of the well into the dusk.

"Should I sneak up to the top of the well and see if I can see the soldiers?" asked Tater, anxious to know if the men were still in the area.

"No," Nahom replied adamantly. "Noises in a well echo. The ladder smacking against the rock wall in here would give away our hiding place. Trust that Seth can lead them away and return here safely, so that we can all go back to be with Alma."

The group waited impatiently as seconds turned into minutes, and minutes turned into hours, with no sign of Seth anywhere. Unable to wait any longer, Squeaks fell asleep. The others watched as the night sky disappeared and the sun began to creep over the mountains.

"Tater, do you have any food left in your knapsack?" asked Butch, as he stomach rumbled from hunger. "I'm absolutely starving."

"All I have is one granola bar. Do you want to share it with me?" Tater asked, holding up the bar for Butch to see.

"Anything would be great," replied Butch, as he held his stomach, trying to get it to stop rumbling.

Tater opened the wrapper and broke the granola bar into two pieces. As his mouth watered from the anticipation of eating the bar, Seth suddenly called down into the well, startling everyone inside.

"Okay, it has taken me most of the night, but I think that I have finally lost those two soldiers."

"Finally, Seth," replied Nahom, jumping to his feet and grabbing hold of the ladder. "I was worried about you. I thought you had been captured."

"Come on, Nahom. Me, captured?" joked Seth, motioning for the group to climb to the surface.

Suddenly, two familiar voices yelled not far in the distance. Seth frantically turned, pretending to be getting a drink and whispered, "I guess I didn't lose them. They found me. Nahom, Ramin, as soon as I am gone, get everyone to safety. Tell my father what has happened. And whatever you do, be very careful, soldiers are everywhere. Word of Alma's escape has already spread through the city, and King Noah is furious."

Just then, the two soldiers grabbed Seth's arm, knocking the bucket out of his hands and down the well. As it fell, Tater reached for the bucket, trying to grab it before it hit the ground and tipped off the soldiers above of the groups hiding place.

"Now we have you, Seth!" yelled Meles. "You thought you could hide from us, but we are to smart for you."

"Oh hi, Aiath, Meles. What are you doing here?" asked Seth, trying to act normal.

"Don't pretend you don't know why were following you," replied Aiath, as he grabbed hold of Seth's other arm.

"I don't have a clue. What are you doing?" asked Seth, trying to act surprised. "I was trying to get a drink before I report to the commander and start searching again today. Let go of my arms."

"We saw you helping Alma and everyone else in prison to escape last night. I think you must be one of his followers," said Meles, with a sinister grin across his face.

"What are you talking about?" asked Seth.

"Don't pretend, we know what we saw," replied Meles.

"I was at home all night," insisted Seth, with an angry look on his face.

"No you weren't! We've followed you all night. That is how we found you here," said Aiath. "You were not at home."

"You found me here because this is my home," Seth replied angrily, pointing to his home across the street. "Now, get your hands off of me. I demand to see the commander right now!" Seth screamed loudly, trying to intimidate the men. "You will not accuse me of something like this."

Aiath was confused. He looked at Meles, sure they had seen Seth helping Alma escape and replied, "We will take you to the commander. He will decide whether you are innocent or not."

The two soldiers firmly took hold of Seth's arms and led him toward King Noah's temple.

"Oh, this is great! What do we do now?" asked Butch

nervously. "You know if the commander doesn't believe Seth and takes him to King Noah, that he will be killed for helping Alma, right?"

Nahom took a deep breath and momentarily looked down at the ground. Wiping a tear from his eye, he replied, "I am afraid we must continue on to Alma before the group travels to the hidden Waters of Mormon. Seth knew the risks of helping Alma, and we cannot stay here any longer. If we are found, we will suffer the same fate as Seth."

"No way, I'm not leaving him to die," protested Squeaks sternly. "There has to be something that we can do."

"I do not know what," Ramin replied solemnly. "Nahom is right - getting the hundreds of faithful followers to the secret Waters of Mormon is more important than saving one person."

"Can't you, as a soldier, find out where they have taken him and what is going to happen?" asked Tater. "We just can't leave Seth behind."

"I suppose that I could, but what good is that going to do us?" Nahom asked angrily. "Seth will be surrounded by guards, they will not leave him unattended."

"If we know where they are going, then maybe we can watch for an opportunity to rescue him," replied Butch. "That would be better than just leaving him here to die."

"I guess I could try to see what information I can find," Nahom hesitantly replied. "I just hope that those soldiers didn't see me last night. If they did, all I am doing is walking into a trap. Ramin, you stay here with our visitors. I will go see what information I can find about Seth."

"No, you will not go alone. I will go with you," Ramin

replied firmly. "The commander will know that something is not right if you go alone. Soldiers are supposed to stay in pairs at all times. You know the rules."

"But…," started Nahom.

"No, I will not let you travel alone," interrupted Ramin.

"If we are caught, your chance for freedom will be gone," said Nahom.

"I understand the risks," replied Ramin. He grabbed hold of the ladder and started to maneuver his way toward the top.

"Ramin, are you sure?" Nahom asked nervously.

Ramin, paused momentarily, nodded softly, grinned, then moved rapidly up the ladder. He was determined to find his friend and return Seth safely to his father.

"Is there anything that we can do?" asked Tater, as he watched the two climb.

"Yes," replied Ramin. "Stay here, and wait for our return. Whatever you do, don't get caught."

"Is there anything that we can do, to help you?" asked Butch.

"Don't get caught," replied Nahom, smiling. "And if we have not returned by dark, make your way along the cobblestone path back toward the forest. Watch for the monkeys, and they will guide you to Helam and the hidden followers of Alma."

"Wait all day?" asked Squeaks.

"Yes, do not try to leave in the light of day. At night, you will at least have the protection of darkness to help you escape safely," Nahom replied firmly.

"You boys, be very careful," added Mrs. M., as she watched them climb cautiously out of the well and into the light above.

"Don't worry about us. I'm sure we'll be back here in no time," called Ramin. The two then disappeared from the group's view into the morning sun.

"I wish I knew what I could do to help them," cried Squeaks as she watched them leave. "I can't bear to just sit here and do nothing."

"I wish I had some more food," said Tater, smiling as he stood holding onto his growling stomach. "We haven't had much to eat for a long time."

"Oh, you're always hungry, Tater," teased Butch.

"Well, I'm hungry too," added Squeaks.

"Well, while we were traveling with the commander yesterday, Seth gave me some of the coins they use in this city," said Tater. "I could carefully find the market and buy some of the bread he gave us yesterday?"

"That's a great idea!" exclaimed Squeaks, rubbing her stomach. "Maybe you can find an apple or some sort of fruit to eat too."

"We're supposed to be hiding," said Mrs. M. "Not running around the city."

"He'll be careful, Mrs. M.," said Butch. "Won't ya, Tater."

"I promise," he replied. "I don't know how much money Seth gave me for sure, but I will see what I can do," Tater said. He dropped his knapsack onto the ground and scraped along the bottom for the coins that Seth had given him.

"Are you sure it is a good idea to leave the security of the well?" asked Butch. "Both Nahom and Ramin said that we should stay here until after dark."

"We have to eat," protested Tater. "I'm gonna waste away to nothing if I don't get something to eat soon."

"I agree, Butch," added Squeaks. "I'm starving."

"You know, Butch, if Tater is very careful, he could get to the market and get back here without being seen," said Mrs. M. "I think if we have to wait until tonight to eat, we'll all be sick."

Butch shrugged his shoulders, looked at Tater and replied, "You know I am starving. Do you really think you can get to the market and back here safely?"

"You know I can," Tater replied excitedly. He quickly grabbed hold of the ladder and swiftly maneuvered to the top of the well. As he reached the opening, he poked his head just above the rock wall. He carefully scanned the area, looking for any sign of the commander's soldiers. With no one in sight, he jumped out and hurried toward the city and the bustling market.

"Why is it so light in here?" asked Butch. "Is the sun directly over us?"

"No, the sun just came up a few minutes ago," replied Mrs. M.

"It looks more like a light—like something is glowing," said Squeaks, as she looked around the walls of the well.

"I think you're right. But what could be glowing?" ask Mrs. M., gazing at the beautiful shadows it cast on the rock wall.

"I know what it is," Butch announced excitedly. "Look, the light is coming from Tater's knapsack.

"Did he leave his flashlight on?" asked Mrs. M., reaching for the pack.

Butch, grabbed the pack and searched for the flashlight. Several seconds passed before he finally said, "No, it's not his flashlight."

"Then what is making the light?" asked Squeaks, trying to see inside Tater's backpack.

"It's the Liahona," replied Butch. He carefully set the leather knapsack on the ground and pulled the Liahona from inside. "We couldn't see it glowing before, because Tater's sack was tied up tight. When he untied it to look for the coins that Seth gave him, he forgot to tie it back up and that is why we can see the light now."

"Oh no! Does that mean it is time to go home?" asked Mrs. M. "Have we done what the Lord sent us here to do?"

"We have helped to free Alma," answered Butch, shrugging his shoulders. "But I didn't think we had done everything that we needed to yet."

"Oh, I hope not, Mom," replied Squeaks. "We're not finished here yet. We might have saved Alma, but we haven't saved Seth yet. And I think he is pretty important!"

"I don't think our journey is over," said Butch, as he looked at the lights flashing on the Liahona.

"Then what is it?" Squeaks asked excitedly. "Is it giving us another clue?"

"I don't know if it's a clue," replied Butch. "But, I think that it's flashing a scripture and some other words."

"What scripture is the Liahona flashing?" asked Squeaks as she rummaged through Tater's knapsack, looking for his scriptures. "I'll read it for us, if you tell me which scripture I'm looking for."

"The scripture flashing is Mosiah 18:12," replied Butch, as he continued to study the letters flashing on the Liahona.

"I found it. Do you want me to read it?" asked Squeaks, running her fingers down the page until she reached the correct verse.

"No, wait. The scripture is changing into symbols - I think maybe they're hieroglyphics," Butch said excitedly, holding up the Liahona for Mrs. M. to see. "Maybe with the scripture, it tells us something else we need to do. Grab that translation paper that we had from earlier, Squeaks."

Squeaks handed the scriptures to her mom and found the paper. "Describe the symbols," she called.

"The first symbol looks like an old shepherd staff. The second symbol is three leaves from a palm tree. The third symbol is half of the sun, and the last symbol is like a square box, only the bottom line doesn't quite close the square," said Butch. He looked up at Squeaks, hoping she could translate the letters.

"The pictures translated spell out *Seth*," she replied.

"What was the scripture that you saw first, Butch?" asked Mrs. M. "Maybe it tells us more."

"Mosiah 18:12," replied Butch. "Do you think it could mean something?"

Unexpectedly, a shadow covered the top of the well. Sure they had been found, the group backed up against the wall, trying to stay in the shadows. Unable to run anywhere and afraid to say a word, everyone watched as the shadow climbed over the edge and onto the rope. Suddenly, Squeaks could smell the sweet aroma of home-made bread.

"Tater, is that you?" she called, excited to eat.

"Yep, and I have tons of goodies," he excitedly replied. "Was everything okay here while I was gone? Did you have any problems? I tried to hurry!"

"Everything was fine here. No one else has returned yet, but we have had some excitement," replied Squeaks, smiling. "We've found a clue, and we're trying to figure everything out right now."

"All right, way to go! A clue. Good job!" exclaimed Tater. He reached the bottom step on the ladder and jumped into the well. Then he handed everyone a full loaf of bread, a small banana, and two tiny berries.

"Was everything all right in the market? Did anyone see you?" asked Mrs. M. She looked up to the top of the well, worried that Tater might have been followed.

"No, the market seemed to be almost empty today. There we no guards or soldiers anywhere, and a lot of the people who filled the market yesterday are staying inside," Tater replied, as he took a bite of his bread.

"Did you hear why?" Butch curiously questioned. "Why was everything so quiet?"

"I didn't want to ask. But from what I could overhear the people in the market place talking about, the news of Alma's breakout has spread all over town. There is speculation that some of his soldiers helped him escape," replied Tater.

"Man, I am so worried about Seth. He could be in real danger," said Squeaks. "We've got to save him as soon as we can."

"Well, this clue might tell us how to help him," said Butch, anxious to continue working on it. "Maybe we should hurry and see if we can figure out the meaning."

"I'll read the scripture," replied Mrs. M. "Mosiah 18:12. 'And now it came to pass that Alma took Helam, he being one of the first, and went and stood forth in the water, and cried, saying: O Lord, pour out thy spirit upon thy servant, that he may do this work with holiness of heart.'"

"I don't understand what the scripture is telling us to do," said Butch. "What does that scripture have to do with Seth?"

"I understand," answered Mrs. M. "I think I know what the scripture means."

"What? What is it telling us?" asked Butch.

"Seth is Helam's son, and it is important that they both be baptized," she replied.

"I bet I know why," said Tater, as he quickly stuffed another piece of bread inside his mouth.

"Why?" Mrs. M. asked anxiously.

"Helam is going to help lead a lot of people from this valley—more than four hundred fifty from King Noah's city alone. Do you think for one minute that he will leave his son here to die?" asked Tater, biting his lip.

"Well, I would never leave any of you," replied Mrs. M. "I'm sure you're right, Tater. If we don't rescue Seth, then Helam will come back. Without Helam's help, those four hundred fifty people may never know the change of heart that comes with repentance and baptism."

"Exactly," said Tater, as he suddenly noticed several carved pictures in the wall.

"Can you see something, Tater?" asked Squeaks.

"Yeah, there are hieroglyphs carved up here on the wall," he replied, as he ran his fingers across the rough rocks.

"Describe them to me, and I will see if I can figure them out," she replied, holding up the paper of translations.

Tater grabbed his flashlight out of his pocket and shined it on the wall. "I'm not sure I can make out all of the pictures. But, of those I can see, the first set starts with a lion, then a rope, a diamond, a hand, and finally what looks like a shepherd's staff."

"Okay…," started Squeaks. "That spells out the word *Lord's*. What's next?"

"The next set of pictures starts with an upside down bowl," started Butch, excited to help. "It's followed by a diamond drawn on its' side, a small bird, and three leaves —I'm not sure what kind they are."

"And I think that describes the word *true*," said Squeaks.

"The next set of pictures seems to be fairly long, so this must be a long word," said Tater. "The first picture looks like a grass weaved basket, two zig zag lines, a hoop shaped rope, and two small birds."

"Wait a minute. You're going too fast," interrupted Squeaks, as she scrambled to find the symbols Tater described. Several anxious seconds passed until she finally looked up at Tater and said, "Okay, keep going."

Tater smiled and again started to describe the pictures. "After the two birds, I can see a sitting lion, three leaves again, the side view of a hand, what looks like a broken pottery dish with a hole in the side, and three leaves again."

Several anxious seconds passed while Squeaks deciphered the symbols. Finally she looked up, smiled, and said, "That word is *knowledge*."

"All right, what do we have so far?" asked Mrs. M., writing down the words.

"*Lord's true knowledge,*" replied Butch. "Are you ready for the next set of symbols?"

"Fire away," replied Squeaks, ready to start.

"Okay, the first picture is a leg from the knee to the foot, followed by a diamond shape, three leaves, two zig-zag lines, a broken pottery dish, and a shepherd's staff."

Only a few seconds passed before Squeaks looked up from her paper and yelled, "That is the word *brings*."

"Shush, Squeaks," insisted Mrs. M. "We don't want to be found hiding down here."

Squeaks nodded, and Tater started with the next set of symbols. "Let's see, the next set of pictures starts with a lion, a small palm tree, a broken pottery dish, a square that is not closed on one side, and an upside down bowl."

"What does it mean?" Butch asked anxiously.

"Just a second," replied Squeaks, as she studied the paper, looking for all the symbols. "All right, I think that word is *light*."

"How many words are left?" asked Mrs. M., as she wrote down the word light.

"Three small words," replied Butch. "The next set of pictures starts with a small bird, two zig-zag lines, an upside down bowl, and a piece of rope."

"That's easy," said Squeaks. "That word is *unto*. Next?"

"Okay, the next set of symbols starts with an upside down bowl, an open square, and three leaves," described Tater.

"Even easier. That word is *the*," Squeaks said excitedly. "And the last word?"

"The last word is two birds, a rope shaped like a hook, a diamond shape, a lion, and finally a hand," described Butch, as fast as he could.

"Okay, first, *w*, then *o*, *r*," Squeaks whispered. Looking up, she exclaimed, "I've got it!"

"Okay, what is the word?" asked Mrs. M., ready to write it down.

"Oh, yeah. The word is *world*," Squeaks replied, smiling.

"Read the entire sentence, will you please Mrs. M.?" Butch asked anxiously.

"*Lords true knowledge brings light unto the world*," read Mrs. M.

"What does that mean?" asked Butch, confused by the sentence.

"I think it means the Lord has revealed true knowledge to Alma. With that true knowledge, the Lord can bring His light unto the world," Mrs. M. replied confidently.

"And without saving Seth, Alma will not baptize Helam. Then they won't be able to lead hundreds of people away from this city," said Butch.

"That's right," replied Mrs. M. "I think the clues are telling us that we have to find a way to free Seth."

"You know, I think that is exactly right," agreed Tater.

"So, what do we do?" asked Squeaks.

"We've got to wait for Nahom and Ramin to return and tell us what they learned about Seth's whereabouts," replied Butch.

"Once we know that, we'll be able to make a plan for his rescue," agreed Tater.

"Yeah, but I wonder where everyone is," said Squeaks. "They have been gone for several hours now."

"You're right. I thought we would have heard from them by now," agreed Tater.

"They did say they would check in as soon as they could," reassured Mrs. M. "I'm sure everything is okay."

"Yes, but I think they would have checked in with us long before now," replied Tater.

"So, then what do you think we should do?" asked Mrs. M.

"I think we need to go to the city and see if anyone knows anything," answered Squeaks. "What if Ramin and Nahom have been captured, like Seth?"

"I guess I could go to the market again and see if the vendors have any more information," suggested Tater. "If they have all been captured, I think the people of the city would know."

"That might be the best idea right now," agreed Mrs. M. "I think if we all go in the market, especially when things are not normal in the city, all of us together would really stand out."

"So, do you think that I should go to the market and see what information I can find?" asked Tater.

"Yes, but be very careful," insisted Mrs. M. "King Noah probably has all his soldiers out searching for anyone who might possibly be followers of Alma. And I'm sure he has spies everywhere."

"My mom is right. Whatever you do, don't trust anyone," added Squeaks.

"Do you want me to go with you, Tater?" Butch hesitantly asked.

"No, I think that will only bring unwanted attention," replied Tater.

"Well, get going already, will ya, Tater," said Squeaks, teasingly pointing to the ladder. "I don't want anything bad to happen to them."

"I'm going, I'm going," replied Tater, smiling.

Mrs. M., Butch, and Squeaks watched as Tater again climbed the rope ladder to the top of the well. The afternoon sun was directly overhead, and the well no longer provided shade or cover to hide in.

Nearly an hour had passed, as Mrs. M. stood and nervously started pacing in a circle around the base of the well. Squeaks and Butch watched her tensely waiting for Tater to return with any word on the whereabouts of their three new friends.

"Do you think they've been caught?" asked Squeaks, as she chewed on her fingernails.

"I hope not, but it's a definite possibility," replied Mrs. M., as she pulled Squeaks hand out of her mouth.

Anxiously, they waited ten more minutes for Tater to

return. Then finally, a dark shadow, blocking the sun's afternoon rays again hovered over the well.

"Tater, is that you?" Squeaks called anxiously.

"Yes," he replied, as he quickly climbed back inside the well.

"Did you find any helpful information?" asked Butch.

"Yeah, a little," he replied, stalling as he cautiously climbed back inside the well.

"What, what already?" Squeaks insisted nervously.

"Okay, this is what I found out," he replied. "According to the people in the market, several of King Noah's soldiers have been captured and are being held in King Noah's private chambers."

"Oh, great. Now what are we going to do?" asked Squeaks. "How do we rescue them if they are being held in King Noah's private chambers?"

"Does that mean that Nahom and Ramin have been captured as well?" Mrs. M. asked worriedly.

"I think so," replied Tater. "As I got the people in the market to talk, they mentioned Seth's name and said the other soldiers were friends of his."

"Everyone that could lead us back to Alma and the Waters of Mormon safely are gone," whined Butch. "What do we do now?"

"Well, according to our last clue, we have to save Seth. Otherwise, his father will never do what is written in the Book of Mormon," said Mrs. M. "So, as far as I can tell, if we want to go home anytime soon, we have to find a way to rescue those boys and get them back to the hidden Waters of Mormon."

"You know what, I bet Seth, Nahom, and Ramin are the reason we were brought to this time in the first place," said Tater. "Not to save Alma."

"I have a feeling that you are right, Tater," replied Butch. "But I still don't know what we're going to do or how we're going to find them."

"Hey, I have an idea," said Squeaks.

"Well, what is it?" Butch asked impatiently.

"Alma knows all the underground tunnels in the city pretty well because he was a high priest. Maybe we should ask him which tunnel leads to King Noah's private chambers. While the King is outside addressing the people about Abinadi, we could use the secret tunnel to free Seth, Nahom, and Ramin."

"Great idea, Squeaks. The only problem is that we don't know for sure where Alma is," replied Butch, shrugging his shoulders.

"Sure we do. He said that he would be going through the city, finding his followers, and trying to get them into the forest where Helam is waiting," she replied.

"We still don't know where in the city Alma is for sure, or even if he is still in the city," Butch replied. "He could have gathered all his followers already and headed into the forest."

"Butch, have some faith please," replied Squeaks. "You know that we have the right to pray to the Lord for help and guidance. Why don't we do that in faith, and maybe we'll be able to accomplish everything that he has sent us here to do," Squeaks boldly replied. "What is that scripture that goes along with the Liahona—Alma 37:40? 'And it did work for them according to their faith in God…,'"

"I agree, Butch," replied Tater. "I know the Lord will help us if we ask. We just need to have faith."

"I think that is a great idea," added Mrs. M. "Especially with the information we are getting from the people in the market. If Seth, Nahom, and Ramin have all been captured, then we have to do something to save them. And standing here doing nothing is not getting us home any faster, nor is it helping Alma to get his people safely to the Waters of Mormon."

"Can I say the prayer?" asked Squeaks, folding her arms and bowing her head.

"That's a great idea," replied Mrs. M., as she, too, bowed her head and folded her arms.

Without hesitation, Squeaks quickly began her prayer. She asked for guidance in finding Alma, safely finding their new friends, and returning them to the Waters of Mormon. She also asked for help in returning home to the Treehouse and possibly being able to do more work for the Lord. As quickly as she had started with her prayer, she ended. She excitedly looked up at her teammates. "Now we'll be able to find Alma," she announced. Then she quickly took hold of the ladder and started working her way to the top.

"I'm not sure it's going to be quite that easy, Squeaks," teased Butch.

"Sure it is. I asked the Lord's help to find Alma quickly, and I have the faith that we will," Squeaks confidently replied.

"Well, so do I," added Mrs. M., following her daughter's lead. "How about you two boys? Do you have the faith that we can get this mission solved and get back to the Treehouse before we run out of time?"

"Well, I know that I do," replied Tater, following closely behind Mrs. M. "Let's find Alma and get this mission solved.

Unsure what else to do, Butch hesitantly replied, "I guess that I do as well."

Chapter Twenty-One

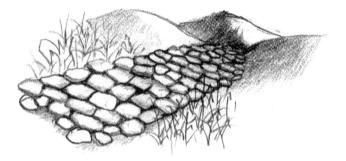

The group scurried along the cobblestone path being careful not to run or bring attention to themselves. But they were anxious to start searching the city for any sign of Alma.

"Tater, is there any chance that you were followed back to the well?" asked Mrs. M., looking suspiciously over her shoulder.

"I doubled back around the house twice, making sure that I wasn't," he replied. "Why?"

"I keep seeing the same man about fifty yards behind us," she replied. "Sometimes, when I look he is there, and other times he isn't."

"I can't see anyone, Mrs. M.," said Butch, looking for any sign of the mysterious man.

"Me neither, Mom," added Squeaks.

Mrs. M. hesitantly looked over her shoulder and was relieved to see no sign of the man. "I guess I'm just seeing things."

"This cobblestone path is going to lead us out of the city. We need to search inside the city limits. I think that is where Alma will be looking for his followers," said Tater.

"You lead the way, and we will follow you, Tater," said Squeaks.

Tater smiled, turned toward the city, and left the cobblestone pathway. He maneuvered through the bustle of the people of the city, watching closely for any sign of Alma. Sure he was still in the city, they continued to search for nearly two hours, through all of the streets and buildings.

Mrs. M. continued to watch behind her, sure a mysterious man was there. A man with dark hair and a wrap over his face, although no one else ever saw him.

"I wonder where Alma used to live?" said Tater. "I think there could be a chance that he might be hiding there. I don't think the soldiers would expect him to go to his home."

"Hey, good idea," replied Mrs. M. "Now all we have to do is figure out where Alma lives."

"No, wait. In all the movies that I have ever watched, the police or soldiers always stake out the house. I'm sure King Noah would have someone waiting and, watching just in case Alma returned," Squeaks said assuredly.

"You know, I think you're right," said Butch. "The soldiers could be watching for him there."

"I have an idea. What about Helam's house?" asked

Squeaks. "King Noah does not know that he believes in Alma's words."

"Yes, but the soldiers just captured Helam's son, Seth," added Butch.

"Yeah, but that doesn't mean he suspects Helam. Alma could be hiding there," replied Squeaks.

"I guess it's worth a try looking," said Tater.

"But we still don't have any clue where Alma lives," said Butch.

"Yeah, but unlike Alma, no one will suspect anything if we ask where Helam lives," replied Tater. "Everyone stay here. I'm going to ask that group of people if they know where Helam lives."

Everyone watched as Tater cautiously maneuvered into the crowd of people. Mrs. M. never let his wavy, blond hair get out of her sight. Suddenly, she spotted the mysterious man who had been following them since they left the well. Leaning over to Butch, she pointed toward the man, as he quickly vanished.

"Did you see him?" asked Mrs. M.

"No, there are a lot of men over there with dark hair and wraps over their faces," replied Butch. "I'm sorry."

"Mom, are you sure you're really seeing someone?" asked Squeaks.

"Positive," she replied boldly. "I know someone has been watching us."

"Do you think he is a spy for King Noah?" asked Butch.

"I think if he were, he would have already had us arrested," answered Squeaks.

"We'll just have to be very careful," said Butch. "I'll help watch, but I really haven't seen anyone."

Mrs. M. rubbed her eyes, wondering if they were not playing a trick on her. Then she watched as Tater confidently moved through the crowd of people. He found a small, elderly man and spoke with him for several moments. As the man turned and disappeared into the crowd of people, Tater excitedly returned to Butch, Squeaks, and Mrs. M.

"What is so funny, Tater?" asked Mrs. M., "What did you find out?"

"One good thing, and one bad thing," Tater replied.

"Bad news first," insisted Squeaks.

"Okay, the bad thing is just what we thought - Seth, Ramin, and Nahom have all been captured," replied Tater.

"How do you know for sure?" asked Mrs. M., suspicious of the elderly man.

"As I was walking through the crowd of people, the man actually stopped me," replied Tater. "He recognized me from the group of followers hidden in the forest and stopped to tell me what was going on."

"Do you believe him?" Butch asked suspiciously.

"Yes, I remembered him helping Helam when we were back at the camp in the forest," replied Tater.

"What else did he say?" Mrs. M. asked curiously.

"He said that Alma was preparing to leave later this afternoon. He has advised everyone who wants to go with him to meet just outside the city at the edge of the forest at three o'clock. From there, he will lead them to the hidden waters," replied Tater.

Chapter Twenty-One

"Does he know where Alma is right now?" Squeaks asked hopefully.

"No, he said that Alma, along with several others, were carefully trying to spread the word to the believers," Tater replied.

"Did he say if Alma knew about Seth, Ramin, and Nahom?" asked Butch.

"The man said that Alma had probably heard, but he didn't know for sure," Tater replied, as he looked sadly down at the ground.

"What, Tater? What's the matter?" Mrs. M. asked worriedly.

"The man said there was nothing that Alma could do about the boys, and that they knew the risks involved with helping him," Tater replied sadly. "He also said that Helam knew. He thought that Helam was heading back to the city to talk to King Noah personally."

"Oh, no!" exclaimed Squeaks. "This is getting worse and worse."

"You're right," agreed Butch. "We saved Alma only to get Seth, Ramin, Nahom, and now Helam caught, and probably killed."

"What do we do?" asked Tater, disheartened by their problems.

"Well, the first thing we do is find Alma. Then we get inside King Noah's temple and find his personal chambers. Once we've done that, we rescue everyone and get back to the forest as quickly as we can," Mrs. M. answered confidently.

"Oh, is that all, Mom?" teased Squeaks.

Suddenly, a familiar voice startled the group. "Well, it seems like we have some more rescuing to do."

Mrs. M. spun around to see the dark shadow that had been following them all morning. "Alma?" she asked.

"Yes," he replied.

"Have you been following us?" asked Butch.

"I had to wait to approach you until I was sure you were not being followed," he replied. "I'm sorry if I frightened you."

"Alma, what are we going to do about the boys?" Squeaks asked nervously.

"I hate to have to leave them, but I fear that we have no choice. I must return to the forest and get everyone to safety before we are all caught," he solemnly replied.

"But…," started Squeaks.

"Don't worry. I would never leave them here for good," he added grinning.

"What if we rescue them and you continue on with your work for the Lord?" asked Butch.

"You have already accomplished what you were sent here to do," Alma answered.

"I'm not sure about that," answered Mrs. M. "The Liahona would be ready to take us home if we had done everything the Lord sent us here to do."

Alma smiled. "The Lord works in mysterious ways. And I am thankful for His help. Do you think that you can save them?"

"I know we can," replied Butch.

"All we need to know is where we might be able to find an entrance to King Noah's personal chambers," added Tater.

Alma thought quietly for several seconds before he

grinned and replied, "I know of a secret tunnel - one that is only used by King Noah and his family. I have been told that the tunnel leads from his personal chambers to a stone somewhere near the marketplace. I believe the stone is close to an old well."

"That doesn't tell us a lot," replied Butch. "How are we supposed to find the right stone in the market place?"

"The stone marking the tunnel entrance has an all-seeing eye carved on the face," replied Alma.

"Somewhere in the marketplace?" asked Mrs. M.

"Not in the marketplace, but close to a well. I've never used or seen the stone before, but I know that the stone pulls away from the wall of the well and is not far from the soldiers' quarters," added Alma. "That way, if King Noah needed to escape from his temple, he could take the tunnel. If his enemies were attacking the soldiers' quarters, he could see it from afar. Then he could escape into the marketplace or the forest. If the soldiers' quarters were safe, he could quickly get inside where they could protect him."

"All right, let's go," insisted Squeaks. "We have four people to save."

"Four?" asked Alma. "I thought there were only three."

"There were, until Helam found out about his son," replied Tater. "A man from the marketplace told me that Helam was on his way back to the city to try to get King Noah to free Seth."

"Are you sure?" asked Alma, surprised by what Tater had said. "I will try to find Helam and tell him that there is a plan to save the boys. Are you sure the man said Helam?"

"I'm positive that is what the elderly man told me," Tater replied.

Alma silently rubbed his chin for several moments. Then he anxiously looked up at the group and said, "I must get to my followers and get them to the safety of the forest faster than I had thought would be necessary. Are you sure that you want to try to rescue these boys alone?"

"Yes, I believe that is the only way we can get home," replied Mrs. M.

"If you are successful, they know the way to the hideout in the forest. We will be there until dark. After that, we will journey to the hidden Waters of Mormon," said Alma. "May the Lord be with you. I pray for your safe return as the forces of evil are against us today."

With that, Alma nodded and pulled his robe tightly around his face. He scanned the area for any sign of King Noah's soldiers, then disappeared into the crowd of people in the city.

The group watched until they could no longer see Alma. Then Mrs. M. asked, "So, kids, where do we start?"

"Yeah, that's what I'd like to know," added Squeaks.

"How are we ever going to find a stone with the all-seeing eye carved on it, that is somewhere near the soldiers' quarters, but we really have no idea where?" asked Butch.

"Did any of you listen to what Alma said?" asked Tater, annoyed by Butch's attitude.

"Sure we listened, Tater," replied Mrs. M. "But it sounds like we missed something that you evidently heard."

"A stone near a well, not far from the marketplace and the soldiers' quarters?" replied Tater, puckering his lips.

"A well?" Squeaks screeched excitedly.

"Yes, a well. Kinda like the well where we hid most of the night," replied Tater.

"All right! Way to go, Tater. We know where that is. Do you really think that is the right well?" Butch asked excitedly.

"It has to be," Tater replied. "What other well is close to the marketplace and the soldiers' quarters?"

"Should we check?" asked Squeaks. "And can we find where the well was?"

"I can find the well—no problem," replied Butch.

"Then we better get out of here, right now," insisted Mrs. M. as she quickly looked away from a group of soldiers in the market.

"Why, what's the matter?" asked Squeaks, quickly scanning the area.

"I think we're about to be caught," she replied. "Or, at least questioned."

Tater, sensing Mrs. M.'s urgency, glanced at the soldiers. Then he started walking back through the city toward the well. "Follow me," he insisted, moving as fast as he dared, trying not to draw attention to the group.

Butch, hurrying to catch his friend, calmly asked, "Do you remember where to go?"

"I think so," Tater replied. "But why don't you help me."

Butch nodded and smiled at Tater. Then he whispered, "Girls, the group of soldiers is following us. We're gonna have to move fast. So, I'm taking the lead back to the well.

Hurry as fast as you can without running. Get as close as you can to Tater and me. As soon as all four of us have rounded the corner of the next building be ready to run."

Mrs. M. and Squeaks, afraid to look and see where the soldiers were, walked faster toward the boys. As they walked around the corner of the next building, Butch took off running as fast as he could. Everyone quickly followed his lead, sprinting to keep up with him.

Nearly half way down the street, Butch unexpectedly turned down a small alleyway between buildings, with everyone following closely behind him.

"Where are we going, Butch?" asked Tater.

"We're gonna hide and find out if the soldiers are following us," Butch replied.

"We kinda know that they're following us," said Squeaks, out of breath.

"Quiet," insisted Butch. "Everyone get behind something and be quiet."

The group scurried to hide just before the group of soldiers rushed down the alleyway.

"Did you see where they went?" asked one of the soldiers.

"No, they were out of sight before we passed the building," replied another.

"This has to be where they are," said the first soldier.

"I don't think so," called another, pointing down the cobblestone road. "I think they headed further down the street. We need to hurry and find them. The commander said we must find Seth's friend. He wants to question him, so everyone follow me," the soldier insisted, as he started further down the road.

The group watched as the soldiers quickly moved out of the alleyway and ran down the street.

Tater carefully moved from behind several large clay pots and cautiously poked his head out into the alleyway. Not spotting soldiers anywhere, he held his finger to his mouth, motioning for Butch, Squeaks, and Mrs. M. to be quiet and stay still. Slowly moving to the main road, he stuck his head around the corner, looking for any sign of the men. Unexpectedly, the group of soldiers were waiting right around the corner for him.

One of the soldiers grabbed his arm and yelled, "We got him! Let's get him to the commander immediately."

"What about the others?" asked another soldier.

"We'll worry about them when the Commander wants them. Right now, we need to get Seth's friend to King Noah and the commander," replied the soldier.

Without another word, the group of soldiers hauled Tater toward King Noah's temple.

"What do we do now?" whispered Squeaks, as a tear rolled down her face. "What about Tater?"

"We continue toward the well," Butch replied quietly, afraid to move a muscle.

"Mom?" called Squeaks. "We're just going to leave him with those soldiers?"

"Butch is right. We continue on to the well, try to find the entrance that Alma talked about, and see if we can save all the boys," Mrs. M. sadly replied.

"What about the soldiers?" Butch asked softly. "Do you think there are more of them waiting around the corner for us?"

"Possibly," replied Mrs. M. "We're going to have to find a different way back to the well. And we won't be able to walk out in the open anymore. We're going to have to find our way there carefully, without being seen."

"But, Mom, what about Tater?" Squeaks demanded angrily.

"We're no match for that group of soldiers. And what good are we to any of the boys if we get caught?" replied Mrs. M. as she cautiously stood up and looked around the alleyway. "Now, both of you follow me. Be very careful. Try to stay hidden as best you can, and let's find another way to the well."

"Okay, Mrs. M.," said Butch. "I think if we follow the alleyway, we can still make our way to the well. We'll just have to maneuver a little further around the buildings and then head toward the edge of the city."

Chapter Twenty-Two

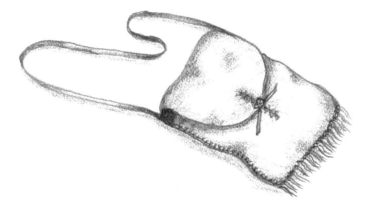

Mrs. M. led the way around the building, trying to guide Butch and Squeaks back to the well. She stayed in the shadows and doorways of the structures. She also hid behind trees, shrubs, and anywhere else that they would not be noticed by the people of the city. Just outside the marketplace, not far from the soldier's quarters, they finally located the well.

"We made it!" Squeaks exclaimed excitedly. "There's the well. I can see it."

"Walk slowly, Squeaks," insisted Butch. "Don't bring any attention to yourself. We don't want to be caught now!"

They carefully moved toward the well. Mrs. M. grabbed the pail that hung from the rope at the top and pretended to throw it to the bottom for some water to drink. Butch walked around the perimeter of the well, scanning for any sign of a stone engraved with an all-seeing eye.

Several anxious moments passed before Butch exclaimed, "It's here. There really is a stone with an all-seeing eye."

"Sssshhhh, Butch," insisted Squeaks. "You're gonna get us caught."

"So, what do we do?" asked Butch, sitting down on the ground next to the stone.

"Alma said something about the stone sliding open," replied Mrs. M., as she pretended to pull the water bucket back toward the top of the well.

"Do you want me to try and slide it one way or the other?" asked Butch.

"Yes, see if you can budge the stone at all," Mrs. M. replied.

Butch pushed on the stone but nothing happened. Scooting to the other side of the well, he again tried to push, but again, nothing happened.

"It won't move," he replied nervously.

"What if I help?" asked Squeaks, sitting down on the ground next to Butch. "Maybe with two of us we can get this stone to move."

Butch smiled, sure Squeaks would not be a lot of help. But the two tried to push the stone.

"Still nothing, Mrs. M.," said Butch. "This stone is too big. We're missing something."

"What?" she asked. "What are we missing."

"I know, I have an idea," said Squeaks. "I bet there is

a secret lever or something that opens the stone."

"Where?" asked Butch. "There isn't anything by the well that you can push or pull."

"Squeaks might have the right idea," replied Mrs. M., nodding. "Can you see anything?"

"I was thinking that maybe the all-seeing eye was pointing to, or looking at, something that would open the secret tunnel," she replied.

"Hey, great idea," said Butch, looking to see where the engraving on the stone was pointing. "I can't see anything except that group of trees. I can't imagine that a secret lever is hidden there."

"I'll go check it out," said Squeaks. She crawled on her hands and knees toward the trees. "I bet in there is a way for us to get inside."

Several nervous minutes passed and nothing happened. "Squeaks, do you see anything?" asked Butch.

Squeaks poked her head out of the bushes and replied, "I found something but…," she paused and then continued, "tell me if anything happens."

Butch watched the stone closely, keeping his fingers crossed for luck. Suddenly, the stone slid open.

"Hey, Squeaks! You did it," Butch called excitedly, as he looked inside the small, square opening.

"Well, don't just look at it," insisted Squeaks, as she quickly crawled back toward the well, grinning from ear to ear. "Get inside fast, before someone sees us."

Anxiously, Butch crawled inside the opening and climbed down the ladder. He was followed quickly by Squeaks and Mrs. M., who scanned the area to make sure no one was watching them.

"How do we close the opening?" asked Butch, as he reached the ground. "We can't leave it open."

"I bet this does it," replied Mrs. M., seeing a small handle at the base of the ladder. She slid it to the right and the stone slowly slid closed.

"All right, it works!" exclaimed Squeaks. "Now we'll know how to open it when we come back."

"There's light in here," said Butch, shocked to be able to see anything.

"Where's the light coming from?" asked Squeaks, as she looked down the tunnel.

"This is King Noah's private tunnel that leads to his personal chambers," replied Mrs. M. "I'm sure that the tunnel is always set up and ready at a moments notice, to accommodate him and his family in an emergency."

"Yeah, and there are torches that are lit about every fifty feet or so," said Squeaks, pointing down the tunnel. "Can you see them?"

"His soldiers probably light them everyday," replied Butch.

"Or they are always lit," said Mrs. M.

"We don't have a lot of time. We better get moving," said Butch as he started to walk down the tunnel toward the light.

"Hold on! Wait a minute!" yelled Squeaks. "What about traps. We've got to watch out for traps."

"I think we're going to be all right in this tunnel," said Mrs. M. "I doubt King Noah would put traps in this tunnel. He's the only one who would be using it and I doubt he wants to worry about falling in to a trap."

"Good thinking, Mrs. M.!" exclaimed Butch, as he started running through the tunnel. "We better hurry. We've got a lot to do to save Seth, Ramin, Nahom, and Tater, before Alma leads his followers to the hidden Waters of Mormon."

Butch, Squeaks, and Mrs. M. hurried through the winding tunnel, grateful for the light. They traveled for nearly a half mile before Squeaks noticed the end of the tunnel, and another ladder in the distance.

"Above us must be King Noah's personal chambers," said Butch, pointing at the top of the ladder.

"What do we do from here?" asked Squeaks. "It's not like we can just climb up the ladder, open the door, and walk into King Noah's chambers. We'll be caught for sure. What is our plan? Do we have one?"

"She's right, Mrs. M., we can't do that," agreed Butch.

"How about if I climb the ladder first?" Mrs. M. offered. "I'll see what kind of opening there is at the top and determine what options we have to enter the room above."

Without waiting for a response, Mrs. M. quickly started climbing the wooden ladder. As she reached the top, she was able to see a large wooden panel, two feet wide by three feet tall. Searching the area for a lever to open the panel, she noticed a switch just to the right of the panel.

"I can see a switch that I think will open the panel," she quietly called. "Instead of switching it, I'm just going to try and push the panel open. Hopefully, I can get it to slide enough that I can see into the room, but not be noticed."

Butch and Squeaks waited impatiently at the bottom

of the ladder, nervously watching as Mrs. M. pushed with all her might, trying to open the wooden panel. Several anxious moments passed before the panel shifted slightly, revealing a bright light from inside the room.

"I got it!" Mrs. M. excitedly exclaimed.

Squeaks and Butch continued to wait as she cautiously pushed on the door, opening it just a little more.

"What can you see?" Butch quietly called.

"Ssshhh," she replied, holding her index finger to her mouth. "People are everywhere."

"Can you see Tater?" Squeaks asked nervously.

"No, not yet. But I can see Seth and several others who have their backs to me," Mrs. M. replied, peering through the opening.

"Can you see King Noah?" asked Butch, looking up the ladder toward Mrs. M.

"I can see the man they all call the commander," she replied, pausing momentarily. "And I can see several men holding spears. They are pointing them toward someone lying on the floor. They must be soldiers."

"Who is lying on the floor? Can you see who it is?" asked Butch.

"Um…," she started. "Give me a second. I can see…,"

"What, Mom? What can you see?" Squeaks anxiously asked. "The suspense is killing me."

"I can see Tater," she replied, gasping in terror. "The person on the floor is Tater."

"Is he dead?" blurted Butch.

"No, he's not dead. But several soldiers are holding spears toward him, and some man in a big robe is screaming something I can't quite understand," she replied.

"I bet that is King Noah," said Butch. "Why is he yelling?"

"I don't know. I can't understand what is being said," Mrs. M. replied.

"What are we going to do?" asked Squeaks, worried about her friend. "You don't think that King Noah would kill Tater, would he?"

"And ruin his personal chambers?" replied Butch. "No way. He'll use Tater and the rest of them as examples, and kill them in front of his people."

"I think we need to wait," said Mrs. M. "Eventually, he will either leave them here or have them sent somewhere else. Either way, we will know where they are and hopefully come up with an idea to save them."

"The problem with that idea, is that we don't really have a lot of time," replied Butch. "And I don't think I have the patience to wait."

"Hold on; something is happening," interrupted Mrs. M., still peering through the small opening.

"What? What's happening?" asked Squeaks.

Mrs. M. watched silently through the small crack in the wooden panel for several moments. King Noah screamed at his soldiers, grabbed something from his throne, and angrily stomped out of the room. Mrs. M. watched as the commander lifted Tater from the floor, pushed him toward the other prisoners, and forcefully threw him to the ground with a big thud.

"Men, do not let these soldiers out of your sight!" he yelled. "King Noah will sentence them in front of the people of this great city, and then their sentences are to be carried out immediately. Is that understood?" barked the commander.

"Something is going to happen really soon," Mrs. M. said nervously. "We're going to have to save them right now. Can either of you think of a distraction - something we could do to get the soldiers out of the room?"

"Is there something we could throw—something that would make them look to see where the noise came from?" asked Squeaks.

"I'm afraid something that simple would only get the soldiers looking around the room," Mrs. M. replied.

"What about smoke or a fire?" asked Butch.

"We can't do that!" exclaimed Mrs. M. "What if we burn down the temple?"

"What about the walkie-talkie?" asked Squeaks. "We could make noise with it."

"No, we can't leave technology from the future in the past," replied Butch.

"Well, that's all the ideas I have. What other great ideas do you have?" demanded Squeaks, with a snooty attitude.

"What if we get the panel opened enough that I can crawl out? Then I could sneak over to where everyone is being held and free them. Maybe then they could over-power the soldiers, tie them up, and we could escape," suggested Butch.

"That will never work," replied Squeaks. "What if you are seen before you get to them?"

"Actually, I think that is probably the best idea,"

answered Mrs. M. "However, I think it is very risky. If you get caught, I'm not sure what Squeaks and I are going to be able to do to free everyone."

"Trade me spots, and let me see what is going on up there, Mrs. M.," insisted Butch.

Mrs. M. nodded and slowly climbed down the rickety, wooden ladder. As Mrs. M. reached the bottom, Butch pushed past her and rapidly climbed to the top.

"Do you think your idea will work?" Squeaks asked in a nervous tone.

Several quiet seconds passed before Butch replied, "I think I can. There are several chairs, a kind of couch, and plants are everywhere."

Without another word, he reached his fingers around the wooden panel and slid it open another eighteen inches. Then he crawled undetected inside the room. Worriedly, Mrs. M. climbed back up the ladder, anxious to see what was happening. She took hold of the panel and slid it nearly closed.

"Good luck, Butch. Be very careful," she whispered through the opening.

She nervously watched as Butch slithered around the area. He quickly moved to the cover of several trees planted in large pots, not far from where everyone was being held. Butch was scanning the area, making a plan for his next move. Then the commander suddenly appeared at the door to King Noah's private chambers.

"King Noah is speaking to his people right now!" he shouted. "Have the prisoners ready in ten minutes. They will face their trial in front of the people. We will let the people decide if they want Abinadi's or Alma's traitors amongst us."

Aiath nodded at the commander, then watched as he quickly returned to King Noah's side. Aiath turned to the other soldiers and said, "I will be back in a few minutes, men. Watch the prisoners closely. I want to hear what King Noah is saying."

Mrs. M. watched as the soldiers spoke amongst themselves. Their attention was away from the prisoners, as they watched King Noah speak to the people. Butch was able to move right next to Seth. Butch whispered quietly, careful not to speak too loudly and get the soldiers attention.

"So, Seth, are you ready to go to the hidden Waters of Mormon?" he asked. He pulled his pocketknife from his pocket and sliced the rope that was tied tightly around Seth's wrists.

"We don't have much time," replied Seth, excited to see Butch. "Get the others untied quickly."

Butch nodded and then crawled on his hands and knees toward Nahom. Slicing through the ropes, within seconds he had Ramin and Tater untied as well.

"How did you get in here?" asked Ramin, glad to see Butch.

"Alma told us about a secret tunnel," Butch whispered.

"Where is it?" asked Nahom, cautiously looking around the room.

Butch pointed toward the potted trees and said, "Over there is our way out. So get those soldiers taken care of, and follow me. We've got to get out of here before the commander returns."

Butch maneuvered slowly through the room, carefully

returning to the wooden panel. He slid it open just far enough to crawl through the opening. Mrs. M., grateful he was okay, hurried to the bottom of the ladder. She watched as Butch waved to his friends, motioning that the tunnel was ready. Then he slid the wooden panel nearly closed.

With the soldiers attention on King Noah, Seth leaned over to Tater and said, "I think the best thing for you to do is get to the secret panel and wait for us there."

"What about you?" Tater asked. "I don't want to leave you here."

"Quiet, traitors," interrupted one of the soldiers, startling Tater and Seth.

They breathed a cautious sigh of relief as the soldiers turned quickly back to watching King Noah.

"Get moving," Seth insisted quietly. "We'll be right behind you."

Tater looked at the soldiers, made sure they were not watching, and quietly slipped toward the potted plants and the hidden wooden panel where Squeaks, Butch, and Mrs. M. waited. Careful to move slowly and stay out of sight the best he could, Tater finally pulled the panel open and slipped inside the tunnel. He made his way down the ladder to where Squeaks and Mrs. M. were waiting.

"You made it, Tater!" exclaimed Squeaks, throwing her arms around his waist.

"Barely," he replied, patting her on the back and smiling.

"What about Seth, Ramin, amd Nahom?" asked Mrs. M. "What are they doing, Butch?"

"It looks like Ramin is going to try to escape next," whispered Butch.

Butch nervously watched as Ramin followed the same path as Tater. He hid behind the couch, to the series of chairs, and then moved behind the potted plants to the hidden wooden panel on the wall. Butch carefully slid the panel open, squeezed to the side of the ladder, and allowed Ramin to move down the ladder to the others.

"One more down," Butch announced excitedly. "Just two more to go."

Everyone waited anxiously as Butch described Nahom's movements as he headed toward the opening. Then Butch slid open the panel for a third time. Mrs. M. breathed a cautious sigh of relief as Nahom made it safely inside the tunnel.

"Seth's last," Butch said quietly.

"Is he close?" asked Tater.

"No, he hasn't even moved yet," replied Butch, shrugging his shoulders. "I don't know why he hasn't moved."

"The soldiers may be able to see him. If they can, Seth won't move. He doesn't want us to get caught," replied Ramin, standing uneasily at the bottom of the ladder.

"How can we help him?" asked Squeaks.

"By waiting here," Mrs. M. replied sternly.

"He's moving," Butch said excitedly. "Not very fast, but he is moving."

Everyone waited as several nervous minutes past. Butch watched Seth's slow progression toward them. Then he slid open the panel for Seth to climb through when he finally reached it.

"Hurry, the soldiers are going to see that we are all missing any minute," whispered Seth. "Slide the panel closed."

Butch waited barely long enough for Seth to get inside the room before he then frantically closed the panel. As the panel slid into place, the wood made a loud 'pop', frightening everyone in the tunnel. Seth made it to the bottom of the ladder in record time. He was followed by Butch, who could hear the soldiers yelling loudly in the room.

"Where are they?" screamed Aiath.

"They were right here," replied one of the soldiers.

"Where did they go?" screamed the commander.

"You let them escape?" bellowed King Noah. "Find them! Find them now! My people are waiting."

"We better hurry; it won't be long before they start searching in here," said Butch, as he hurried down the ladder.

"Thanks for saving us," started Ramin.

"There's no time for that now; you can thank us later," said Mrs. M., as she hurried the group through the tunnel.

The group quickly followed, sure at any moment King Noah and his soldiers would open the hidden panel and enter the tunnel. They raced as quickly as they could through the winding tunnel. Then Tater suddenly said, "I think I can hear someone behind us. They must be in the tunnel."

"How much further do we have?" asked Seth.

"The end of the tunnel is only another hundred yards or so," replied Butch, panting to catch his breath. "Then we have to climb a ladder similar to the one we climbed down earlier. The opening is at the well where we hid over night."

"The well?" asked Seth. "By my home?"

"Yes, the well," replied Mrs. M., looking over her shoulder. "And Butch is right; we have to move faster. I can hear someone following us."

Moving as fast as they could, they finally came to the ladder at the end of the tunnel. Mrs. M. and Squeaks climbed first. Mrs. M. quickly flipped the lever and the stone slid open, revealing the bright afternoon sunlight outside. Without worrying about who might see them, they quickly crawled outside and waited for everyone else to climb to safety before King Noah's soldiers caught up with them. Ramin climbed out, followed by Butch, Nahom, Tater, and finally Seth.

"There they are. They are escaping. Hurry men, catch them."

The group looked back to see several soldiers running toward them. Seth took the lead and yelled, "Everyone, follow me!"

The group ran as fast as they could to keep up with Seth. He dodged around people, animals, and trees running through the city, trying to stay out of view of the soldiers. He led the group behind buildings, down alleyways, and finally to the edge of the forest.

"Where to from here?" asked Tater, glancing over his shoulder.

"Deeper into the forest to Alma's hideout. But first, we have to make sure no one follows us," replied Seth, gasping for breath.

"That's right, we don't want to lead King Noah's soldiers directly to Alma and his followers," said Nahom.

"How do we do that?" asked Squeaks, sure the soldiers were still behind them.

"We've got to make it to our secret hideout and wait for the soldiers to move somewhere else. Then we can continue on to Alma's hideout, where we took you earlier today," answered Ramin.

"Well, we better hurry. I can hear the soldiers screaming in the distance," said Mrs. M., looking back toward the city. "They're not far behind us."

"You're right!" exclaimed Seth. "Come on, we have to stay ahead of them. Everyone, follow me."

Seth ducked under the leaves of a willow tree and quickly disappeared into the thick brush of the forest.

"Come on, we don't want to lose him," said Tater, moving as fast as he could to catch up with Seth.

The group rapidly maneuvered through the thick grasses, trees, and bushes deeper into the forest, struggling to stay ahead of King Noah's soldiers. When Seth reached a stream, he turned and ran upstream. They all struggled not to fall on the round pebbles that lined the stream banks.

"We've got to get away from this stream," called Butch. "We're leaving hundreds of footprints in the sand and rocks."

"We are," said Nahom, pointing ahead of the group.

They came upon a beautiful tree. The tree's fragrance was sweet and seemed to spread throughout the area. Seth paused at the base of the huge tree and waited for everyone to catch up with him. As soon as everyone was there, he cautiously scanned the surrounding area. Sure none of the soldiers were close, Seth placed his back against the tree and took four large steps into the brush. Directly in front of him, he came upon a large, mossy mound. Grabbing a broken tree branch from the ground, he pried the edge under the thick green sod, revealing a vault-like box. Ramin and Nahom loosened the enclosure and suddenly exposed a large round hole.

"Quick, everyone inside," demanded Seth, pointing to the hole in the side of a moss-covered mound.

"What is this?" asked Tater.

"A safe hideout," replied Ramin. "We have used this hideout several times to throw off King Noah's soldiers. Now quick, get inside."

"This feels more like rabbit's house on Winnie the Pooh," said Squeaks, as she climbed through the hole.

"Whatever it is, it is safe for now," replied Mrs. M., completely out of breath. "I wasn't sure I could go on running one more minute."

"You're not that old, Mom," teased Squeaks.

Mrs. M. smiled and counted as everyone entered the hideout. Then Seth slid the covering back over the hole.

"Now what do we do?" asked Butch, trying to look around the small dirt hideout.

"We wait," replied Nahom. "Seth will watch through a crack in the cover and tell us when it is safe to leave."

"What about Alma?" asked Squeaks. "We're supposed to meet Alma."

"Did you see him?" Seth asked quietly.

"Yes, that is how we knew about the secret tunnel we used to rescue you. Alma told us where it was," she replied.

"Did he say anything else?" asked Ramin.

"Yes, he did," replied Butch. "He said he would gather the followers that were ready, and they would leave the city at three o'clock."

"It's past three now," replied Nahom. "After all of that, we have missed him."

"No, not yet you haven't," interrupted Mrs. M. "Alma also said, if we didn't meet him by three, that you would know the way to the secret hideout in the forest. From there, right around dark, he will lead his followers to the hidden Waters of Mormon."

"That doesn't give us much time," said Nahom. "We have got to hurry, or we'll never make it to the hideout before dark."

"We can't leave while the soldiers are so close," replied Seth. He motioned for the group to be quiet, as he pointed to the soldiers right outside the small hideout.

Suddenly, an unexpected bright light filled the small hideout.

"What is that?" Seth whispered angrily. "Tater, is that your light? Turn it off!"

Tater, sure his flashlight batteries were dead, shook his head. "It's not my light, I don't know what it is," he replied.

"The light is coming from your bag," replied Ramin, pointing.

Tater pulled off his knapsack and frantically motioned for Butch to help.

"Hold the flap down, and I will try to squeeze the

material together until the coast is clear," Tater whispered, as he wrapped his hands around the contents of the bag.

Butch helped hold the flap closed, and they nervously waited for the soldiers outside to leave.

"What is the light from?" asked Butch.

"I think it's the Liahona," replied Tater.

"Is it time to go home?" Squeaks asked excitedly.

"Possibly," replied Tater.

"But we haven't returned the boys safely to their father yet," whispered Mrs. M.

"That may not have been what we needed to do," reasoned Tater. "They seem pretty capable once they are in the forest. Maybe our job was to free them from the commander and King Noah. We have done that, so maybe now it's time to go home."

"Pull it out so we can see what is flashing," insisted Mrs. M.

"Wait a moment," said Seth. "The soldiers are just starting to leave. I don't want to be caught after all of this."

"What do you mean, 'go home'?" asked Ramin with a confused look on his face.

"We may have completed the mission that the Lord sent us to do. If so, it is time for us to go back to our time," Mrs. M. replied quietly.

"We won't see you again?" asked Nahom sadly.

"Not unless the Lord sends us back to your time," replied Squeaks.

"I'll miss you—all of you," added Seth. "The soldiers have gone for now. What does your Liahona tell you to do?"

Tater laid the bag on the ground and carefully opened the flap. Reaching inside, he grabbed the Liahona and lifted it out for everyone to see.

"It's flashing something," Mrs. M. said excitedly. "What is it flashing?"

Tater turned the Liahona enough to see the flashing inscription. Then he turned to the group and said, "I guess it's time to go home."

"Tell Alma goodbye for us, will you?" asked Squeaks, as she moved closer to Tater.

"And your father as well," added Mrs. M. "Tell him thank you for believing in us."

Suddenly, bright light filled the room, followed by complete darkness.

Chapter Twenty-Three

"Where are we, Mrs. M.? Did we go home?" Butch asked nervously.

"I don't know," she replied. "It feels like we're somewhere I've never been before," she replied, as a crash of lightning flashed and thunder boomed over their heads.

"I know where we are!" Squeaks shouted excitedly. "I've been here before."

"Where are we?" asked Butch, sure that Squeaks had no idea.

"We're inside the Treehouse," she confidently replied.

Tater looked around as another flash of lighting sprayed through the holes and crevasses in the tree. "Hey, I think Squeaks is right."

"How do we get out of here?" asked Mrs. M., ready to be done with the mission.

"At the bottom of the tree, there is a small, secret entrance that we'll have to climb out of," replied Butch, as he cautiously maneuvered his way to the bottom of the tree.

Hurriedly, the group climbed out of the opening at the bottom of the tree and found themselves surrounded by a late summer rain, thunder, and lightning storm.

"When we go inside, remember that my dad's home and he probably doesn't know anything about where we have been," said Squeaks. Then she took off running toward the back door.

"Well, he will know in a minute," replied Tater. "We're all in Book of Mormon clothes still."

"That's right, we left our modern-day clothes back with Helam," said Butch sadly.

"Everything will be all right," said Mrs. M. "We'll just have to explain why we are dressed this way."

"Oh I'm not worried about that," replied Butch. "I'm sad I left my favorite hat there."

Mrs. M smiled. "We're home!" she called surprising the rest of the Team when she suddenly threw open the sliding glass door and walked into the kitchen.

"All right, you made it!" declared Bubba. He grabbed Squeaks and gave her a bid hug.

"We sure did," replied Butch, "and just in the nick of time."

"The nick of time for what?" asked Dad, unsure what they were talking about.

"In the nick of time to get his surprise, right?" asked

Hero, trying to keep the Liahona a secret.

"That's right," agreed Mrs. M., as she gave Hero and Bubba a big hug. "That was a grand surprise."

"Will someone please let me in on the secret?" asked Dad, feeling somewhat left out. "And why are you dressed like that?"

Mrs. M. smiled as she threw her arms around Dad's neck. Then she whispered in his ear, "I promise I will fill you in on the secret later."

"Is anybody as hungry as I am?" asked Tater, holding his starving stomach. "All I have had to eat today is bread."

"A whole loaf of bread," Squeaks added teasingly.

"That's still not enough for a growing boy," said Aunt Maggie, as she held up two homemade pizzas fresh from the oven. "Dinner's ready; come and eat."

Relieved to be safely at home, Mrs. M. sat down at the kitchen table and let out a long sigh.

"So tell me, sis, did you have fun on your mission?" asked Aunt Maggie.

Mrs. M. looked up, smiled, and quietly replied, "You will never believe all that we did, the people that we met, and places that we've been. I can't wait to tell you everything."

"Neither can I," Aunt Maggie whispered back, as she gave her sister a hug. "I'm glad you made it home safely."

"So, was everyone okay here while I was gone?" asked Mrs. M., as she sunk her teeth into a warm slice of pepperoni pizza.

"No, Dad was a little worried," replied Hero.

"Worried about what?" asked Mrs. M.

"He hates it when we have a secret that he doesn't

know about," teased Hero. "I think he has tried for the last two hours to get Aunt Maggie to tell him what our secret is."

"No, not Dad," laughed Mrs. M. "Was everyone else okay?"

"Yep, we're all okay," reassured Stick, as he sat down at the kitchen table.

"Tater, don't you have something that I need in your pack?" asked Mrs. M., holding out her hand.

Tater smiled and nodded. Then he handed Mrs. M. his pack.

"I will be right back," she said. She quickly finished her last bite of pizza, stood up from the table, and disappeared down the hallway.

"Mom, don't let anyone like Dad see where you are putting that," called Hero, teasing his dad.

"We don't want any of our secrets revealed again," called Bean, smiling.

"Don't worry, Team. I know exactly where to put this so that no one can find it," called Mrs. M. She disappeared into her bedroom and quickly closed the door.

Determined to hide the Liahona so that no further missions could happen without the proper precautions being taken, she slipped the Liahona back into its treasure-box container and looked around her room. At first, she thought of putting the Liahona into her cedar chest, but then thought better. She contemplated putting it under the bed, but was sure that Dad would check there. Then she had a great idea; she remembered a saying that she had heard as a little girl. "'Things are always safest when they are hidden in plain sight.' "I know where to put this," she said to herself.

She quickly pulled the stool from her closet and arranged the small, ornate box on her shelf of knick-knacks. Smiling as she stepped off of the stool, she gazed upon the box. She was sure that no one would even suspect that the Liahona was safely hidden inside. Then, she returned the stool to her closet. Opening the door to her bedroom, she walked back to the kitchen as quickly as she could.

"So, sis, come into the living room and tell me about your day," said Aunt Maggie.

"We're gonna go up to the Treehouse for a little while before everybody has to go home for the night, Mom," said Hero. Then the Team quickly disappeared out the sliding glass door, through the rain, and into the safety of the Treehouse. Everyone on the Team had already ran out of the house before Mom even had a chance to reply.

"I'll be in to talk in just a minute," called Dad, as he slid the glass door closed. "I'm going to clean up the dinner mess."

Mom kissed him softly on the check and whispered, "Thanks." Then she walked into the living room.

"Now's my chance," thought Dad. He cautiously tiptoed down the hallway, heading straight for his bedroom. "I know I can find what she was hiding. I know all of her secret hiding spots."

Dad scanned the room. First he checked under the bed, then he looked inside the cedar chest, finally he checked the bathroom, the clothes closet, and the linen closet.

"Where did she put it?" he thought to himself. He scanned the room, unable to find the secret. "She's never good at hiding stuff."

Standing in the center of the room, he started to study everything for something new. He tried to see anything that he had not seen before. Suddenly Mrs. M. walked in the room, startling him.

"What are you doing?" she asked, smiling.

"Nothing," Dad replied, grinning from ear to ear.

"You'll never find it," she teased, as she turned and headed back toward the living room and Aunt Maggie.

"We'll just see about that," thought Dad, as he continued to search the room, more determined than ever.

Several anxious minutes past, with still no sign of the secret Mrs. M. had hidden. Smiling, Dad had an idea. He ran to the kitchen, retrieved the walkie-talkie, and then returned to the bedroom. He cautiously pushed the talk button, being careful to make sure Mom and Aunt Maggie could not hear him. Then he called for Hero and Bubba.

"Boys, boys, can you hear me," Dad whispered.

"Sure, Dad. What's up?" asked Hero.

"I need some help. Could you carefully get to my room without anyone hearing you?" Dad asked.

"You mean so Mom can't hear us?" teased Bubba.

"That's what I mean," laughed Dad.

"We'll be right down," replied Hero.

Afraid Dad would find the Liahona and suddenly be in a lot of trouble, the boys left the Team and hurried toward his room.

"Do you think he found it?" Bubba asked worriedly.

"I sure hope not," Bean replied, startling the two boys.

"What are you doing here?" asked Hero.

"I figured you two would need help explaining what

the Liahona was and how it worked," replied Bean, smiling. "Besides, I thought if you ended up having to tell him about the Liahona, and I was there to confirm your story, he would be more likely to believe you."

The three kids sneaked through the house toward Dad's room and quickly slipped inside the door.

"So, what can we help you with, Dad?" asked Bubba smiling

"I can't stand not knowing what's going on. So, you kids need to help me find this secret your mother is hiding," replied Dad.

"We can't ruin Mom's secret," insisted Hero.

"Then I will have to continue to search for it until I find it," answered Dad, looking around the bedroom.

"How about we sit on your bed, and if you find it, we can help you understand what it is?" asked Bubba.

"What would be hard to understand?" Dad asked curiously.

"Dad, the secret is the treasure that we found from Moroni's treasure map," explained Hero. "And I'm afraid that you could really be in trouble if you find it alone."

"I guess you're right, guys. You better stay right there, 'cause I'm not gonna stop looking for it now," said Dad, more determined then ever to find the Team's treasure.

Hero, Bubba, and Bean sat down on the bed. They watched as Dad scoured every inch of his room, searching for the hidden treasure. They were amused as Dad became more and more frustrated, unable to locate the mysterious secret. Several nervous minutes past before Bean spotted the treasure box ingeniously hidden on the shelf as decoration. Nudging Hero, she carefully motioned up to where the box was hidden.

"Should we just show him?" she whispered.

"Do you want to end up on another mission?" squeaked Hero, surprised by her suggestion.

Bean shrugged her shoulders and smiled. "You know, I think traveling back to Book of Mormon time is scary. But the one thing I do like is how much fun it is to meet the characters I've read so much about all my life."

"Me, too," replied Bubba, grinning. "You know, it might be fun to go on a mission with Dad."

Hero looked up at the box and shook his head. Then he slowly started to stand up. Looking down toward Bubba and Bean, he asked, "Are you sure you want to do this?" "Sure," replied Bubba. "We can do it again." "We did great the first time we went on a mission," replied Bean. Hero again shook his head and whispered, "If we did so great, then how come you were captured?" "Come on, Hero. Where's your sense of adventure?" she teased. "You know, Dad, this treasure might totally change your life," said Hero. He slowly moved toward the shelf and started reaching for the box.

After all...if the Lord provided a way for you to travel back in Book of Mormon time, wouldn't you keep going back?

About the Author

Although born in Provo, Utah, Tina spent most of her life in San Diego, California. Her writing is strongly influenced by her hometown experiences and her large family whose flair for story telling never ends.

As a direct descendant of Heber C. Kimball and Orson Pratt, the stories told to her by her parents about them encouraged a fascination with the Book of Mormon, Church history, and the adventures of the early saints.

Tina Storrs Monson currently lives in Draper Utah, a suburb of Salt Lake City. She attended Brigham Young University where she met her husband, Kreg. They have been married for eighteen years and have five children.